CALLISTO:
BLOOD MISSION

CALLISTO:
BLOOD MISSION

SIMON CLARK

DARK MOONS

ISBN: 978-1-957121-66-6

Text © 2023 by Simon Clark

Cover art by M. Wayne Miller © 2023

Interior and cover design © 2023 by Cyrus Wraith Walker

Copy Editor: F. J. Bergmann

Editor and Publisher, Joe Morey

DARK MOONS

Dark Moons is an Imprint of
Weird House Press
Central Point, OR 97502
www.weirdhousepress.com

For Joe Morey. In gratitude for planting the Callisto seed and for encouraging me to grow his idea into a fruitful—and decidedly otherworldly—novel.

CONTENTS

ONE

SOMETHING DEADLY THIS WAY COMES

Dan Karlton sat in his office, waiting for eleven a.m. Eastern Daylight Time. He glanced at the laptop's clock, which told him it was five minutes to four p.m. here in the UK. Therefore, he was ahead of the New York office by five hours. Dan hoped that the video call wouldn't be a long one. He'd promised to take part in a darts match at the Elsie Tavern at six.

In her office, the project manager watched a livestream from a news channel. The woman was fascinated by the progress of the Rib as it had made the ten-day journey back from Callisto to Earth.

She called across the passageway to where Dan sat at his desk: "Hello, Dan."

"Hello, Shaz."

"You begun the video call yet?"

"It's due to start in a few minutes."

"When do you go back to America?"

"End of the month."

"I'll miss you, Dan. You're one of the good guys."

"Cheers, Shaz. And you're one of the good gals."

Shaz Chandler was in her early thirties, wore her dark hair short and had the most striking almond-shaped eyes that Dan had ever seen. Her olive-brown skin always seemed to have an enchanting glow all of its own, and she had a single dark freckle in the center of her right cheek. Sometimes she cheerfully referred to the freckle as "the bullseye." Maybe that was a dash of grim humor, Brit-style. Dan could never work out if she meant that was the target to aim something at. A bullet? A cream pie? A kiss? But he did appreciate her lively sense of humor, and her wit was quick and slick, and it always made Dan laugh. Shaz now held up the tablet so he could see the screen, though he couldn't make out much detail from this distance.

She said: "They estimate the Rib will reach Earth tomorrow."

Dan smiled. "You wouldn't get me on one of those things. Not for all the gold in the world."

"You're AB positive, aren't you?"

"Uh?" Dan was momentarily distracted by the notice onscreen, announcing the meeting would be starting soon.

Shaz spoke louder. "Your blood group? AB positive?"

"Yeah, sure."

"So people with your blood group amount to only three percent of the world's population."

"I know what you're hinting at." He smiled. "And the answer is a muscular 'no'."

"You're thirty-eight. The prime of your life. You should be lusting for adventure. The Rib Caucus is crying out for AB plus folk. The salary is phenomenal."

Rain clattered at the window—the sound was like sharp claws tapping at glass—and the breeze quickened, drawing out a long, low howl as it blew against the tall building, which overlooked city streets far below.

Shaz grinned. "The salary for an astronaut is ten times what you're earning."

"You'd never get me on a Rib."

"Think of the adventure."

"What? Riding in a capsule bolted onto a Godawful lump of alien technology? With nobody knowing how its propulsion system works? And nobody can steer the thing? It just blasts off, goes hurtling hell-for-leather to Jupiter, then comes back."

"It goes to Callisto, Dan."

"Whatever." He grinned back at Shaz. He liked her, and they always enjoyed their conversations that were woven through with bright laughter. "You won't get me within a hundred miles of a Rib. Evil things, they are."

"Ah, well," she sighed. "Seeing as you won't be exchanging your life as a structural engineer for that of an astronaut, heading into the great blue yonder, I'll bring us back to Earth with a bump. Have you made the calculations yet for the supermarket newbuild? Greg needs the percentage of roof that can accommodate solar panels. Build budget is capped as per contract."

"I'll run the numbers tonight. When they're done, I'll lob copies at Greg as well the quantity surveyor and the architect."

The onscreen countdown to the meeting had begun. *Sixty. Fifty-nine. Fifty-eight …*

Wistfully, Shaz looked at the screen. High-orbit satellites tracked the Rib as it prowled from the darkness of deep-space. "I'd go," she murmured. "But I'm O-type. They only want people like you, Dan—with a nice, juicy AB plus."

The countdown to the meeting relentlessly ticked away the seconds: *nineteen, eighteen, seventeen.* Dan glugged from a water bottle on his desk. Straightened his tie. Shaz switched off the livestream of the approaching Rib. A vessel that looked, to Dan, like something out of a particularly horrific nightmare. Bizarrely, it resembled part of a ribcage that had been torn from a human being. Rain pounded the glass. Dan glanced out of the window as he began positioning himself in front of the webcam. The summer afternoon was a gloomy one. The city lay beneath a dense layer of cloud. Humidity levels were high enough to be oppressive.

The Rib was still a million miles from Earth. Yet preceding it was an altogether more lethal traveller, comprising of twenty tons of iron ore. And that was the moment the asteroid struck the Earth's atmosphere. The time was five seconds to four.

Dark cloud boiled away beneath the hammer blow of interplanetary rock, striking the Earth at ten thousand miles per hour. Once dark cloud was instantly and violently transformed into blinding white incandescence … and nothing was ever the same again.

TWO

BLOOD ON BONES OF STEEL

First, the flash. It was so bright he felt as if it had seared his brain, penetrating right through to its bloody core.

Then movement.

Thunder.

A whirlpool of sound and movement. Dan Karlton's desk leapt from the floor, where it crashed—*smack!*—into the ceiling, shattering the neon strip-light, which showered him with razor-sharp fragments that filled his hair. Dust didn't merely billow—it punched him in the face with the savagery of a fist. With the dust came fragments of concrete, hitting the tender flesh of his face with stinging force. Trying to protect his eyes by slamming his hand to his face, while peering out through the narrowest of gaps in his fingers, he headed for the door. To his horror, he saw that Shaz had been thrown to the floor. Liquid smeared her forehead—red and wet.

Where there had once been floor-to-ceiling windows, there was now only an empty void. Blinds were flapping with a violent snapping sound as storm-winds blasted through. Dan panted for breath, yet every intake of air sucked tiny splinters of concrete down his throat into his lungs. Those sharp fragments stabbed into the lining of his throat. The pain was immense.

Shaz yelled: "What happened? A bomb? It must be a bomb, right?"

Blood spurted from a gash in her scalp, releasing a fresh river of crimson down over her face. The whites of her eyes flamed bright from a bloody mask.

The entire building convulsed. Hideously, the once solid floor beneath his feet appeared to turn into soft rubber that constantly rose and fell. The floor was splitting ... opening dark ravines, through which plumbing pipes and cables could be seen.

The floor sagged.

Moving downward.

Sounds louder than thunder. *Rumble! Snap! Crash!*

His colleagues' screams ripped through the filthy air. Instinct shrieked at them: *Escape! Escape! Get out! Don't die in here!*

Dan leaned inward through the doorway, his hands thrusting out to Shaz, who'd begun climbing to her feet—she was reaching out to him. Fear blazed in her eyes.

"Grab my hand!" he shouted through the choking dust.

That was the moment the entire façade of the building peeled away from its steel skeleton. Suddenly, behind Shaz, there were no walls, no window frames, no cladding. The face that the building had presented to Manchester for twenty years was gone. Dan gripped the doorframe as he leaned further into the office, his hand stretching out. His fingertips brushed the fingertips of her outstretched hand.

There was a loud snapping sound and then the floor abruptly dropped away from beneath Shaz. The woman became a whirling figure of arms, legs, fluttering black hair—then the shocking flash of her upturned face as she looked back at him, with eyes that were round, white, and blazing with terror.

More debris cascaded down, blocking his view of Shaz as she fell. And concealing her death from his eyes when her body slammed into the rubble at the foot of the now-ruined building.

The destruction didn't end there. With the steel bones of the building broken, by the impact of whatever had struck it, the integrity of the structure was broken. Partition walls collapsed, electricity cables snapped, and they shorted out in explosions of sparks that were so bright he was forced to scrunch his eyes to slits. Gobs of molten copper from burning cable seared holes through his clothes before inflicting painful lesions in his flesh.

As he ran back along the corridor to the main office, a doorframe burst under the savage pressure as the entire building deformed and distorted. A yard-long piece of the doorframe punched outward into his mouth. The merciless blow ignited napalm flashes of agony inside his skull. His tongue instantly found the jagged surfaces of broken teeth.

The building was collapsing around him. Walls vanished, revealing open views of the faraway Pennine hills. He scrambled over a floor that shifted and tilted until he was running uphill. There were smashed computers, phones, broken coffee cups, scattered architectural schematics of warehouses, office blocks, supermarkets. There were upended Styrofoam models of shopping malls, with tiny silver figures to represent shoppers. Then there was the dead face of Jack Mackintosh staring up at him from a halo of shattered concrete. One side of his head was a sickening mush of exposed brain. Arteries, resembling strands of soft spaghetti, hung out from the creamy pink mass.

Dan was reduced to nothing more than a beast, driven by the instinct to outrun Death—he became a terror-struck creature that blundered along: grunting and snarling and clawing through the dust-filled air.

Do not die.

Stay alive.

Find the safe place.

With the building collapsing around him, there was no place safe from harm. And yet …

… and yet his experience as a structural engineer punched a single word through his brain. *ELEVATOR.*

Get to the elevator. No. Not as a means of escape. The elevator shaft in this building comprised a tube of reinforced concrete that rose from the basement up to the twentieth floor—which was the very one he fought across now. The floor beneath his feet continued to become deformed as steel reinforcing rods snapped within the concrete, giving the impression that what had once been a solid, immovable mass had dangerously become as flexible as rubber. Behind him, sections of floor—ten feet by ten feet—simply tore away before plummeting to the ground far below.

Dan fought his way forward through cascading debris. The once horizontal surface of the floor had reached a thirty-degree angle. Desks, chairs, filing cabinets, corpses flowed past him in a torrent down the incline. Objects repeatedly crashed into his body, threatening to carry him away to bloody destruction. The swirling fog of dust grew so dense he could no longer see any of his colleagues. The screams, though ... he heard their screams. He glimpsed blood on a desk that tumbled by, end over end, missing his own head by inches.

Then he was at the elevator doors. They were closed, yet dust jetted through where the twin doors met: an updraught must be rushing up the shaft as if it were a chimney, drawing dust up within its hollow core. With that updraft came the stink of burning plastic.

Dan, with utter determination, pushed his back against the hard outer wall of the elevator shaft.

Just then, the entire building in front of him peeled away. Tons of concrete and steel thundered to the ground, far below his feet. He now stood on a platform of concrete that extended out by three feet from the shaft—the steel reinforcing rods in this part of the floor beneath him benefitted from being embedded into the vertical structure that carried the elevators. There was nothing but open air in front of Dan now. Birds whirled in panic against the boiling fug of smoke and dust.

Beyond the front of the platform, on which he stood, there was a long drop to the heap of rubble beneath him, the remains of the building. The steel bones of the skeleton that once had supported the office-block were bright red. Freshly painted with the blood of hundreds of people who had crashed downward, striking the metal spars on the way down.

The dust slowly began to clear, to reveal what remained of buildings and streets. The city had become a grim terrain of absolute ruin. And in the centre of that barren landscape was a gaping wound in the earth. Dan's blood turned cold. Because he had realized he was looking at a crater that was perhaps a quarter of a mile in diameter.

A sparrow, exhausted by the calamity that had struck Manchester, alighted on the jagged platform. A fellow survivor from the day an entire city died.

THREE

TANZANIA

Seventeen months later.

The Tanzanian landscape was as flat as a table top. Very green. Very wet. And made wetter by the current downpour of rain, accompanied by a rumbling drumbeat of thunder—all this accompanied by flashes of lightning that were a brownish red.

Dan Karlton had never seen lightning that was the color of congealing blood before, but then he'd never been to Africa before, so perhaps that type of lightning wasn't so unusual here. He'd been on the bus for an hour after disembarking from the plane. There was still another twenty minutes before they reached the picturesquely named Skyway Village. This was the residential complex for astronauts and workforce employed on Project Skyway.

The bus passengers were jet-lagged, some were already asleep, their heads nodding to the rhythm of the bus as it moved along an undulating road, built in one heck of a hurry through a vast swamp. Dan felt his own eyelids droop as he gazed out at lush greenery, where wading birds moved on their rigid-as-stilt legs through ponds of greenish water, their long beaks probing downward into the goo for whatever it was they ate.

Humidity made breathing difficult. The smell of cigarettes still clung to smokers' clothes. That stale odour mingled with the stench of vegetation that rotted in the swamp.

Dan thought: *This is a green hell. Why did I agree to this? At night, the place is going to become mosquito central.* He gazed at his reflection in the glass, seeing scars of old wounds that had been carved into his face during that horrific day when hell had arrived in the city of Manchester. He was immediately drawn back to the moment when the sky had appeared to catch fire, just before the asteroid punched into the ground at ten thousand miles per hour. The resulting shockwave had flattened buildings, and it had damaged the office block where Dan had been working. Half of the building had sheared off before plunging down into the street, taking floors, walls, ceilings, and dozens of coworkers with it.

And Shaz, of course.

The instant he closed his eyes he saw her face again—shrinking in size as she fell. She was still looking up at him, her eyes all but screaming out her terror ... and knowing that what awaited her now was a vicious blow of all-engulfing agony as she impacted the ground ... followed by death.

Dan's mouth was dry. He ran his tongue over freshly capped teeth. The dentist had adroitly repaired the damage wrought on his incisors during the office block's collapse. Though it was beyond the wisdom of medical science to repair the wounds to his mind, so brutally inflicted on that summer's day seventeen months ago.

The rumble of the bus faded as memory drew him down a dreadful pathway, back to when he clawed his way across the office floor as it sagged when steel reinforcing rods snapped inside the concrete. Then the cascade of all that furniture rushing by him. The pain of being struck by debris, the thunderous cacophony of destruction, the tiny splinters of concrete ripping the membranes of his throat as he gasped for air. And the apocalyptic terror ... the sheer terror that felt as if bloody chunks were being torn from his heart.

Dan opened his eyes. His reflection in the window was superimposed over passing marshland. Suddenly, the bus sounded loud again, tires swishing through rainwater puddles. Lightly, he touched the scar that ran down one cheek, from beneath the right eye to the bottom of his jaw. A chunk of concrete, as sharp as a Neolithic hunter's axe, had etched that memento of the worst day of his life.

Dan realized that a face looked back over the seat in front of him. A round-faced guy, with short black hair and a black moustache, was subjecting him to intense appraisal. Dan had noticed the man waiting for the bus. There had been a blue Skyway jacket over his arm, which marked him out as a fellow crew member. Dan didn't react to the judgemental stare, other than giving a small nod in greeting. They were fellow astronauts, after all. The guy might even be in the next cabin when the time came to hit the great void of outer space.

The man nodded back. He smiled, though it was more a grim tightening of the lips, rather than an expression of happiness. "Spiro," he said by way of introduction.

"Dan."

Dan held out his hand. Spiro half stood in his seat so he could reach back and shake Dan's hand. The grip was a formidably strong one.

Spiro gave Dan that judgemental stare again before saying, "Well. This is it."

"This is it," Dan said in agreement.

"What made you sign up?"

"People I knew died. So I realized I had to do something."

"My wife and kids were killed when the August rock hit Corfu. We both worked at a hospital there. I was away on a fishing trip, therefore ..." He shrugged. "You can guess."

The bus rumbled on. Reddish-brown lightning flickered on the horizon. Children standing on a patch of grass at the side of the road watched them pass by.

Spiro sighed. "Those kids aren't old enough to know when rocks weren't tumbling out of the sky to blow us to shit. Not like us. We knew a peaceful time before the asteroids started falling like fucking rain." Spiro's expression revealed that awful memories were threatening to bite their cruelly sharp teeth into him, so he rubbed his face—made an attempt at a grin, and said, "The job application was so damn easy, wasn't it? As soon as they saw that my blood group was AB plus they sent me to the training camp. Say … Do you know any of our fellow astronauts on the bus?"

"Nope. All strangers."

"Yeah." Spiro looked uneasy. "In my opinion, our training was scant to say the least. I know how to put on a suit, regulate oxygen flow, set the heating controls, and how to attach the piss pipe … oh, that rubber O-ring nips, doesn't it? But as for maintaining life-support on the Crab, I just don't have a clue."

"They'll have specialist crew members for that. What's your role?"

"Paramedic. And you?"

"Structural engineer."

"Wow, Dan." Spiro was surprised. "Are we going to be building stuff on Callisto?"

"They just said they needed a structural engineer."

The mood on the bus changed as Skyway Village drew nearer. Heads were lifting up, all signs of tiredness evaporating. Passengers were pointing out signs for Sky Port, and suddenly everything started to become that bit more real. A gritty reality at that, which made everyone appear suddenly uncomfortable in their seats. Six weeks from now, they'd be climbing onboard one of the Crabs that piggy-backed a hunk of alien technology. And nobody knew how that alien technology worked … or what it was made of, or even how to navigate the monstrosity. The Rib was an impenetrable enigma.

Dan knew that something unpleasant was about to happen. Every mile ramped up the tension. He began to feel sick with nerves. Passengers started to become agitated. They were running their fingers through their hair. The driver repeatedly glanced in the rearview mirror—she knew that her passengers were becoming more anxious with every mile that passed.

A guy with a shaved head and wearing sunglasses, even though there was no sunshine, abruptly stood up and waved his arm to attract the driver's attention.

"I've changed my mind," he said. "Stop the bus. I want to get off."

The driver called back in tones that were polite, yet tight with tension: "Sit down, sir."

"I want off this fucking bus! Fucking now!"

"Sir, I can't alight passengers here. You must go on to your destination first."

The guy stepped out into the aisle between the seats. His knuckles turned white as he clenched his fists. Spiro glanced at Dan, as if to say, 'He's going to turn violent'.

All the passengers watched the man now. They'd picked up on the man's aggression that seemed to spread out through the air, touching everyone onboard, making them wary—and to expect that fists would be flying soon. Dan slid sideways into the empty seat beside him. By this time, the guy was moving along the aisle toward the front of the bus. He thrust his face forward. Veins stood out in his neck. The muscles in his body were tensing. Adrenalin must have been spurting through his veins.

"Hey, stupid!" he yelled. "I'm telling you to stop this bus. I'm getting off."

"No, sir. Please sit down."

"I'm not going to Skyway. They can fucking stick that dump up their backsides!"

He began to shrug off his jacket.

Dan murmured to Spiro, "Looks like he's getting ready to attack the driver."

The guy was now five feet from the front of the bus. His voice rose, as if incredulous that his orders hadn't been instantly obeyed. "Hey, stupid! I'm not going any further."

The driver's patience evaporated. She twisted her head back so she could glare at him as the bus rumbled along at fifty miles an hour. "We're not going to the village ... we're going direct to the launch site."

The man erupted. "Fuck! No way! I'm going home! I've changed my mind!"

"Sit down! You'll upset the other passengers."

The man paid no heed to anything about upsetting the passengers. He hurled himself at the driver, knocking her sideways in the seat, so her head slammed into the side window. Despite what must have been a painful blow, the driver held onto the wheel. At either side of the road were glistening stretches of mud that smelt like dead beasts were rotting there.

The guy's yells were a wordless outpouring of rage. He hauled at the steering wheel, like he was intending to make a U-turn at fifty. The driver, meanwhile, struggled to keep a tight grip on the wheel. Nevertheless, the bus weaved, hurling people from one side of the bus to the other. Bags, jackets, laptops—they cascaded down from the overhead rack. The other passengers shouted in alarm, but none appeared to relish the prospect of tackling the troublemaker.

Dan, however, moved along the aisle, tapping Spiro on the shoulder as he went, and hoping that Spiro understood that was code for 'follow me'.

The driver yelled at the man to let her go. The man did not back down and there was a battle for possession of the steering wheel. The bus roared along the highway, lurching from left to right. Sometimes a tire ripped through grass at the side of the road, sometimes the bus veered toward one of the muddy lagoons before the driver managed to win control of the steering wheel, bringing the bus back onto a straight line at the centre of the road.

Dan saw a convoy of trucks approaching. Instantly, he pictured the bus slamming head-on into the lead truck, and the vehicles being engulfed in a fireball, resulting in the drivers and passengers being burned to death in the midst of this evil-looking swamp.

Dan pounced on the guy who fought with the driver.

Dan yelled, "Let go of her! You'll get us all killed."

The man raved. He swung his arms wildly as he tried to simultaneously grab the steering wheel and push his hand into the driver's face. Spiro tried to get hold of the man's hand but was shrugged off.

Tires screeched. The water alongside the highway drew perilously close. The convoy of trucks thundered toward them; their drivers frantically began pounding their horns. It became the bellow of brutish creatures that demanded their share of the road.

Dan chose his moment.

Balling his fist, Dan punched the guy in the centre of his face—a punch so hard that a spike of fire rammed up Dan's forearm.

The guy slumped backward over the dashboard, blood venting from his nostrils in a sticky river of red.

Immediately, the driver braked hard, bringing the bus to a skidding stop on a triangle of grass beside the road. The convoy passed by, horns blaring, lights flashing, the faces of drivers glaring out through side windows.

When the guy had fallen back onto the dashboard, he'd somehow activated the radio. A newsreader was in the process of delivering another depressingly regular account of destruction. "Reports are coming in of yet another asteroid striking the Earth. New Zealand authorities say that a large asteroid has impacted South Island in the vicinity of the city of Nelson. There are no confirmed casualty figures at present, but early reports suggest that the loss of life is substantial."

The troublemaker had dropped down into a sitting position on the floor next to the driver. He shook his head, dislodging strings of blood from his nose.

He muttered: "I don't want to go. Please don't make me go."

FOUR

N'DARBI

Spiro finished tying the knot in the sling behind Dan's neck.
"How does that feel, Dan?"

"Not bad. And thank you."

"You're more than welcome." Spiro smiled. "Gives me a chance to refresh my paramedic skills." He took a peek at Dan's hand that had begun to swell. "You dished out a helluva punch there. I don't think anything's broken, but they'll X-ray the hand as a precaution."

Dan sat in the Sky Port lounge, which largely consisted of lots of plastic seats in a row, with a table nearby where there were sandwiches, cakes, and a line of jugs that contained coffee, hot chocolate and tea. Bottles of cold water sat on another table. Passengers filed in from the bus. They patted Spiro and Dan on their backs and told them they were heroes.

One of the passengers, a woman with short grey hair, said, "We don't have to worry about Flinders anymore. They already shipped him back to the airport." She shook her head. "If that's a typical example of our crew, then God help us. What a flake."

Dan disagreed. "He was scared. Come to that, I'm terrified."

Spiro nodded. "We all are."

The woman scowled. "Well, I'm not."

After she'd gone, Spiro murmured to Dan: "If she's not scared, then that scares me. The prospect of being lobbed into space should terrify anyone. Am I right, Dan?"

"You're right, Spiro." Dan smiled. "Shall we grab some snacks before … huh, I'm not actually sure what's coming next, are you?"

"Nope." Spiro led the way to the drinks. "But something's changed, hasn't it? We should be going to Skyway Village to be assigned our accommodation. Why are we at the launch site?"

"They might be giving us a conducted tour first."

Spiro looked doubtful. "Yeah, maybe. Though a doctor should check your hand."

Dan shrugged. "It doesn't hurt that much now. It's probably just bruised."

He poured himself a coffee as the bus passengers, in their blue jackets, began to cluster around the tables, helping themselves to sandwiches. Dan counted fifteen of them—a mixture of male and female, all different ages, and nationalities. Then Project Skyway was an international effort, with disparate nations cooperating in the face of a Global crisis. Over a million had died so far, ever since the asteroids had begun falling out of the sky several years ago. At first, the rocks had been no larger than a truck and had incinerated themselves in the Earth's atmosphere, in fiery displays of self-destruction. Then the asteroids became bigger, which meant they didn't fully burn up in the atmosphere. Most had plunged harmlessly into oceans or into remote desert areas or mountain ranges.

Then an asteroid had plunged into the atmosphere before exploding into fragments—many of these were big enough to smash into the Earth. North America had suffered badly. One chunk of rock had flattened half of Boston. Several smaller towns, west of the city, had been completely wiped out by these death rocks.

Dan sipped his coffee while moving toward where sandwiches were heaped onto serving platters. Spiro had already piled sandwiches onto a plate, together with cubes of yellow cheese.

At that moment, a tall woman in a dark business suit, gold rimmed glasses and strikingly high stilettos strode across the floor. She slowly clapped her hands.

"Good afternoon and welcome. My name is N'Darbi. May I have your attention, please?"

Everyone politely turned toward her.

N'Darbi smiled, though Dan sensed the woman was deeply uneasy—and in a hurry, despite her not trying to show it.

Spiro nudged Dan with his elbow. "Looks like we're going to get the welcome-to-the- trip-of-a-lifetime speech."

"Ladies and gentlemen. Fellow astronauts. Please take a seat." N'Darbi waved her hand to a line of twenty seats arranged in front of a TV screen. At present, the screen was black, simply reflecting the images of men and women as they began putting their plates back down on the table.

"Please, bring your snacks and drinks." The woman was visibly tense. "I do need to tell you something of great importance. However, we don't have a great deal of time."

Dan noticed that the others had picked up on her anxiety—they shot questioning glances at one another as they took their seats.

One woman said, "Madam, we've all had long flights. Isn't there any chance we could check into our accommodation first? I promised I'd call my sister when I arrived."

"There will be plenty of time for that later."

People muttered amongst themselves. They'd been promised time in their rooms to rest, take showers, call home. Now this ...

Whatever "this" was—though Dan's gut told him they'd soon hear N'Darbi utter, "I'm afraid I have bad news."

Spiro was clearly thinking the same, because he whispered to Dan: "Someone's up a creek without a paddle, aren't they? Or, to put it bluntly, the shit is just about to fudge the fucking fan ... pardon my multiple use of the letter 'f.'"

Dan whispered back. "Yep ... and fudge the fan fucking big-time."

N'Darbi began knitting her fingers together like she didn't know whether to talk to her audience or start praying.

As it turned out later, Dan Karlton realized that prayer might have been good for their immortal souls ... considering the horror-show that was going to unfold before the light finally died on what was to be the grimmest of days.

FIVE

IT BLEEDS GOLD

Dan sat there in the company of Spiro and what would be his other crewmates. N'Darbi, neatly clad in her business suit, with a pencil inserted through the tightly woven plaits on top of her head, glanced at her wristwatch, then licked what appeared to be very dry lips, before nervously smoothing down her skirt with both hands—and both hands were trembling.

Thunder rumbled. Rain abruptly fell hard on the steel roof above their heads—a frantic drumming sound. Some of the people coughed, not really to clear their throats, but a nonverbal question that demanded, "Are you going to tell us what's happening or not?"

N'Darbi glanced at her watch again. Finally, she nodded as if relieved that this was the designated time to begin.

She began speaking in clear tones that rang with authority. "Ladies and gentlemen. Firstly, I will swiftly go over events of the last six years. Secondly, I will explain your purpose here. That is to say, I will describe your mission. Thirdly, I shall inform you about what you will be doing this afternoon."

"Finally," muttered a guy further along the line.

N'Darbi continued: "Six years ago the three Ribs, which the entire

21

world is now familiar with, were discovered when drought conditions lowered water levels in the marsh that surrounds this launch site. When scientists examined the Ribs, they quickly concluded that they are examples of extra-terrestrial technology—this was the first discovery of objects that prove that life exists elsewhere in the universe. Initially, experts concluded that they were machines of great antiquity. And that they no longer functioned, as they appeared to be completely inert." N'Darbi knitted her fingers together—her subconscious urge to pray, if that's what it was, was a powerful one. "Ladies and gentlemen, four years ago, information being streamed from a satellite in orbit around Jupiter revealed that the planet's gravitational field had significantly, and inexplicably, weakened."

A grey-haired woman raised her hand. "Madam, we know all this. The media has been reporting it for years."

"Please bear with me, Lady Stainforth—for reasons that will soon become obvious, a great deal of information about the situation in the Jovian system has been kept secret from the public."

The mood of her audience became more serious.

Lightning flared against the windows: a vicious red color. Then came the crash of thunder, the frenzied pounding of a demonic fist against the steel walls—or so it sounded to Dan, who momentarily closed his eyes. Instantly, he was locked into that dreadful moment when Shaz fell—just before his fingers could close over her hand, so he could pull her to safety. He saw the fluttering of her black hair, her oval face turned to his, her terrified eyes … and he hated himself. He'd failed her. Now, if he could atone for his pathetic failure to save her life by embarking on this … this suicide mission … then all well and good.

Though everyone had been assured this was not some one-way death flight, Dan could not help but consider it to be one. Would any rational human-being allow themselves to be locked into a big metal can that was strapped to an alien spacecraft? Which would then soar away into deep space. You might as well program the satnav to guide you to your grave.

His heart thudded—a deeply ponderous sound, which hinted that it might come to a juddering stop at any second. He thought about his mother and father, and his sister. And her kids, Billy and Meesh, who loved spending time with Uncle Dan. And there was Shaz again, burning bright in the centre of his mind's eye. She was forever falling. Her eyes were always locked on his.

"Dan ... Dan."

He opened his eyes to see Spiro looking at him.

"Are you okay, Dan? I thought you'd died on me there."

"Uh ... fine, Spiro. Jetlag, that's all."

N'Darbi was looking at Dan. "Are you all right, Mr. Karlton?"

She knows my name, he thought—she'd probably been studying their records before they arrived. *We're the poor fools that are going to ride the ship of the damned.*

Spiro indicated Dan's arm that was supported by the sling. "My friend hurt his hand earlier. A doctor should examine it, and he needs painkillers."

"Soon, Mr. Balouris. I must finish speaking to you all first." She then continued in those clear tones: "The result of the weakening of Jupiter's gravitational field is that it introduces chronic instability to the orbits of millions of asteroids between the orbit of Mars and Jupiter." She raised one hand above her head. "Julia, run VT." Instantly, the huge screen behind her burst into life, showing footage of asteroid strikes on the Earth—these images were largely captured by CCTV and phone footage. After that, came news coverage of the terrible results of those immense space rocks plunging into cities. Against this backdrop of destruction—of mutilated figures lying in streets or amid the rubble of buildings—N'Darbi became a towering silhouette, standing before all those horrific images as the footage rolled. There was no sound from the TV and she provided the voiceover.

"Initially, the asteroids that detached from their usual orbit, and headed toward the Earth, were relatively small and were incinerated by the friction effect of our atmosphere. However, larger asteroids began to reach us. This resulted in horrendous devastation. Impact craters a mile across were created. Hundreds of thousands of people have died. What the public does not know is that there are much larger asteroids approaching the Earth. We aren't sure of precise numbers, but they exceed ten thousand."

Nobody moved. Everyone seemed to be holding their breath. Their eyes were fixed on the woman. Dan could sense the anxiety all those men and women felt. At that moment, the tension became so intense he wanted someone to yell or throw a chair, anything to break that dreadful spell that tightened muscles to the point that his stomach ached.

"These are extinction events," N'Darbi told them. "That is to say, they will be if just one of those asteroids were to strike our planet. If that should occur, then more than ninety percent of all lifeforms would become extinct within a matter of months. Only rats, cockroaches, and smaller species would survive. Humans would certainly die out completely. And, no, before you ask, we don't have enough missiles to either destroy all those asteroids or even nudge them off course." Rain pounded against the metal roof, an urgent rhythm, like the God of Death was trying to attract their attention. "You all know about the events that occurred after the discovery of the three Ribs in the swamp. Just days after their discovery, one of the Ribs, which we call Rib One, simply rose into the air, before accelerating away from the Earth. Tracking satellites traced its route to Jupiter where it landed on Callisto. After thirty hours on Callisto, it returned to Earth, landing in the exact spot where it had lain for many thousands of years. A week later, Rib Two repeated the actions of Rib One—undertaking a high speed visit to Callisto, followed by a rapid return to Earth. The Rib's homeward journey took ten days. Therefore, the velocity of the Ribs defies explanation, indeed it defies imagination. After all, can we even begin to imagine what marvellous engine drives the Ribs at such speed? You know what came next. Scientists attached what were termed 'Riders' to the Ribs—these were packages of instruments. As we suspected, Rib Three departed the Earth in the same manner as the other two Ribs. Rib Three returned within twenty days. The Riders were detached and the data they harvested was studied, confirming that the destination had been the Jovian moon of Callisto. Callisto is the second largest of the Jupiter moons.

It appears to consist of rock and ice, though we now believe that there might be a liquid ocean beneath the surface." More lightning flashed—becoming a violent, bloody-red in color. This prompted N'Darbi to speak faster, urgency giving her words a compelling rhythm. "And you know we attached habitat pods known as 'Crabs' to the Ribs. These are crewed by volunteers. It's common knowledge that the first crewed mission to Callisto departed on Rib One, and it flew to Callisto and back in a matter of days. What did happen, unfortunately, was that everyone who has a blood group other than AB positive became unwell on the journey. Other blood types, due to some effect we don't understand, didn't allow the usual absorption of oxygen into the bloodstream. This meant that the astronauts who didn't have AB positive blood simply fell asleep for the entire journey, there and back. Hence, we only recruit people, like yourselves, who have the requisite blood type."

Spiro raised his hand. "Are you going to tell us what's gone wrong? Because something has gone badly wrong, hasn't it?"

"First, I will tell you what has gone right. Later missions to Callisto, using Crabs piggybacking on the Ribs, have revealed that there are structures embedded into the surface of Callisto. And I must stress that all the crews returned safely, though they remain in quarantine, which is understandable. Those brave men and women have gathered valuable information. And, most importantly, they have discovered that one of those buildings has a gravitational pull all of its own. And here we are forced to make a leap of imagination, because we do not have sufficient factual evidence. Nevertheless, experts have developed a hypothesis that these artificial structures, which appear to form a city, are responsible for generating what was once a gravitational field of immense power, which, in turn, fed into the Asteroid Belt, which held asteroids in their orbit, thus preventing them from drifting toward the Earth. However, it is believed that whatever alien technology generates the gravity has become faulty. The machine is breaking down. Hence, the weakening of the gravity that once surrounded the Jovian system. So, I now arrive at the point where

I state your mission. You are to travel to Callisto. You will examine the gravity generator, if that's what it is, and you will repair it, and ensure that the gravity begins to flow again."

At this, everyone rose to their feet shouting.

Lady Stainforth flung up her arms in astonishment. "How can we do that? How do we repair alien technology?"

"Impossible," shouted Spiro.

Others shouted pretty much the same thing. "We don't even know how the Ribs work. So how are we going to repair something that generates gravity?"

"This is crazy!"

"All we'll succeed in doing out there is dying."

N'Darbi raised her hands, a plea for silence. When there wasn't silence, she yelled with a ferocity that was electrifying. "You must succeed! If you fail, every human being on Earth will be killed. That will be the end of your friends, families—everything. The first of the extinction-event asteroids will, we believe, strike the Earth fifteen months from now."

Everyone stopped shouting. There was dead silence.

Silence, that is, apart from the slow rain. A grim sound, truly not unlike the fingers of skeletons tapping on the door of a tomb.

When nobody else spoke, N'Darbi surged on against the backdrop of TV footage, showing rescue workers carrying away body bags from the wreckage of a school. The body bags were full of rounded, lumpy objects. Parents who had survived the asteroid strike were weeping—though the images remained without sound. Something that made the silent weeping appear even more dreadful and heart-breaking.

"Yes," N'Darbi told her audience. "Something has gone wrong. Half of the crew that were supposed to depart on Rib Two have upped and left. Regrettably, their courage has deserted them. Their cowardice will forever be a scar on their lives."

Dan stood up. His injured hand was throbbing, yet the pain seemed so insignificant now.

He said, "Just hours before a Rib lifts off, it begins to vent metal in liquid form. This pours out of fissures in the flanks of the structure."

N'Darbi gazed at Dan. Her eyes didn't blink once. "You are correct, Mr Karlton. Liquid gold vents from openings in the Ribs. A process known as Visceral Extrusion, but everyone calls it a 'bleed'."

"Is there a bleed present now?"

"Yes. That's why I am going to take you out to Rib Two. We estimate liftoff could occur at any time within the next five hours."

A large door slid to one side at the far end of the building, revealing a pair of open-backed trucks. On the horizon, lightning constantly flashed— it resembled stalking figures of red fire that prowled the swamp. As if in search of prey.

SIX

SUSPICIOUS HEARTS

The open-backed trucks were accessed at the rear by a short ladder bolted to the metalwork. Seating was a series of benches running from one side of the truck to the other. Dan chose a bench at the back of the truck. Spiro sat alongside him; the man's large brown eyes scanned the cloud that covered the sky.

"At least it stopped raining," Spiro said. "Though, they could have provided buses. These trucks just reek of military service, don't they?"

Dan, despite the heat—and the smothering humidity—began to shiver as his blood turned cold. Instinct was telling him to be on his guard. *Not everything is as it seems. Beware … beware …*

Dan murmured, "Where has everyone gone? Why is it so quiet?"

Spiro was looking increasingly worried. "I don't know. But something isn't right here, is it?"

Soon, Dan's fellow crew members were on the trucks. Slowly, the big machines moved off. They picked up speed, gliding away from the big tin shed that served as the departure lounge, and then they headed across an expanse of blacktop toward a deserted road that ran in a straight line through the malignant-looking greenery of the swamp. There were thousands of marshy ponds stretching as far as the eye could see. Clouds of insects hung above brown water that no doubt contained enough bacteria to kill a person stone dead within the week, if they were foolish enough to drink even so much as a cupful.

The stink of mud filled Dan's nostrils. A stench so powerful that its flavor of rotting vegetable matter crept over his tongue and down the back of his throat to the extent he found himself repeatedly swallowing lest the sandwiches and cake he'd eaten in the departure lounge might violently return along what was normally the one-way-street of his gullet.

Spiro fanned his face with his hand. "What a stink. I figure that marsh must be an elephant's graveyard or something. I remember when I treated my first case of necrosis—this place smells just the same as the poor guy's neck when the fissure opened up."

Spiro was swallowing, too: the stench made everyone nauseous.

Dan began to speak. "Okay, I get why they recruited you for the mission. You have medical training. If we get sick, you make us well again, but why do they need me? I'm a structural engineer."

Spiro shrugged. "There are people from all kinds of professions that are making the journey. Electronics specialists. Scientists of all kinds."

"It seems to me, they've put a bunch of disparate individuals together in the hope that somehow we can repair a gravity generator, which will return the asteroids to a stable state."

A woman on the bench in front of Dan abruptly turned to face him. Clearly, she'd been listening to the conversation. "We've been lied to, haven't we?"

"Have we?"

She gave a sharp nod. "I was talking to a techie on the plane. He's thinking of bugging out, because … you know the crew of the last mission to Callisto—the ones that arrived back here back in June?"

Spiro nodded. "Yeah, they were on every news program for a week."

The woman's eyes narrowed. "Actors. They never went to Callisto at all."

Dan saw that the woman believed what she'd been told. But there must be millions of conspiracy theories out there about the entire situation with the Ribs and the asteroids.

Spiro had been thinking about what she'd said. "Surely, if the crew of Rib One had been actors or stooges or whatever, there'd be people out there who'd know who those fakes were?"

Dan said, "He's right. The public would soon know that the Caucus were trying to deceive everyone."

The woman gave a knowing smile. "The truth will come out within days. That's why they're rushing us out to board the Crab now before their lies are exposed."

Dan was puzzled. "I don't get it. What have the Caucus got to gain by fabricating reports that a crew travelled to Callisto before coming safely back to Earth again?"

Suddenly, she grabbed hold of Dan and Spiro's hands then pulled them closer to her as she whispered, "The reason is obvious ... shockingly obvious. The reason they are parading a bunch of fake astronauts in front of TV cameras is because when the Crab returned to Earth, it was empty. Its crew remained on Callisto. And nobody knows what has happened to them."

SEVEN

FIRST SIGHT

The woman's revelation that the crew was inexplicably missing from the returning Crab, which was attached to a Rib, left Dan with plenty to think about. He sat on the bench at the rear of the truck, the warm air blowing in his face—it carried the thick, cloying stench of the swamp, which stretched out for miles in every direction. The electric motor of the truck had become a mournful drone, which accompanied their journey toward the alien spacecraft.

What if the Rib made a one-way journey this time?

Of course, the popular belief was that extra-terrestrials had built the Ribs, and then left them on Earth as a means of transport for human beings to visit the creatures, which, scientists theorised, inhabited Callisto. A picture was painted by the media of benevolent creatures that cared deeply for their human neighbours on Earth. With loving care, they would carefully ship men and women to that far-off moon of Jupiter with the intention of ... what? To joyfully greet their human neighbours? To share their technological knowledge? "Here's a cure for cancer, and why not swallow the pill of eternal youth as well?" That was the kind of hopeful speculation being bandied about.

In reality, nobody knew of ET's motivation. The only salient facts were these: One: alien technology had been discovered in the form of three Ribs. Two: that, one by one, the Ribs had flown to Callisto before returning several days later. Three: Governments had cooperated to an unusual degree. They had funded the construction of a spaceport in the swamp, in close proximity to the Ribs, and had instructed scientists and engineers to build habitat pods. These became known as Crabs, due to their silvery legs extending out to cling to the Ribs.

Dan knew that the alien craft defied all attempts to discover their nature. No tool could cut into the material that formed the exterior of the Rib. Sonar and radar didn't penetrate the structure. Ribs didn't react to chemicals. They revealed no trace of electrical activity. Their temperature always matched that of their surroundings.

The Ribs were dead—yet they lived. That was the bizarre truth of the matter. Only when they approached the time when they would ascend into the heavens did they perform something that was officially termed Visceral Extrusion—this was when liquid gold dribbled from small holes that speckled the body of the Rib. Of course, scientists had tried to insert tubes that were tipped with tiny cameras into those holes, but they'd only penetrate the Rib to a depth of no more than ten inches. Cameras revealed nothing but a slender cavity. Then the cavity narrowed to the point where the tube couldn't be coaxed inward any deeper.

The woman who'd revealed the disturbing story about the return of a Rib that was devoid of crew had moved to another bench, where she whispered into the ear of a woman with red hair and striking green eyes. The woman with the red hair kept shaking her head. Dan suspected that she didn't believe the tale of the empty Crab. Then did he believe what the woman had told him? Footage of cheerful crew members stepping out through hatches after the voyage appeared convincing, as did black streaks on the silvery Crab, supposedly caused by extreme heat when it plunged into the Earth's atmosphere at five thousand miles per hour. After re-entry, the Ribs decelerated, and then gently carried their piggyback rider down into the marsh again, to the exact same coordinates where lift-off had occurred.

The teller-of-tales returned to her bench, this time bringing with her a guy of around forty. He had a shaved head and neat goatee beard. The guy's expression was grave—clearly, he'd heard the scare story, too.

The woman sat on the bench, then leaned closer to Dan and Spiro. "This is Hassan. Oh, I'm Katrina by the way."

Dan nodded. "I'm Dan. This is Spiro."

Hassan said, "Katrina has revealed to me that after a crewed expedition to Callisto the Crab was empty when it returned to Earth."

Spiro shrugged. "Though there's no proof that the Crab was empty, is there? Those people we saw on TV, who were filmed leaving the Crab, might genuinely have been to Callisto."

Hassan whispered in a conspiratorial way: "Admittedly. There is no proof yet that the Crab returned empty. However, do you know why you are seeing only small numbers of ground crew here?"

Spiro shook his head.

Hassan continued: "Because the workers are ... what is that American phrase? Ah, yes ... bugging out. Ground crews are bugging out by the dozen. Many believe that getting too near the Ribs is dangerous."

Katrina gave a sharp nod. "People are saying that those things mess with your mind."

Dan heard a rumble of thunder. The storm was returning.

Spiro frowned. "Mess with your mind? How?"

Hassan leaned closer as another peal of thunder rumbled ominously across those bleak acres of oozing mud. He said: "Over the last few weeks, I've done some detective work, emailing people who once worked here. They say that it feels like shadows begin to fill your head. You become depressed. Bad dreams come at night. People warn that if you remain in close proximity to the Ribs you start to have terrible thoughts."

Katrina said, "Hassan and I have decided to quit."

Hassan grimaced. "After all, do you really believe we are being sent to Callisto to repair a gravity generator that will stop asteroids from reaching Earth?"

Spiro's patience started to wear thin. "Are you saying that we're being delivered to the aliens as some kind of sacrificial offering? Do you think they're going to eat us? Or impregnate us with their devil spawn?" Spiro laughed. "My friends, you have been listening to too many conspiracy theories."

Hassan and Katrina glared angrily at Spiro.

Hassan wagged his finger. "Half of the original crew, who were part of this mission, have gone home. Every day, launch-site workers pack their suitcases and rush to the airport. Something is very wrong here. And, if you ask me, downright evil."

"Our mission," Dan said, "is to try and save the lives of everyone on this planet. If there's even the slimmest of chances we can prevent the end of the world by climbing onboard one of those Crabs, isn't it worth the risk?"

Before Hassan or Katrina could even begin to answer Dan's question, Spiro suddenly pointed at something out there in the swamp.

"There they are." Spiro had breathed the words in a way that could be described as religious awe. His eyes were actually bulging with amazement as he uttered: "The Ribs. Just look at the size of them."

The trucks glided along the road toward where the nearest of the three Ribs lay. By now, it was just over a mile away. The truck's passengers stared at the alien craft as they slowly approached. Of course, Dan had seen the Ribs many times before on TV, and in magazines, and on countless websites. Social media had spawned billions of words of opinion about those alien machines.

But this was the first time that Dan had seen a Rib with his own eyes. He'd not expected to feel a physical reaction when seeing one of those things. But this felt like a punch in the belly. He actually recoiled. The structure was, indeed, shaped like a human rib. It curved up at both ends, and was very nearly black in color, yet having reddish tints—though in the gloomy light that filtered through the thick cloud, these tints were a deep, deep red. Dan could easily recite facts about the Ribs: three point eight miles long. Half a mile across at its widest. The surface on the top of the Rib was largely smooth, yet had subtle undulations, such as bulges, together with linear features that could be likened to those depictions of bicep muscle found in medical textbooks.

The underbelly of the Rib was entirely different. It presented a scarred face to the world. A face riven with jagged fissures that extended to a depth of thirty feet into the body of the craft. This surface, and it was the same with all three Ribs, had some people speculating that the Ribs had taken part in a ferocious battle millions of years ago. The underside had been clawed by something of immense destructive power. Blast craters had been ripped into its uniquely tough surface. On the underside of the Ribs, there could be found radiating lines of yellow, as if left there by explosions.

And yet the Ribs had survived.

Also, there were indications that this alien device had at least some capacity to self-heal. All the 'wounds' inflicted by what must have been formidable weaponry had scabbed over as a result of that process of Visceral Extrusion. Liquid gold had flowed into the fissures, craters and assorted ravines to partially fill them before setting to a hardness that defied any human attempt to even cut away the tiniest of samples for examination in a laboratory.

Yes, the Ribs were remarkable. They were astonishing. They amazed scientists and the public alike.

And the Ribs were awful.

They were somehow dreadful to look at.

They were as wrong as seeing a kitten that had been born with two heads.

Dan thought: *I don't want to go anywhere near that thing. It isn't a machine. It's a monster.* And yet that's where he was headed. Riding in the back of a truck, beneath skies that boiled with thick, dark cloud. Flashes of lightning prowled across the stinking morass of the swamp. The lightning cast salvos of electrical fire down into the stark terrain of mud and water and evil-looking swaths of thorn trees.

Dan Karlton felt a powerful urge to leap from the truck, then run hard and fast, back toward the airport. And yet he sat there, staring at the monstrous object, as the vehicles drew ever closer. Everyone else did the same. Hassan reached out to Katrina, and they both held onto each other's hands with a desperation that made their bodies visibly tremble. Ten minutes ago, they'd been strangers. Now, Dan saw that they clung to one another's hands, like two children who'd just discovered a maggot-infested corpse during what should have been their lovely woodland walk.

The trucks pulled onto a concrete apron close to the Rib. The steel Crab—which was an oval capsule a quarter of a mile in length—gripped onto the underside of the Rib that rested on concrete blocks the size of houses. These blocks had been installed on the landing site during the Ribs' flights to the Jovian system to prevent the Ribs sinking into the mire again (taking the Crabs with them), which would have necessitated their excavation from deep mud. Indeed, this area of swamp had been drained, yet the ground was still mushily soft.

Hassan's eyes were bright with horror. "The work was conducted in such a rush that fifty people died in the construction of the Rib harbours. The bodies of many of those men and women are encased in the cement. They didn't even pause construction to retrieve them."

The trucks stopped a hundred yards from the Rib. The alien machine possessed a menacing charisma all of its own. Dan couldn't put what he experienced into words exactly, but it was as if a gloomy halo surrounded the Rib. An aura of shadow that extended outward, creating a dark stain in the air all around it.

Before Dan and the other crew members had even climbed down from the back of the vehicle the trouble began. First shouting, then the violence.

EIGHT

THE EXTRAORDINARY POWER OF FEAR

S labs of dark cloud pressed down from the sky. The weather was absolutely oppressive, inducing the ominous sensation that a huge weight
was about to fall on everyone as they climbed down from the trucks. Dan
sucked in a lungful of air that was so humid that it felt like inhaling warm
liquid. He was panting as if there wasn't enough oxygen in this place. He
noticed that Spiro stood there with his hand on his chest. He, too, was
finding the simple act of breathing had become laborious—in fact, painfully so.

Dan's heart thudded as it drove what felt like sludge, rather than blood,
through his arteries. A sharp pain flared in his right eye. A sensation that
disturbingly echoed that of a steel needle being pushed into the centre of
his right eyeball, and through the back of the socket, deep into his brain.
An awful sensation. One that begged the question, was he suffering a brain
haemorrhage? He rubbed his forehead, trying to dispel the pain.

"Tension headache." Spiro grimaced. "I've got it, too."

Hassan and Katrina hurried across the concrete apron to where
N'Darbi stood in her heels and business suit, doing her utmost to appear
a commanding figure who was calmly in charge. Yet failing. Even from
where Dan stood, he could see the way her eyes darted nervously in the

direction of the Rib. Those 'bleeds' had painted yellow stripes of liquid gold down its sides here and there.

Perhaps as many as a hundred men and women in hi-viz vests, which were a brilliant orange, dashed around an assortment of vehicles, ranging from large trucks to small golf-buggy-size carts. They all moved in a way that could be described as frenzied. Their activity was chaotic, and Dan immediately sensed that they weren't an experienced workforce. Some unloaded boxes of food from a truck. Several workers carried these boxes to the Crab that was pretty much at ground level, with hatches left open wide to receive supplies and its crew. One guy on the back of a truck was clearly eager to get the job done then get the hell out of there. He began throwing boxes of food out for his colleagues to catch. Many of the boxes missed the outstretched hands and fell onto the ground where they burst open, scattering cans, packets, bursting plastic bottles, which released brightly colored sauces and drink onto the concrete. Katrina and Hassan began arguing with N'Darbi. Dan couldn't hear what was being said, though the furious gesturing hinted powerfully enough that Katrina and Hassan were denouncing the entire operation, while no doubt demanding they be returned to the airport as soon as possible. N'Darbi repeatedly shook her head while pointing at the Rib.

A woman of around sixty bustled up. She wore a dayglo orange vest with the words *Team Leader* on the back. Above those words, someone had added *I'm Gen* in black marker pen.

"Astronauts," she panted. "Hey, astronaut guys. The rucksacks are over there. Collect the ones that are yours and take them onto the Crab. Hurry. There's not much time left!"

Spiro caught the woman by the arm. "Miss. What the hell's happening here?"

"Ha! Isn't it obvious? Most of the Launch Handlers quit last week. We flew in replacements, but nobody knows what they're doing. No time for training. No time for anything but more of this fucking chaos." She abruptly yelled at a man who was dragging a heavy sack toward the front of the Crab. "No! I've already told you. Foodstuff goes in the stern hold. No, the stern is that way. To your right!"

The guy stopped hauling the sack. Briefly, he stared up at the Rib, his eyes watery with sheer horror. Then he abandoned the sack and ran to the truck that Dan had arrived on. There he scrambled into the back and hunkered down as it pulled away, heading back to the Sky Port buildings.

"You see?" The woman's breath smelt of whisky. "Absolute fucking pandemonium." She clapped her hands to attract the crew's attention. "Everyone! Find your rucksacks. Get on the Crab! It might liftoff from the harbour at any moment! You need to board—now!"

Then what had been a deeply troubling situation became nightmarish.

Lightning flickered on the horizon—bolts of fiery red blazed with their own dangerous power. Dan realized that the storm was getting closer. And they were exposed in a very flat landscape.

Spiro had picked up on the very same thing. "Hey, N'Darbi, do people ever get struck by lightning here?"

"Never mind that. Just get yourselves on board. We need to run final habitat checks before the hatches are closed."

The pain in Dan's head became even more cruel. He clenched his fists as a spike of agony drove through his eye, right through his brain, to dig deep into bone at the back of his skull.

"What's happening to me?" He gave an animal grunt of pain.

At that moment, the atmosphere changed. A sense of imminent violence crackled on the air. Dan glanced at Spiro, and he had the sudden and overwhelming fear that the man would punch Dan in the face. That he'd attack with demonic ferocity.

That's crazy, he told himself. *Spiro's a nice guy.*

And yet …

Dan was gripped by the certainty that Spiro would kill him. He glanced around—other people were reacting in the same way. A sense of impending threat bit deep into their bones. They looked around with frightened eyes. Some of the workers began shouting angrily. Those that had been unloading food supplies from the truck started throwing punches at one another. A woman leapt into one of the golf-buggy carts and accelerated away, heading back toward Sky Port. One of the crew members, who had been on the truck with Dan, abruptly sprinted toward the golf-buggy, jumped on the back and clung on tight. He stared back at his colleagues as he was carried away.

Spiro grunted—a sound that actually gurgled thickly in his throat. "Uh … is paranoia contagious? Right now, I don't feel safe. I can't shift the feeling that people are going to attack me."

"Same here."

Dan found his gaze drawn to the monstrous form of the Rib. "It's true, isn't it? That thing can get inside our heads."

Spiro nodded. "And we all thought Satan was the guy with the forked tail and the horns. But that thing's Satan, isn't it? Or as near as damn it …"

By now, most of the ground crew were either running back along the road, or they'd grabbed vehicles and were powering away. One driver lost control of a truck. It skidded off the road to plunge into a muddy pond, hurling brown spray into the air. Nobody seemed to care. Leastways, nobody stopped to find out if the driver had survived the impact.

Gen, the woman who smelt of whisky, shouted, "We have movement! The Rib has lifted eighteen inches above base line." Then she took a huge breath of air before screaming, "Get on the fucking ship! It's going to leave!"

Dan Karlton ran to where the rucksacks had been carelessly dumped onto the concrete. Spiro followed. Soon they were rummaging through the bags, until they found theirs. Most of the other crew members did the same. However, Katrina and Hassan were shouting at N'Darbi.

"We're not boarding the Crab," they were yelling. "We're going home. We quit!"

N'Darbi paused, staring hard at them, then she uttered a chilling prophecy. "If you don't board the Crab now, then you will, likely as not, die here in the next five minutes. You don't want to be within a mile of that Rib when it breaks free."

NINE

RUSH

Dan Karlton hurtled into the vortex of people that were screaming as loud as they could. They were either berating anyone who got in their way or yelling at drivers of vehicles to stop and let them climb onboard, so they could flee this living hell that had erupted on the concrete apron beside Rib Two.

Dan realized that he was being hampered by the sling as he tried to haul his two rucksacks from the heap of bags. Quickly, he pulled the loop of fabric from his neck and tossed the sling aside. After grabbing his bags, he headed for the Crab, where an open hatchway revealed a void that was black with shadow. This had all the blood-chilling unease of approaching a tomb whose door had inexplicably swung open.

Hassan and Katrina grabbed their bags. They ran the other way, however, gesturing frantically to a van that hummed by at dangerous speed. It was weaving across the ground, trying to avoid hitting ground crew in their hi-viz vests. The ground crew, in turn, frantically gestured to drivers to slow down, so they could tumble onboard. Some succeeded, others were left behind. Several men and women had leapt onto speeding trucks only to be flung off again—people were tumbling across concrete with bone-snapping force. Nobody paused to check on the injured people who lay screaming on the concrete—there was purely this instinctive drive to go—to run—to get away—to escape—to leave that loathsome slab of alien devilry behind.

The team-leader, Gen, furiously beckoned her own people. Her body language screamed panic. "Everyone! Get on the fucking Crab. It's twenty-five inches above base line. The fucker is beginning to fly. Hurry, get on the Crab. That goes for everyone—supply staff, ground crew, astronauts, every fucking one."

Her cuss-driven orders began to work. People who were there purely as ground crew to service the Crab began to scramble through hatchways into the silvery pod that had been built to house the astronauts.

Dan had reached the entrance to the Crab. The sight that greeted his eyes was a strange one. Foam mattresses were fixed to the floor with straps of wide fabric. While bolted to the ceiling were tables and chairs. Dan noticed Spiro looking at the surreal position of furniture on the ceiling.

"Didn't they tell you?" Dan said. "The Crab falls within the Rib's gravitational field. By the time it reaches space, 'up' flips to 'down'."

"They cut my introductory training period short. All the instruction I got centred on how to operate the sickbay."

Yells of "Stop!" drew Dan's attention to where Hassan and Katrina ran out in front of the last truck to depart the launch site. They waved, shouting pleas for the driver to stop, so they could climb on that final escape vehicle. The driver aimed straight for the couple, accelerating all the time, the engine rising to a painfully loud howl. Hassan and Katrina dived aside just in time. They both sat where they landed on the concrete, staring in disbelief as the truck sped off toward the road. There was still a couple of dozen people milling around the apron, unable to decide whether to run toward the Crab, or take their chances on foot, hoping to reach a safe distance from the thing before it unstuck itself from the concrete blocks.

N'Darbi still beckoned people, shouting to them that they must climb onboard the Crab.

Gen's shout cut through the babble of voices: "Forty inches above baseline! The fucker's rising faster. Get on ... or get ready to die!"

Spiro grabbed Dan by the elbow, then drew him inside the Crab. The downward facing tables and chairs were now directly above their heads—a decidedly weird arrangement that only added to Dan's unease, as if, literally, his world had suddenly turned upside down. Some of the astronauts had, as their training dictated, laid down on the foam mattresses and were strapping themselves in tight, ready for take-off.

Dan shouted to N'Darbi, "You too, Miss. Get onboard!"

N'Darbi stared at the people still out there on the apron, then threw out her arms in despair—she'd done her best to save their lives. A moment later, she stepped onboard.

With a grim glance at Dan, she hissed, "My blood group is O. They rejected me for the flights, so, for me, this is going to be rough." She turned to Spiro. "You're the medic. Therefore, you'll need to take care of the non-AB plus folk."

"I'm one of the medics."

"No, you are *the* medic. Ballam and Singh never left the airport this morning. They bought tickets home."

A huge thudding echoed through the craft—the sound of a monster fist pounding metal.

Spiro reacted with shock. "What the hell? Explosions?"

N'Darbi shook her head. "That's the Rib waking up. Somewhere inside that thing, the motor, or whatever passes for a motor, is beginning to run up to speed." She called through the hatchway, to those still on the apron. "You've got less than twenty seconds! Get on this thing!"

Some did heed her plea—they ran to the Crab, leapt through the hatch, then moved to the far wall of the cabin. Their eyes were huge with fear.

Dan thought: *They never volunteered for space. But they're going anyway. They must be scared out of their wits.*

N'Darbi spoke quickly to Spiro. "The de-oxygenation effect kicks in quickly. All those who aren't AB positive will become comatose within minutes. You'll need help to put everyone into a bunk, then mask them and feed them pure oxygen. That will keep them alive, at least. Me included."

Gen had boarded the Crab, too, where she remained in the doorway. When anyone got close enough, and who appeared to dither, unable to decide whether to board or not, she grabbed hold of a fistful of their clothes, then with a fierce strength dragged them on board, with a cuss word and a "I just saved your freaking life. You can thank me later."

Openly now, she reached into her back pocket, pulled out half a bottle of Scotch before sucking hard on the glinting neck of the bottle. Dutch courage, Dan realised. Booze helped damp down the panic she must have felt. Then everyone was feeling the contagion of panic, too.

Soon the cabin was getting crowded. People either had that fixed stare of someone in shock, or they muttered to each other—a mixture of anger and fear. The members of the ground crew in the cabin were stunned to discover that they'd become accidental astronauts.

Then came a huge shriek of a sound—like a slab of metal being torn apart by a monstrous force.

Spiro gasped in astonishment. "We're going!"

Gen leaned out through the open doorway to shout at those on the apron as the Crab rose slowly from the ground. "This is your last chance! Jump on board!"

A guy with short silver hair did grab the chance and leapt upward, his top half curling forward through the open hatchway. Dan grabbed him by the arms and dragged him into the cabin. As he did so, he saw Hassan and Katrina run toward the Crab, obviously deciding, at last, this would be the way to save their lives.

Katrina leapt upward. The Crab had reached a height where only her fingertips reached the edge of the floor between the cabin and outer hull. Lightning fast, N'Darbi and Gen grabbed her wrists, before hauling her on board. The Crab began to vibrate with such force that a thunderous knocking echoed through the steelwork. Hassan jumped toward the hatchway, which was now some distance above his head. He misjudged and fell back.

Spiro yelled, "Again! Jump higher."

Hassan shrugged off the dead weight of his backpack. He jumped once more, his hand swimming forward through thin air. Dan caught his wrist. Hassan's free arm frantically waved above his head. Gen grabbed his forearm. Dan nodded at Gen.

"Count of three. One, two, three. Pull!"

Panting, his shoulders hurting so much he'd swear that tendons were ripping free of their anchor points on bone, he and Gen heaved. Inch by inch, they dragged the big man onboard.

By now, ten or more ground crew had decided to board the Crab. Most, however, couldn't jump high enough. Then some did the craziest thing of all. Because they couldn't reach the hatchway, they climbed up a latticework of metal that ran up the flank of the Crab. One, two, three, four men and women had begun to scale the latticework as if it was a ladder. Grim-faced, they clung tight with both hands to metal struts that formed a criss-cross structure. They pushed their boots deep into the recesses, hanging on for their lives.

One guy succeeded in reaching the open hatchway.

"Pull me in!" he cried. "Pull me in! Please, I don't want to die."

Dan and Spiro grabbed a hand each. They hauled him inward. Within a moment, his arms were fully in the cabin, then head, then the upper part of his torso.

He shrieked, "Pull, you fucking useless bastards. Get me inside!"

Nobody operated any controls that Dan could see. However, that was the moment the hatch slammed shut with huge force.

Suddenly, pulling the guy was easy because the hatch had cut through his torso, just beneath his ribs. The man's eyes became glistening disks of horror as he jerked his head downward to see that he'd been neatly cut in half. The bottom half of his body was already falling toward the ground. His top half slid along the floor—and like a slug leaves a trail, so did the open wound beneath his ribs. Though this was no silver streak. This was red—a crimson trail of his lifeblood.

The man gurgled—a thick, wet sound. With surprising force, he yelled, "Oh, God!"

Then what remained of his body convulsed; his jaws champed—a reflex action—they champed hard enough to sever his tongue, which slipped (a pink pellet of an object) from his lips and onto the floor. Then his eyes drifted out of focus as his heart stopped beating.

Despite the gruesome spectacle, most people didn't even look at that half-man horror on the floor. They'd clustered up to the windows where they pointed out at the men and women that gripped the lattice structure. Dan went to the window. The Rib, carrying the Crab, had begun to accelerate vertically at such a speed the vast body of the Rib created a vacuum, which sucked the people that had been on the ground up with it for a distance of a hundred feet or so before the suction weakened enough for them to fall back to Earth—a lethal distance.

The men and women on the latticework moved their mouths, apparently yelling for help. Their expressions bled sheer terror. Their eyes blazed with panic. Abruptly, the Rib accelerated to an even greater velocity. There was no sensation of travelling at high speed in the Crab. All was eerily quiet. Yet the ground fell away, roads became grey lines running through green swamp. Buildings at the space port were little silvery boxes, mere children's toys at this altitude.

Outside on the lattice, it must have become a maelstrom of agony. The slipstream was so fierce that one of the men was peeled away from his handholds. He went whirling away into a terminal death fall. A second later, a woman followed—her hair was billowing, a pennant of shining yellow.

The Crab, gripping tight to the disfigured underbelly of the Rib, ascended through cloud. The murk instantly obliterated any view of the doomed people clinging to the metalwork. Five seconds later, the Crab emerged into brilliant sunshine, the sky was darkening from pale blue to dark blue as the altitude increased at breath-taking speed.

Dan saw that one woman remained clinging to the lattice.

Hassan began punching a button at the side of the hatch, but the lock mechanism didn't respond. "Open it up! Let her in!"

N'Darbi gripped his shoulder. "The hatch can't be opened manually. Even if it could, we'd all be killed."

The woman outside curled her body around the latticework. Her eyes fixed on the faces of the people who looked out through the glass. Nothing could be done to save her.

Dan knew that she should not die alone. He realized he was duty-bound to be there for her in her last few seconds of life. She clung on. Even when she became terrible to look at.

People in the cabin gasped. They pressed their hands to their mouths in shock as they watched the ghastly effect of the thousand-mile-per-hour slipstream was having on her body.

And on her face. The savagery of the airflow began to remove her nose and then her lips from her skull. As simple and as brutal as that. Then the slipstream ripped away her face, leaving bare bone, from which drops of blood flew at such a speed they were just blurry specks. Her eyes blazed into Dan's eyes. He remembered the way Shaz had looked back at him when she'd fallen to her death as the building had collapsed. Out there, the woman's eyes bulged from her skull—two balls of glistening gel. Then, mercifully for her, mercifully for everyone, she suddenly released her grip on the latticework and the rush of air swept her away, and out of sight.

After that, there was silence, which was eventually broken by the sound of men and women as they began to softly weep.

TEN

THE CORPSE IN THE DRIVER'S SEAT

Beyond the windows, the sky turned from deep blue to black. The men and women who'd trained for the mission began to lie down on foam mattresses that were fixed to the floor. Quickly, they buckled the restraining straps across their bodies.

The air smelt of swamp mud—a portion of the atmosphere above that waterlogged land had been captured when the hatch doors had shut with explosive speed.

N'Darbi had buckled restraints onto the top half of the cadaver. The raw opening at the bottom of the chest, where the hatch had sliced through, was an awful thing to see. Dan, though he tried not to, saw plenty of gruesome details. The pale nub of the spine poking through what resembled a mass of raw beef, the sagging blue bag that was a lung, prolapsing through the wound. The pale tube of an artery. N'Darbi tugged a blanket up and under the restraining straps to conceal the grim relic of dead flesh and bone.

A few of the astronauts helped the accidental travellers, telling them to lie down on the foam mattresses before strapping them in.

Already, the Crab had begun lurching as it rose with the Rib, high above the Earth.

Spiro chose a mattress beside where Dan was buckling himself in.

Meanwhile, a woman in a hi-viz vest, marking her out as ground crew, followed Spiro's instructions.

"Secure the straps over your legs," he told her, "then lie down and fasten the straps over your chest. The ride's going to get bumpy, isn't that right, Dan?"

Dan nodded. "We've not hit the zone yet where we experience g-force, but it will come."

Within three minutes, everyone had strapped themselves in, so that they now occupied long lines of mattresses. Most gazed up at the peculiar arrangement of tables, chairs and other items of furniture, fixed to the cabin ceiling. Dan counted thirty men and women in the cabin—an area that would become a lounge area during the flight. Far off, came the sound of pounding again—as if a huge fist slammed into a metal slab. A pounding that had an after note of a chime that slowly decayed on the air, which smelt so strongly of mud and of wild creatures that lay rotting in that oozing mass of the swamp. Some ground crew began to complain that the straps were too tight, and they didn't see the reason why they had to be restrained in that way.

The complaints stopped when the floor convulsed beneath them. For a second, an upward force tried to hurl everyone to the ceiling. A second later, the force switched to a downward pressure—a huge pressure at that, as g-force slammed everyone back down so violently there was a loud "*Uph!*" sound as breath was knocked from lungs.

Dan grimaced. The weight on his chest was immense—this was a result of the Rib accelerating to a huge speed, carrying its parasitic Crab with it, which consisted of a pod that held a few dozen people in an oval-shaped structure that contained communal areas, cabins, passageways, food stores, tanks of drinking water, fuel cells and the precious machines that would provide the very air that they would breathe for the duration of their expedition.

As Dan lay there, the pressure eased gradually. The sky beyond the window was dark. Not a trace of stars, nor even a glimpse of the Earth as it undoubtedly became a sphere in the sky. He wanted to see the Earth because the darkness beyond the window had become frightening in its intensity. It spoke of a vast emptiness where a human being could die in a split-second.

Dan found himself remembering a recurring dream that he'd experienced in his early teens. Night after night, he would dream that he stood looking at a car in a dark street. For some reason, a rotting corpse sat in the driver's seat, its clawed hands gripping the steering wheel; its dead face was turned toward Dan, patiently waiting for him to reach a decision. Even though he was revolted and terrified by the corpse, which stared at him with bulbous eyes that were entirely white in color, he would climb into the passenger seat, close the door.

The corpse would start the engine and then steer the car away along the road, accelerating steadily until buildings flashed by in a blur. Dan knew the corpse drove him away from what had become an unpleasant home life, ever since his mother had lost her job when the factory she worked at went bust. When the teenage Dan was awake, life had become a nightmare. He'd been forced to go to a different school, which he hated, because the kids mocked his accent. They'd gang up and throw punches at him for the most ridiculous of reasons. "We don't like the color of your shoelaces." Bang! "Your hair smells disgusting." Bang! "Your mother is a whore!" Bang! Fists would smack into his mouth and into his nose on a weekly basis.

To obliterate his misery, he once drank vodka he'd found in a cupboard at home and made himself so sick that his mother had to rush him to hospital. He still recalled how her eyes bled shock and remorse as medical staff pumped the vodka out of his stomach.

A day after his trip to the hospital, he was once again walking into the valley of death that was his school. "Karlton, why do you wear such a stupid shirt?" Bang! "My dad says he saw your mother bare-assed in a drug-dealer's car!" Bang! Bang! His nose got bloody once more. His bruised eyes would swell until they shut.

So, when he dreamt about the corpse in the driver's seat, he quickly reached the right decision during the witching hour as he slept. He gratefully climbed into the car. Smiled at the corpse, and old Billy Dead Bones (as Dan came to call his macabre chauffeur) would drive him away from high school hell.

The metalwork of the Crab made deep groaning sounds as if in terrible pain. The stresses of acceleration were immense. He gazed up at the metal ceiling. Just for a moment, (as if he'd developed X-Ray eyes) he almost believed he could see through the metal, and then through the outer shell of the Rib, and into the midnight dark heart of its infinitely mysterious core.

And sitting there, looking back at him, was the corpse in the driver's seat. The grim figure had returned. Old Billy Dead Bones. And Billy was steering the Rib into the deadly vastness of space. At that moment, the corpse nodded back at Dan Karlton, acknowledging that the adult Dan had made the right decision. It was time to make that final journey into endless night.

Dan realized he was dreaming again. That he'd fallen asleep on the mattress. He sensed that the corpse in the driving seat was taking him on a journey to a remarkable destination. Perhaps it was at this destination where he'd discover his fate or his destiny. But the final destination was, indeed, coming—and his dreaming self, hoped he would be ready for what he'd find there.

ELEVEN

S-CAVE

Forty-eight hours after take-off, and already a routine had established itself on the Crab for its passengers. Ten of those passengers had been unwilling ones. They'd been ground crew who'd been forced to board the vessel—either that or face certain death when the Rib began its ascent. The suction was created when the massive object moved skyward and was powerful enough to carry anyone in the vicinity upward for several dozen feet before dumping them fatally back to Earth.

All but one of the ground crew had blood types other than AB plus. Their blood couldn't absorb sufficient oxygen, due to some inexplicable effect of the Rib. Those individuals had quickly lapsed into a coma, their lips were turning blue as the oxygen depleted in their bloodstream. Dan had helped Spiro get the affected people onto bunks. Thereafter, Spiro had strapped masks to their faces, which supplied pure oxygen to the corpse-like figures. Though they didn't fully recover consciousness, their breathing became more relaxed. The blue tints left their lips, indicating that oxygen levels had risen in their bloodstream. Most could answer basic questions, such as "Are you feeling comfortable?" or "Do you feel any pain?" with grunts, and a shake or nod of a head.

N'Darbi was one of the people stricken by the effects of de-oxygenated blood. As Dan had pulled a blanket up to her chin, she had reached up to grip his wrist, then pulled him closer.

Dragging aside her oxygen mask, she whispered, "Mr. Karlton …"

"Call me Dan."

She nodded. "Dan. Lovely Dan. Lovely trustworthy Dan."

He smiled back at her, thinking that the lack of oxygen had made her woozy.

"Dan." Her grip tightened on his wrist. "Dan. You are trustworthy. I'm sure of it. But there are people onboard who I … who I don't trust. Not … at …" Her chest began to rise and fall in an exaggerated way as she fought to suck enough air into her lungs.

Dan placed the oxygen mask over her mouth again. She took several deep breaths, pulled the mask aside, and whispered in a way that was so grave shivers trickled down his spine, like drops of ice-cold water were crawling down his back.

"I won't be functional for a few days," she whispered. "Not until we reach Callisto. So, I won't be able to protect you and those in the crew who sincerely wish to complete this mission and save all those … all those people on Earth from the big asteroid that will, inevitably, strike our planet." She was becoming breathless again, her lips tightening as she sucked in huge quantities of air. "Dan, there are bad people onboard. I can't … can't identify them, because … I don't know who they are. But intercepts reveal there are spies … saboteurs. Evil people … So, be very careful. Always be vigilant. Don't trust someone just because they smile and are nice to you.…" Her voice slurred as her brain became starved of oxygen. "Be vigilant. We are in danger here. From … snakes in the grass …" She gave a drunken-sounding chuckle. "Also … you weren't warned about a strange talent of the Ribs… there is something within them that can look into your mind. Whatever they see inside your head, they have the power to make real. Beware of your own thoughts, Dan. The Rib can turn them into reality. Those funny thoughts that you think are private and yours alone might well end up sneaking up behind you to tap you … on the … shoulder.…"

"Miss N'Darbi. I don't understand. What do you mean? How can they make our thoughts become real? Miss N'Darbi ... can you hear me?"

"Problem, Dan?"

Dan glanced back, seeing Spiro standing at the cabin door. "Uh, Miss N'Darbi keeps pulling the mask off."

"I'll apply a sedative patch. She'll sleep then."

Spiro stepped into the cabin. He quickly repositioned the mask over her face before tightening the straps. He stared down at her thoughtfully for a moment. Her breathing gradually became regular once more.

Dan said, "She's fallen asleep. She should be all right now."

"I'll still apply a sedative patch. It might be dangerous if she paws off the mask when there's nobody here." Spiro paused for a moment. "What was she telling you, Dan? I heard her say something about your thoughts becoming real."

Dan shrugged. "If you ask me, the low oxygen levels were causing her to hallucinate. That can happen, can't it? Not enough oxygen reaching the brain can lead to someone not able to tell the difference between dreams and reality?"

"Sure, it can." Spiro raised N'Darbi's closed eyelid to check her pupil. "Ah, our patient's doing okay. I'll go get the patch, then she's guaranteed a nice, long sleep."

"Spiro."

"Hmm?"

Dan had planned to tell Spiro about N'Darbi's warning about spies and saboteurs, though a sudden instinct for caution stopped him dead.

Spiro's brown eyes fixed on Dan's face. "You were going to tell me something important, weren't you?"

"Yes." For a moment, he desperately clutched for alternative subjects. Then he smiled. "The good news is that N'Darbi and other non-ABs will recover when the Rib lands on Callisto. Apparently, their blood oxygen levels will then return to normal. But then you probably already knew that, didn't you?"

"Indeed I did, but good news like that is worth repeating." Spiro's warm smile was a broad one as he patted Dan on the shoulder. "Uh, I've another piece of good news. Cookie's bringing fresh donuts into the lounge at one. Best get there in plenty of time before they're all gone."

Dan never did get his fresh donut. Instead, he received an order from the captain that was far from pleasant.

As he was heading to the lounge, Captain Flynn poked her head out through her office door. Flynn had already been on board the Crab several hours before its departure, so Dan and his crewmates didn't even know who their captain was, let alone meeting her before being hurled out into the depths of space.

Captain Flynn was aged about sixty. She wore a pale blue all-in-one jumpsuit, which served as her uniform. Her rank was printed in gold letters across her back. There was a line of medal ribbons stitched to the uniform above her breast pocket. Evidently, Flynn had been in a branch of the U.S. military—other than that, he knew very little about her. Apart from her habit, that is, of calling people "soldier," whether they'd ever worn a uniform or not.

"Hey, soldier." That was how she addressed Dan as he walked along the corridor.

"Yes, Captain?" he answered.

She stepped out of the cabin. Her long hair was iron-gray in color. It had been plaited into a thick cable that hung down her back, as far as her knees: something which prompted several crew members to snigger and call her Rapunzel behind her back.

Flynn spoke briskly: "You're the structural engineer?"

"Yes, Captain."

"It was explained to you that you'd be on S-Cave duty."

"S-Cave? Sorry, I don't think ..." Dan shrugged in bewilderment.

"Typical." Captain Flynn scowled. "Sadly, your training, and that of your comrades, has been rushed to the point of negligent inadequacy. I'm not blaming you, soldier. However, I'm concerned that the decidedly rudimentary training program you underwent could be dangerous for everyone. Alas, too late to remedy that now. So ... the S-Cave."

Dan felt his heart sink as he suspected that bad news lay ahead. "If you don't mind me asking, Captain. Where is the S-Cave?"

Silly question. Dan Karlton had no sooner asked, "Where is the S-Cave?" when he guessed the answer before Captain Flynn could tell him.

In this instance, leaving the Crab fifty million miles from Earth did not require Dan Karlton to don his spacesuit. A flexible hose, which was big enough to accommodate a steel ladder, extended from the Crab for a distance of thirty feet, until the other end of the hose entered the S-Cave that, in turn, penetrated the interior of the Rib. There were fissures, gullies, craters, and pockmarks galore on the underside of the Rib, yet only one of those features formed what could be described as a cave.

Dan had covered the basics of space travel during what had been a distinctly hurried training course to become an astronaut. And he'd discovered that other astronauts, who crewed the space stations, referred to individuals that would specifically travel in the Crabs as Rib Rats. A term that was generally acknowledged to be nothing less than mockery by the people who considered themselves to be bona fide astronauts, and who dismissed the Rib Rats as poorly trained buccaneer characters, who had shamelessly grabbed the opportunity to earn huge salaries with minimal effort.

Dan, however, in his heart of hearts, truly believed in the mission to Callisto. If there was a one in a million chance that they could repair some alien gizmo that manipulated gravity within the Jovian system, which would prevent asteroids crashing into the Earth, then he'd give it his best shot. He only had to close his eyes ... and he was back in the office building again, its floor sagging beneath his feet, walls collapsing, clouds of dust billowing: and there was always Shaz in the centre of his memory—her eyes becoming twin pools of terror as she nearly—very nearly—grabbed his hand before slipping from him, then plunging down toward-

"You okay, soldier?"

"I'm fine, thank you, Captain Flynn."

"You look a bit peaky, like you feel nauseous."

"Just nerves," he said. "I'll be okay."

Dan stood in the airlock—that strange limbo zone between the air conditioned safety of the Crab and the deadly vacuum of outer space. Flynn's life-size head and shoulder image filled a screen on the inner airlock wall.

Flynn said, "I regret your additional duties weren't explained to you. That you'd be required to visit the S-Cave every forty-eight hours to check for new anomalies within the structure. Don't worry. Air quality and oxygen levels are checked automatically. Ambient temperature is equal to that of the Crab's interior."

Dan nodded. "I understand. I'm ready to make the checks as soon as you open the airlock door."

"Opening the hatch now."

He heard a click, then the hiss of hydraulics as a hatch opened inward.

Flynn continued in calm tones: "You'll see handholds in the wall of the airlock. Use those to climb into the connecting flex-tunnel. Then use the ladder to access the Rib and the cave. There are no windows in the tunnel. What you will see is the expansion ring at the end of the tunnel that locks it in place inside the cave. There are instruments in the cave, placed there by our scientists, to monitor the environment: constantly checking for any changes in temperature, integrity of the structure, appearance of biological matter and so forth. Okay ... ready when you are, Dan. Safe journey."

"Thank you, Captain."

Dan used recesses in the wall to climb down and out through the hatch into the flex-tunnel, which was pretty much like entering an inflated balloon—albeit a balloon that was long and thin—he determined the tunnel to have a diameter of no more than five feet.

Quickly, he descended the ladder, which was a rigid structure. The climb of forty feet was strenuous enough to set his heart pounding. Meanwhile, the bag on his back clunked against his spine; the strap over his shoulder began to chafe until the tender skin became sore. Gravity was the same as that of the Earth's. At that moment, he wished the Rib would dial down the G to allow him to float down the inside of this damn sausage.

And what about micrometeorites? It would only take one the size of an apple seed, traveling at fifty thousand miles an hour, to puncture this flimsy sheath. Hell, come to that, the micrometeorite could blast right through his skull in a nanosecond, spraying his brains all over the wall.

"Fuck," he muttered. "Fuck, fuck, fuck. Don't think about stuff like that."

But he did think about the potential threat of tiny pieces of stone slamming through this absurdly flimsy tube—gruesome images of splinters of rock blasting holes through his eyes, face, throat, torso, genitals, hands, gut, had neatly ignited his imagination—and those images accelerated his movements until he scrambled down the ladder.

Moments later, the walls turned from white to very dark red. Freestanding lamps illuminated the cave. He reached out ... touched the red surface with his bare fingers... his fingertips were now touching the 'meat' of the Rib ... with explosive speed, he flinched back.

Just the action of pressing his skin against the alien substance of the Rib was enough to jangle his nerves to the point his heart felt as if it would explode. Touching the Rib was nothing less than visceral. As powerful an experience as thrusting his fingers into the wet belly of a man ten weeks dead—a rotting monstrosity. Dan pressed his hand to his mouth. His entire body shook. Thoughts rampaged through his head in a way that was utterly irrational and utterly violent. His own brain was thrusting wild scenarios through his head.

Hands will erupt from the wall. Drag me in.

A terrible face will flash from the shadows.

I'll die alone in this cave. Flynn tricked me. I shouldn't be in here. N'Darbi warned me about evil players ... this is Flynn's way of murdering me....

Dan saw himself there in the cave, which formed an undulating gut that ran through the body of the Rib. Moreover, he saw himself as a poor wretch of a man … one so frightened his face had become an animal snarl. Then his knees were buckling until he crouched in the middle of the cave, with one hand pressed against his mouth.

"My fingers … I'm touching my mouth … and I've just touched the wall."

He spat so loudly the sound went echoing through the cave, distorting and mutating into something that became a thunderous hog-like grunt—the echoes continued for way, way too long before transmuting into a long, drawn-out hiss that hovered on the still air before it slowly died.

Dan reached into his pocket, dragged out a wad of tissue, then he rubbed his lips so hard that blood filled his mouth. The blood smeared his tongue: he could taste it—a bitter tang as if the flavor of the stuff that flowed in his veins was mutating in this alien environment.

He found himself imagining that he floated in space, some distance from the Rib, and he was looking back at the alien craft, with the silvery Crab fixed underneath. Then he imagined he could see through the substance of the Rib, gazing right inside the thing. He saw the worm-like shape of the S-Cave. He saw himself crouching inside the cavity that penetrated the Rib. He'd become a parasite inside the gut of the monster. It was Dan Karlton that had become the loathsome thing. A nasty, nasty germ that must be expelled from a perfect machine.

A hand made of shadow touched his shoulder. With a yell, he clawed at the hand.

There was nothing there beneath his fingers, other than his own shoulder. Dan closed his eyes. He forced himself to breathe in a controlled way. Deeply inhale. Hold until the count of three.

One. Two. Three. Then slowly exhale. He knew he must marshal his thoughts. Because should he lose control, then death would find him quickly. All too often, soldiers in battle died when panic overwhelmed them. Sailors in storms were the first to lose their lives when fear stifled their ability to make the right decisions.

"Do your duty," he told himself. "Be professional. Be methodical. Doing your work will stop you being frightened." He took a deep breath. "After all, you are only being frightened by what you have imagined while you've been in here."

Nevertheless, he recalled N'Darbi's words about the Rib having the ability to turn thought into reality. He bit his lip hard enough for the pain to override mental images of blood-red tentacles snaking from the walls to wrap their loathsome flesh around his throat.

"Work." He stood up. "Firstly, measure the width and height of the cave, where markers designate specific measurement points."

Quickly, he pulled a laser measure from his bag. That done, he moved along the cave, which gently turned to the left as part of its S-shape configuration. Freestanding markers on small tripods indicated where he should measure. Now, with brisk efficiency, channelling twenty years' service as a structural engineer, he made the measurements. Height. Width.

He pulled a tablet from the bag, then checked the table of figures onscreen. "Height unchanged. Width unchanged."

But did scientists expect that the rock-solid cave might expand or contract? Evidently, they did. Hence his mission here today. He took photographs of the walls at specific locations—the photographs would be compared with ones taken on a regular basis since the cave had first been explored. Forensic examination of the images would determine if any changes to texture, color and so on had occurred. Moving with brisk confidence now, Dan Karlton walked along the S-Cave, following its curves until he reached the end of the cave, which, according to the record, was precisely one hundred and eighteen feet from start to finish.

The cave ended in a clot of solid gold. Possibly, the cavity had been much longer. However, molten gold had, at some point long ago, flowed in and blocked the passageway. And though gold is a famously soft metal, this substance defied all attempts by engineers to bore into it, melt it, or even scrape away a few atoms for analysis.

Dan stared at the plug of glittering yellow that prevented him from moving deeper into the gut of the Rib. He reached out. Touched it. Then he closed his eyes. His heart pounded, thrusting blood through his body ... blood which was turning darker, as death prematurely congealed that vital fluid ... the fingers touching the gold were stinging as if hot needles were driven into the flesh. A sharp pain tore through his forehead. His stomach muscles clenched so fiercely that he grunted.

He opened his eyes and he saw shadows pouring out from the walls.

"No." He pulled his hand away from the golden barrier. "I won't let you poison my mind." He took a deep breath, then shouted: "Do you hear me? My name is Daniel Karlton. You will not use my own thoughts to erode the human being that I am!"

Dan shoved the laser measurer and tablet into the bag. After that, he marched back through the cave to the ladder that led through the flex-tunnel. Eight minutes later, he stood in the airlock, listening to the whisper of air as valves made the slight adjustment in air pressure between the cave and the Crab. His ears popped and he opened his jaw wide in a pretend yawn. His ears popped again and felt normal, no discomfort.

Captain Flynn's face appeared onscreen to his left. "Everything go okay, solider?"

"Fine." He smiled. "No problems, whatsoever."

"Some people find the S-Cave unsettling. Several have even compared the cave to a haunted house. That they sense a hostile presence there."

Dan's smile became even broader. "I didn't notice anything unusual. All readings are exactly the same as last time."

Dan knew that he must not show any sign that he'd been frightened. If he did, the other crew members would be sympathetic toward him—however, they'd also stop trusting him to be even remotely reliable. When the door opened, allowing him to leave the no man's land of the airlock, and to re-enter the Crab, he found Spiro waiting in the corridor for him.

"I wanted to tell you in person," Spiro said. "Two of the non-ABs have died. One was ground crew. The other was Miss N'Darbi. They must have pulled off their oxygen masks."

TWELVE

SPACE DAYS

One thing is true: life demands routine. Meals eaten at the same times. Go to sleep at the same time for the same number of hours. Human beings impose a rhythm on their lives. Timetables. Schedules. Procedure. All part of the *Homo sapiens* instinct to create order out of chaos.

These thoughts flowed through Dan Karlton's head as he helped himself to breakfast from the buffet that Cookie had set out in the canteen. Spiro waved to him from the table they habitually favored—the one against the window. For all they could see through the window, they might have been gazing out at a wall that had been painted black. Experts speculated that these alien craft possessed a dark aura—a kind of halo of shadow that blocked any view of the stars. Dan still hadn't even snatched a glimpse of the Earth as the Rib carried them through the Solar System. Come to that, the sun only revealed itself as a smudge of light far, far away. Also, the shadow halo blocked all radio signals. The folk in the crab couldn't speak to Mission Control, and Mission Control was effectively on mute.

Dan sat down with his breakfast roll—this comprised a large pancake that neatly parceled chopped fried eggs, sausage, potato and mushrooms. It tasted good. So good, in fact, that he devoured this delicious, buttery-yellow parcel every morning.

Spiro said, "I've booked us into the gym for the eleven to twelve slot."

Dan nodded. "Cheers. I'm back on the weights today. Maybe try and firm up some arm muscle."

Spiro buttered a slice of toast. "Pub quiz starts at twenty hundred hours. They've got the usual silly prizes."

"If you want the voucher I won for a head massage, it's yours—gratis."

Spiro chuckled. "I'll pass on that, thanks. Hey, Dan, while I remember, I found squash rackets and balls in the aft cargo bay. There's space there for a game, if you want to give it a try later?"

"Sure. I could do with some real exercise." Dan lifted the wrap to his mouth, took a bite. Paprika tingled across his tongue. "Hmm. Cookie is getting even better at making these."

"Did you know that Cookie is actually a member of the ground crew that jumped onboard as we were lifting off? By sheer chance, he's an AB plusser like us."

A thought occurred to Dan. "What were you doing in the aft cargo bay? There are no medical supplies kept there."

"There are chemicals, though." Spiro grimaced as if his toast had suddenly become bitter in his mouth. "Specifically, formaldehyde, which preserves ..." He grimaced again.

"Flesh." Dan nodded.

"Initially, I thought that N'Darbi and the other guy who died—his name is ... was ... Schwab ... well, I thought they'd get a space burial. You know, glide them out through one of the airlocks. Which happened to the guy who was cut in half by the hatch."

"That's what I'd heard."

"Change of plan. Captain Flynn decided we're going to keep the bodies and bring them back to Earth."

"So you're preserving them in formaldehyde?"

"Yep, both bodies are soaking in the same bath in one of the spare cabins on B deck."

The image of two corpses floating in clear liquid in a bathtub was so strong in Dan's mind that he put the breakfast roll down on his plate. Suddenly, the juicy filling didn't seem so appealing.

"It gets worse, my friend." Spiro's expression revealed he had some bad news to deliver. "After the two corpses have been steeped in that witch's brew for the rest of today, I have to haul them out, dress them—to maintain proper dignity of the deceased—then Cookie is going to use his gear in the galley to shrink-wrap the bodies in plastic. After that, we must somehow drag them through that pipe you use to reach the Rib."

"What? You're going to store bodies in the S-Cave?"

"Yep. The captain is adamant that the Crab doesn't become a morgue."

The routine continued. Dan shaved. He stuffed clothes that needed washing into a laundry sack that bore his name. So often at these times, he'd find himself thinking, *Here we are, flying through space, and we still do the same mundane chores we do on Earth.* The morning shave. Sorting laundry. Hunting for the rogue sock that's vanished—the rogue sock often turning up in the sleeve of a sweatshirt, or in the folds of the bedding on his bunk. And then there was the eternally recurring human habit of gossip. He encountered another gossipmonger when he went to the storeroom to collect a new razor. A man by the name of Garner was there. He was a tall guy with a head that had become completely bald at the top, leaving a ring of black hair around his skull, so that he resembled one of those monks from the time of yore: the kind with a tonsure shaved into their scalp. As usual, Garner wore spectacles with dark blue lenses that gave him the air of being a villain from a movie.

As Dan searched the shelves, hunting for a box that contained packs of wet-shave razors, Garner did the conspiratorial thing of looking over his shoulder at the open doorway that led into the passageway.

"Dan, did you hear about Mahoud and Sinita? They're now sharing the same cabin. Kelly says that the noises that come through the wall from their cabin into hers have to be heard to be believed. All night, every night. It's a wonder they can stay awake during the day."

"No, I hadn't heard." Dan found the box of razors.

"And the scientist we have onboard. Did you know that he's a botanist?"

"No."

"Why do we need a scientist that specializes in plants?"

"The Caucus must have chosen him for a reason."

"Do you think they're expecting us to build a settlement on Callisto? With fields and crops and stuff?"

Dan shrugged. "Maybe earlier expeditions revealed evidence of plant life."

Garner went on to detail the crew's discontent that a botanist had been chosen over what they considered to be a useful branch of science, such as physics or electronics—a discipline that might result in the gravity machine being fixed. Then Garner had a surprise in store for Dan. Suddenly, he grinned and whispered in salacious tones: "And you should know something else. Something that affects you, Danny Boy."

"Uh?"

"Captain Flynn. She's taken a liking to you."

"What?"

Dan stared at Garner in astonishment. The man's eyes were concealed behind blue-tinted glass, so Dan couldn't tell if Garner was being serious, or if he was taking the piss.

"Yes, Danny Boy, that's what everyone's saying. What? Don't say you hadn't picked up on the way she takes hold of that big fat wodge of hair of hers when she talks to you and begins stroking her fingers along it? Danny, when she talks to you and strokes the plait she is symbolically stroking your—"

"Okay, Garner. I get it."

"Word is that you are a fortunate boy. Flynn treats you like a favorite. Just don't forget your friends when she instals you into her deluxe cabin. They say that it has a glass roof, so you can gaze up, after making sweet-sweet love, to gaze at the stars."

"Now, you are taking the piss." Dan bluntly changed the subject. "Whoever organized this storeroom did a crap job. Where's the shaving foam? I've been using ordinary soap ever since we've been on this tub."

"Stocking the Crab for the trip was chaotic, to say the least. We're fortunate there is enough food. If we'd taken off before they'd got the nosh onboard, we'd have starved. The Crab would have returned to Earth full of skeletons. Ah, there's the shaving foam. In the white carton by the loo rolls. Thank Heaven, they remembered the loo rolls. Oh, did you know about Geraldine?"

Dan listened politely to a tale of a banal love triangle. Because he knew that if crew members stopped being polite to one another the rot of poor morale would soon set in. One thing they didn't need, umpteen million miles from Earth, was for discontent to descend into internecine strife.

THIRTEEN

OH, SEDITION … YOU POISONER OF CIVILIZATION

Later that day, Dan realized that not only could poor morale be dangerous on the Crab: sedition was, too. And now he experienced the perfect example. Certain individuals believed that anonymous men and women had murdered N'Darbi and Schwab, and that a replacement captain should be installed. That kind of talk was absolutely toxic in this enclosed society on a vessel speeding through interplanetary space.

Dan had been helping Spiro, by going from cabin to cabin where the ground crew, those who didn't have the necessary AB positive blood group, lay comatose in the bunks, where they were fed oxygen twenty-four hours a day to prevent them from dying as N'Darbi and Schwab had done—their heart muscle had fatally deteriorated for want of sufficient oxygen.

Dan entered the cabins on the right-hand side of the corridor, Spiro those on the left. Dan checked that the oxygen masks were snugly in place. He also did a visible check to ensure that chests steadily rose and fell with no sign of panting or any indication of respiratory distress. Each patient wore a wristband with a small screen that revealed their pulse rate. This wristband was paired with the vessel's onboard computer that would signal an alert if the pulse became too rapid or two slow. All the pulse rates ranged between a safe beat of between fifty and seventy a minute. Spiro had also instructed Dan to check for any sign of vomiting. Fortunately, everything appeared as it should. Some of the patients were linked intravenously to saline. Spiro would also check catheters and waste bags. Dan's last patient was Gen, the ground crew boss, the woman who'd clearly used whisky to keep the horrors of the Rib at bay. The woman lay there, the coma softening her face into something that could be described as serene. All her facial muscles were perfectly relaxed now that her worries lay submerged in an ocean of sleep. He repositioned the mask slightly where it had slipped down her face a little. Then checked the pulse reading. Fifty-five—AOK.

"Will she be the next to die?"

Dan turned, on hearing the female voice.

"Katrina? Looking for Spiro?"

Katrina stared in through the cabin doorway at him.

"I'm looking for you," she said.

"Oh?"

"N'Darbi and Schwab died because their oxygen masks were removed, leaving them to suffocate."

"The masks weren't removed, Katrina. Not deliberately, anyhow." He gently smoothed the hair away from Gen's face, ensuring that no strands had gotten under the mask to impair the seal and let cabin air to enter, rather than pure oxygen.

Katrina stepped into the cabin—she closed the door behind her, an action that told Dan that she wanted to speak in private.

She said: "N'Darbi was murdered, because she knew that the first crewed mission to Callisto returned without the crew."

"Everyone saw the crew leave the Crab after it landed."

"They used actors. Hassan discovered that some of the so-called crew didn't even have AB-plus blood."

"You already told me that when we were on the truck, heading to the Rib."

"Don't you believe what I'm telling you?"

"Honestly, Katrina, all I can say is, that like nearly everyone else on

Earth, I saw it on television—the astronauts coming out of the Crab, waving to the cameras, then they were bussed away to the quarantine centre."

"Before N'Darbi became unconscious, she confided in someone on this ship that the previous crew had been stranded on Callisto. And that we are a crew of expendables, trained in a rush, and sent out, just to see if we make it back to Earth."

"You're saying that we've been sent on a suicide mission?"

"As good as."

"Aren't we supposed to be finding the gravity machine that's supposed to exist? That's our mission, isn't it? Fix the machine. Restore gravity. Save the Earth."

"If you believe that, you'll believe the moon is a honking great chunk of smelly cheese."

Dan stared at Katrina. When the crew of any ship, whether it's one with sails or a spaceship, starts telling each other that their voyage is doomed, either due to the commander's negligence, or that crew members have begun murdering each other, then morale plummets and discipline will swiftly break down. Dan eased the sheet up to Gen's chin before tucking a loose flap of the fabric under the mattress, though he knew she was oblivious to his attempt to ensure her comfort.

Katrina said, "Some of us are meeting in Hassan's cabin tonight to talk about this—we need to decide on a plan of action."

"What plan of action can you take?" Dan heard the note of exasperation in his voice. "Nobody is steering the Rib. Nobody human anyway. We can't decide to turn around and go home. The course of this thing is pre-set. Our destination is Callisto. That's the bottom line."

"But we can choose who is in charge."

"You're planning to get rid of Captain Flynn?"

"Shush." She put her finger to her lips. "We've got to be commanded by someone we all trust."

"Okay, who do you trust?"

"Some of us have already been talking." She gazed at Dan in such a direct way that a shiver ran down his spine. "Everyone mentions your name, Dan. We trust you."

Katrina suddenly opened the door. She'd delivered the message that she'd needed to impart, now she wanted to leave. Perhaps before he could protest against what, to him, was an exceedingly dangerous (and irrational) plan to stage some kind of mutiny and instal him as captain.

Dan lunged forward, grabbing her wrist. "Wait."

"Dan, I'm in a hurry. I need to help out with a stock-check ... there isn't as much food in the stores as we thought."

"I need to ask you something."

"And I need to go—now."

"No. You said N'Darbi confided in someone that the Crab attached to Rib One came back to Earth empty. Who did she tell?"

"Isn't it obvious?"

"Not to me, it isn't. Give me their name."

"Just think who is perfectly placed to kill sleeping patients."

"Tell me."

"It's—"

Abruptly, she clamped her lips shut as a figure moved along the corridor behind her.

She shot a hard glance at Dan, then she painted a warm smile on her face as she turned to the figure. "Hello, Spiro. I'm trying to convince Dan to partner me in table tennis. Hassan has arranged a tournament."

"Table tennis?" Spiro caused his eyebrows to rise in a theatrical way, as if to say, Who are you kidding?.

In a flustered sort of way, Katrina said her goodbyes before rushing away.

Spiro winked. "You and Katrina? Oh, my friend, I didn't see that romance coming. Everyone was saying that you and Captain Flynn were getting to grapple beneath the covers."

Dan laughed. "You heard the rumor, too? Why am I the only one who never heard the rumor that Flynn is getting all dewy-eyed over me?"

Spiro put his arm around Dan's shoulders. "If you want any advice about the art of love, just you ask your Uncle Spiro."

Spiro was still laughing as he left the cabin.

Dan watched the man head off to check on the next sleeper. He knew only too well the name that Katrina was about to reveal as the murderer. Dan didn't believe it for a moment. Spiro just wasn't the kind of guy to kill another human being. Even so, the seeds of suspicion had been sown. Dan switched off the cabin light, plunging Gen into a darkness that must have matched the inner darkness of her mind, down in the depths of the coma. After that, he told Spiro that the sleeping patients he had checked were well … he hoped that particular state of affairs would remain that way.

FOURTEEN

THE SHRINK-WRAPPED DEAD ...

Dan had not gone to the meeting where there was to be a secret discussion about the possibility of him replacing Flynn. Dan absolutely did not want to become captain. He'd not told anyone else about that murky conclave of conspirators. As far as he knew, the only people at the meeting were Katrina and Hassan. So, Dan pretended everything was normal. Well ... near normal. The captain had flirted with him in the canteen yesterday. Dan liked her, though he realized all too keenly that if he embraced an intimate relationship with the commander of the ship that would set him apart from the rest of the crew. Eternally in human society there is always the 'us and them' situation. If he literally climbed into bed with Captain Flynn, he would be joining the 'them' camp. And if the relationship turned sour. What then?

Dan walked along the corridor to the lounge. Most of the crew were there—they were either talking, playing cards, or drinking various kinds of liquor that had been smuggled onboard. Lately, the atmosphere had become increasingly tense. Some of the crew bore the wounds of fistfights on their faces. Conflict over sexual partners, gambling, or petty irritations erupting into all-out battle had become common lately.

Bit by bit, Dan had begun to suspect that theirs was indeed little more than a suicide mission. That the Caucus's plan was to gather up a group of misfits, desperados, and money-hungry losers, then load them onto a Rib that they knew would depart for Callisto soon, then see if that pathetic array of individuals actually returned. He knew that Katrina and Hassan believed that the real mission to fix the gravity generator, if such a thing did exist, would take place on the next flight of a Rib after Dan and his colleagues returned. If they returned.

Yes, they did have one fully qualified scientist on board, yet he had his own desperate reasons to be here. Rumor had it that he was injecting heroin on a daily basis, and the only reason he'd joined the expedition is because he'd been facing a jail sentence for a crime he'd committed (the crime wasn't known for sure, but there was plenty of whispered speculation amongst the crew). So … all in all, the motley collection of men and women that partied, gambled and fought amongst themselves didn't inspire any confidence that the mission would be even remotely successful.

As Dan walked through the lounge, Garner, the man with the blue-tinted spectacles, grabbed his arm, while gesturing at the table he sat at with a bottle of bourbon in the centre. Two more men sat at the table with him.

Garner's fingers curled around Dan's forearm. "Danny boy. Won't you join us for a drink?"

"Sorry, I've got work to do."

Garner sneered. "Work? Nobody's got work. We're just here for a ride. Do you see any of us doing any work? At any time, day or night?"

"I need to run checks in the S-Cave."

"Ah, extravehicular activity."

The other two guys laughed, and one said, "Dan's one of the good boys. He always does what he's told."

Garner smirked. "Yeah, because he's the apple of Captain Flynn's eye."

Another guy nodded. "Dan's one of her favorites. You got one of the deluxe cabins, didn't you, Dan-oh?"

"No, it's the same kind of cabin as yours."

Garner let go of Dan's arm with a shrug. "Well, you be a good boy, Danny. Run along, do your work. Make Flynn proud of you."

Dan was tempted to volley back a couple of adroitly chosen swear words, but he sensed that behind the bourbon-fuelled leg-pulling there was pent-up aggression smoldering that could, if he didn't choose his words carefully, erupt into violence.

Therefore, Dan opted for diplomacy. "It'll take me an hour to run the checks. When I'm done, I'll join you for a drink. Sound good?"

Garner smiled a boozy smile. "Sure. We got plenty of bourbon. And you can share your dirty secrets about sexy Captain Flynn."

Dan made sure his laugh sounded authentically good-natured. "Why not." Though, in truth, he didn't have secrets to share about Flynn. "Of course, you're welcome to join me in the S-Cave, if you're in the mood for a change of scene."

One of the guy's visibly shuddered. "What? Go inside that lump of alien crap? Not a chance in hell. Every time I go to sleep, I have nightmares about that thing." He picked up his glass and took a meaty slug of liquor. "Thing is, I'm sure it's putting nightmares into my skull. The things I see … just awful." He shuddered again.

Dan aimed to lighten the mood with a joke, "Okay, if I'm not back in an hour, send in the search parties."

The three men didn't laugh. It seemed to Dan that they were sinking deep into their own troubling thoughts. Dan offered them cheerful farewells, but they barely responded, other than to give a cursory nod. Just mentioning the Rib to people these days was guaranteed to submerge them into a gloomy mood. Maybe alcohol was the antidote the crew were reaching for. Though the amounts they were drinking would lead to creating more problems than it solved.

Dan headed toward the airlock. Yeah, he had nightmares, too, though he wouldn't share them with Garner and his cronies. Last night, Dan had dreamed about N'Darbi and Schwab lying in their makeshift morgue. The dream came back to him now so strongly that his blood turned cold, because that's where he was headed: to the S-Cave where the pair had been temporarily laid to rest.

Dan Karlton saw the pair the instant he entered the S-Cave. Freestanding lights on tripods illuminated the bleak scene with a light that was so cold and so bright that it triggered a needle-sharp pain above his eyes that ran deep inside his skull. The pain made him grunt.

Dan, nevertheless, pulled the laser device from his bag and began taking measurements.

However, the two objects lying side-by-side on the floor had their own morbid grip on his attention. He found he repeatedly glanced at the two corpses lying there, almost like a pair of lovers lying asleep in their bed. The harsh light revealed every dreadful feature. The man and the woman had been dressed in their uniforms. After that, they had been placed in bags made of clear plastic, then the air had been sucked out through valves near their feet, this effectively shrink-wrapping their bodies, like they were two pieces of raw meat, ready for placing on a supermarket shelf. The vacuum must have been perfect because the bag had contracted into a hard shell around the bodies. The compressive force of the plastic had distorted the faces of N'Darbi and Schwab in a horrible way, drawing back their lips into a snarl that exposed their teeth.

Though he tried not to, Dan found himself moving closer to those gruesome relics of humanity. He could see that between the plastic and the faces there was a smear of pink fluid—possibly a chemical preservative. N'Darbi's eyes were shut. One of Schwab's eyes was open, yet it was horrifically distorted by the effects of the shrink-wrap. The white of the eye had turned blood red. The pupil had expanded into the colored iris, so that it seemed a large black disk centred the eye—an eye that appeared to stare at Dan, as if the dead man knew that there was an intruder in their tomb. The effect was horrific. The pair of corpses resembled modern versions of Egyptian mummies—the same human shape bound in a tight wrapping—yet this wrapping was transparent.

"I'm sorry this happened to you both," muttered Dan, trying to release the tension building up inside of him with an apology. "You shouldn't have died. Spiro and I did our best to keep you both alive."

The eye with that terrifying heart of darkness within it stared up at Dan.

The stare forced more words from Dan's mouth. "With all my heart, I wish I could turn the clock back and make you live again."

He forced himself to look away. Methodically now, trying to use his work to distract himself from the shrink-wrapped dead, he moved deeper into the cave, where he recorded measurements at the designated points marked by free-standing signs. He used the tablet to take photographs of the cave walls for comparison with earlier photographs. The S-shaped curve of the structure meant that the two corpses were soon out of sight. Nor could he see to the end of the cave.

At that moment, he envied his crewmates in the Crab. They played cards, made love, or sipped their liquor—an idle life of pleasure. A surge of bitter fury swept through him. Why did they have it so easy? Here he was in the awful gut of the Rib. The sense of being alone in this morbid place drove cold tides of fear through his body. The harsh light made his eyes hurt. The alien monstrosity that enclosed him triggered a primordial instinct to scream and run—*to fucking run back to the Crab*. No living person belonged here. This place was hostile to human beings. A certainty took root in his brain—small at first, then swelling and swelling inside his head until he clamped his right hand to his forehead: he was convinced his skull would burst, flinging out blood, brain, and creating a Godawful fucking red mess over the walls. He closed his eyes for a moment. He could hear the ponderous thud of the pulse in his neck.

When Dan opened his eyes, he recoiled from what surrounded him. What looked like flashes of crimson lightning sped through the walls of the cave. They were so much like the stalking columns of lightning that he'd seen blazing down from the sky into the swamp. He now wondered if the Ribs, themselves, had conjured the lightning to prowl the horizon before Rib Two had lifted-off from the launch site. Dan took a deep breath. He was determined to continue his work. If he fled back to the Crab now, then he knew that fear would become his master. The notion of seeing himself as a coward was repellent to him and would redefine the image he had of himself. And that new self-image would be far from pleasant. Okay, it was an ego thing for sure—but, in his eyes, he'd become the guy who always ran away. Therefore, he walked boldly forward, intending to reach the end of the cave—there he'd make the final readings before returning to the Crab. With his courage intact.

Lightning flashed in the walls. He walked with the tablet raised to eye level, filming the apparitions, and sweeping the tablet slowly from left to right to capture those spurts of blood-red running through the structure's fabric.

He thought: *You're seeing something that nobody else has seen before. This is scientifically valuable.* There was no way of telling if the tablet's camera would capture the full strangeness of the lightning flashes, because it seemed to him that the walls of the cave had become as clear as glass, and he was seeing those bursts of red coming from a great depth within the body of the Rib. The possibility that the Rib might be a hollow shell was somehow dreadful in its own right. He found himself wondering if the Rib was something like a vast tomb rocketing through space. The image of dead things that had never breathed the air of Earth, and which now lay in their flying tomb, had a powerful effect on Dan. His muscles tensed so much that he felt them compress the soft organs inside his body. His lungs suffered from the pressure the most. He struggled for breath. His chest ached. His eyes felt as if thumbs were pressing into the sockets in such a powerful way he grunted with pain.

Then he realized what he was experiencing. In some inexplicable way, he was feeling what those two shrink-wrapped corpses back there would feel if they still had living nerves and a living brain. He had the disturbing sensation that some substance was shrinking tight around him. A powerful force compressed his body. He tried to inhale deeply, but the vicious pressure on his ribs meant he could only draw in sips of air. Green sparks flew inward through his eyes. Oxygen starvation? Had the air inside the cave become toxic? Would he be choked to death in here? Drowned by poisonous fumes leaking from the walls.

Die, Dan, die.

The pulse in his neck seemed to chant the words.

He turned the last corner in the cave.

The gold plug …

The shining mass of yellow metal that sealed the end of the cave.

It was gone.

Die, Dan, die.

"I can't breathe."

A monstrous weight descended on his chest. Crushing his heart into a small crimson pellet that didn't have the strength to pump blood through his veins—that's how it felt to him, even though the notion was utterly irrational. Yet, despite everything, he kept moving toward the part of the cave where the gold plug should be. He held up the tablet, filming everything.

Scientific evidence.

Data.

Information.

This would be useful in the right hands.

He moved beyond where the obstruction had once been and continued into a section where no human foot had trod before. Red lightning smeared the walls.

The blood-red flash revealed a seated figure. Beside that figure was an empty seat.

The empty seat was for Dan to occupy. He knew it.

He knew because here was that dream again. The dream that had haunted him in his teens—the night terror with the rotting corpse that drove the car. In the dream, he'd climb into the passenger seat, then the driver would accelerate away, taking him to who knows where. Dan moved closer to the dead driver. Rotting claws of hands gripped the steering wheel. The same dreamcatcher hung down from the rearview mirror. Dan saw the gleam of dashboard lights that illuminated a face that was rotten … wormy … a face set with two bulging eyes that were sacs of fluid. Wet lips formed a vicious snarl, revealing teeth that glinted.

The driver's waiting for me....

Now, that section of cave really did resemble the interior of a car—there was a dashboard, a steering wheel, the dreamcatcher dangling from the rearview mirror. *And Old Billy Dead Bones is waiting. All I have to do is sit beside him. And then we drive....*

But drive where?

What is the final destination?

DEATH.

Because Death is everyone's final destination.

Dan was running now. Away from the corpse driver. His heart was thudding painfully. His breath produced loud gurgling sounds in his throat. His eyes still hurt—the harshness of the light felt like knife points being pushed hard into the centre of both eyes. Even breathing had become a cruel act of torture.

He approached the shrink-wrapped corpses. The bag that contained Schwab burst open, his arms flopping out with explosive speed the instant the compressive effect of the plastic membrane was released. The pink chemical that coated the corpse sprayed out: a harsh chemical stench filled Dan's nose, and gouged into the soft tissues of his throat, making his trachea instantly sore with such an intense burning sensation that he flinched back, coughing.

Schwab sat up. His dead face was disfigured and ugly beyond belief. The head whipped around so that the single eye, which had remained open, was fixed on Dan.

Dan continued running.

However, the corpse's hand flashed out—fingers curled around Dan's ankle. They held on tight. They were an anchor of dead flesh that prevented Dan from reaching the umbilical tube that would allow him to reach the safety of the Crab. A place where men and women laughed and made love and didn't even know—and couldn't even guess—what ordeal Dan now faced. The dead hand of Schwab pulled Dan off balance, so he flopped chest down onto the cave floor.

Red lightning pulsed in the walls. There was a palpable sense of being inside the beating heart of the god of terror.

Dan yelled—a sound that mated pain and despair.

Because the dead hand gripped Dan's ankle—and slowly, and horrifically, pulled him back to where the corpse lay—its single evil eye burning with hatred as it stared at Dan.

The dead envy the living. The dead hate the living.

Those were the words that pounded through the soft, wet pulp that was Dan's brain as the dead man's head suddenly swung forward. Its bottom jaw was dropping down to create a huge, gaping mouth.

The mouth clamped onto Dan's throat. Teeth dug into soft flesh.

Agony exploded inside his head—a napalm burst of light that engulfed his mind with pain.

After that ... darkness.

FIFTEEN

AIRLOCK

Hassan's boots smacked against the floor as he ran for his life.

Men and women screamed their rage at him. When he glanced back, as he raced along the corridor, he saw faces twisted with hatred, their eyes glinted, and there was a sense of turbulent movement as the mob pursued him.

As he ran, he yelled back over his shoulder: "Listen! I was trying to save you!"

This only provoked furious yells of "Catch him!" "Don't let him get away!"

But where could he run? The Crab was an oval-shaped vessel a quarter of a mile long. Beyond its steel walls there was only cold vacuum.

Garner ran ahead of the mob. He bellowed, "You'll pay, Hassan! You're not going to get away with this!"

The end came with shocking speed. Hassan cut along a corridor to his right—only to find it blocked by angry crew members. Moments later, Garner and the bulk of the mob ran into the corridor behind Hassan.

Trapped. He turned round and around, hands out, as he implored them to listen to him. The mob closed in from both directions—they walked slowly now. Violence painted the very air—it was as if the atmosphere had become electrically charged.

Hassan tried to reason with them. "Please, listen. Yes, I was attempting to detonate the explosive bolts that hold the Crab to the Rib."

"If you'd succeeded," Garner snarled, "we'd all be dead by now."

"No, you wouldn't." Hassan tried to maintain eye-contact with as many people as possible, hoping that would be enough to discourage them from attacking him. If you face your assailant, they're less likely to assault you—that's the theory, he told himself.

Taneesha glared at him. "Hassan, why did you try and jettison the Crab? We'd have drifted in space until the air ran out."

"No, that wouldn't happen," Hassan told them. "The Crab is fitted with its own emergency propulsion system."

"Liar."

"I'm telling you the truth," he insisted. "There is a secret propulsion system and guidance program that automatically returns the Crab to Earth orbit if the Crab separates from the Rib. Okay, we are at the limits of our own technology here. The Crab's rocket motors aren't as effective as whatever powers the Rib, but we would safely return to Earth orbit in a matter of months. After that, conventional rocket-powered shuttles would ferry us back down to the planet's surface."

"You take us for fools." Garner's mouth formed a snarl as he spat out the words. "We've all undergone the same training course. They would have told us if there was an automatic system to get us back to Earth if we had to ditch the Rib."

A guy with a red beard bunched his fists, like he was ready to start punching. "There is no secret propulsion system. Hassan was trying to murder us. This would have become our coffin."

Garner pulled off his spectacles—his eyes were lit with a terrible fire that blazed there. "Get him out ... get him out!"

Garner suddenly spun around and slammed his fist against a sensor next to a steel door. On the door, black words were stencilled over white. **SECONDARY AIRLCOCK. NO ENTRY WITHOUT AUTHORISATION.** The door slid open to reveal the bare cell of the airlock. The outer door was a black oblong embedded into the flank of the Crab.

Taneesha's eyes were flashing with something close to ecstasy. "Get him out!"

Bloodlust gripped the mob now. They weren't individuals capable of rational thought. They'd collectively become a vicious beast that lusted for destruction.

Taneesha pointed at Hassan. "Grab him!"

The mob surged forward. Hassan screamed, kicked out. But strong hands gripped his limbs so fiercely he cried out in pain. Though he writhed, and begged for his life to be spared, they pushed him into the airlock. The guy with the red beard punched Hassan in the stomach—a savage punch that knocked the air from him, causing him to double-up, and robbed him of his ability to fight back.

Seconds later, the airlock door closed—it shut the mob out. And it shut Hassan in.

Hassan pounded at the sealed airlock door. "Don't you understand? I was trying to save you. The Rib is going to take you to Callisto, but it won't bring you back. The people who went out on the other Rib never-"

The outer airlock door opened with a speed that was nothing less than brutal. Water vapour in the air condensed the second it struck vacuum, creating a flurry of white mist. Hassan was spat out of the airlock, carried by a punch of air as it vented into nothingness.

His hands frantically clawed at the vacuum, as if he could swim through the murderous emptiness, and back to the ship. Utter cold froze his face. The skin split—deep cracks opened in his cheeks, radiating out from his nose. His tongue, driven by a spasm of pain, thrust out through his lips. His lungs ruptured, casting out blobs of glistening red from his mouth.

The man's eyes only possessed the power of sight for one more second. Then they were gone, vomiting from the sockets as they became liquid. For another eight seconds, his heart continued to beat in his chest: testimony to the surprising resilience of the human body. Even in the most brutally hostile of environments. Then, finally, his heart stopped. Hassan had become merely an approximation of flesh in human form, as the vacuum, and temperatures cold enough to turn oxygen to liquid, destroyed his body.

The corpse drifted away from the Crab. And darkness consumed what had once been Hassan.

SIXTEEN

WORLDFALL

The face looked back at him from the mirror. He touched the marks on his throat. They stung so much he flinched. For a moment, he looked around at his surroundings without really comprehending where he was or how he got there.

Then it all came rushing back—a torrent of awful memory.

The corpse with the yawning mouth. Teeth biting into his throat.

Dan Karlton gulped in a lungful of air. He spasmed as if electricity tore through his body. Then he staggered backward where he dropped down, to sit on the edge of his bunk. His fingers were probing the bite marks in a way that mingled disgust with fascination.

This felt like waking from a nightmare. A fear sweat broke out on his face. He didn't remember how he escaped from the corpse that had grabbed hold of him. All he remembered was scrambling back into the airlock.

Dan blundered into the bathroom, twisted the taps of the shower, getting the flow as hot as he could—near boiling hot. Steam billowed in the shower cubicle. He wanted with desperate urgency to scald away every trace of the corpse's mouth from his face—every gob of spit, every smear of saliva that had dribbled from the dead mouth. Fully clothed, he lumbered into the shower—he was crying out as scalding water pummelled his face. But he didn't quit the stall. He'd clean every square inch of his body. As the water gushed down, he peeled off his clothes as if they were contaminated. The sopping garments were destined for the trash, come what may. No way would he ever wear them again, not after they'd been slobbered over by that vile cadaver.

And he would never reveal to anyone what had happened.

They'd tell him he was insane. He'd be injected with sedative, locked in the cabin, given a plastic spoon to eat his meals with, because they'd fear he'd hurt himself with metal cutlery. He'd be a prisoner until they returned to Earth ... if they returned to Earth.

Dan couldn't bear that. He didn't want to be alone here in this tiny cabin with his thoughts. Because he now realized that N'Darbi had told him the truth. The Rib had the ability to turn thoughts into reality. That ability included the tangible manifestation of nightmares, too. He didn't want to see the horrific content of his night terrors come padding out of the darkness. Because they would lay their monstrous hands on him as he lay sedated on the bed. Alone. Helpless. Easy to kill.

Dan woke on his bunk to the sound of Captain's Flynn voice blasting, hard and loud, from the PA speakers in his cabin.

"Ladies and gentlemen, the end of the journey is in sight. We are approaching Callisto. Soon we will be in zero-g. Of course, we have no control over when weightlessness will occur. That's all down to the capricious whims of the Rib. Therefore—as quickly as you can—secure all loose items, lock off bathrooms and the galley. I repeat: secure all loose items in cabins and in communal areas, otherwise there will be a blizzard of crap that will knock holes into your faces when we hit zero-g. It's impossible to be exact about our ETA. However, it's likely to be minutes, rather than hours. This is it, my gallant comrades; we're going in."

SEVENTEEN

THIS IS IT … WE'RE GOING IN

Don't walk! Run!

Those must be the words crashing through every crew member's skull as the Crab began to tremble, as the stresses of deceleration tested the integrity of the vessel's structure.

After securing loose items in the cabin, Dan sped along the corridor to the lounge where (as his training dictated) he was required to bolt loose items of furniture to the walls in their designated places. Other crew members would be in the galley packing away sharp knives into drawers, locking food cans in cupboards, emptying sinks, gathering up food and plates from work surfaces—all this before zero-g catapulted every unsecured item through the air. Those items would become dozens of rogue missiles that were likely to cause injury.

Steelwork groaned as he wrestled a table to the wall before clamping it in place.

Spiro, meanwhile, would be in the cabins, checking that patients were strapped to their bunks.

Captain Flynn pumped urgent instructions through the Crab's PA. "Close covers on all trash receptacles. There is an unattended refreshment trolley in the stern corridor on A deck. Dock it in the nearest available storeroom. Remember, ladies and gentlemen, first we get zero-g. Then gravity flips before landing and the ceiling will become the floor again. Vomit bags—grab 'em if you think you'll need them. Spiro Balouris, disengage sickbay locks—it needs to autorotate as gravitational direction switches."

Garner helped Dan upend a freestanding sofa against a wall where it would be held by restraining straps.

Garner stared at Dan's throat. "Are those … my God, they are … teeth marks. How the hell did you get teeth marks all over your throat?"

The corpse of Schwab bit me, that's how. Dan absolutely wanted to fire those words at Garner, the infuriating shit, but the last thing Dan needed right now was compulsory psychological evaluation. Yeah … it'd be like: "Daniel, do you often imagine that dead people are biting you?" Then there'd be speculation about how poor, deranged Daniel Karlton faked a set of fang marks on his throat. And, of course, he could show everyone the footage of the cave lightning storm that he'd recorded on the tablet but, equally, everyone would suspect that he'd faked that, too.

Dan, therefore, did a good job of pretending to smile. "How did teeth mark get on my throat? You tell me, Garner."

Garner helped Dan strap the sofa in place. "Dan, I know your terrible secret."

"Oh? Vampires? Monsters?"

"Nope. Things are getting frisky with you and the captain. But, dear oh dear, she has a different idea entirely when it comes to bestowing love bites."

"Yeah—things did hit erotic overload."

"Hey, Dan-Oh, you must bring out the beast in women. Be sure to get some cream for those bites from Spiro. They broke the skin. Looking sore, my man." He laughed. "I dread to picture the state of your cock. Probably hanging by a sticky thread." He laughed again. "What did you say to Flynn, when she was chewing your flesh?"

"Buckle it tighter."

"You said *what?*"

"This strap, Garner. Buckle it tighter, because if this thing breaks loose, it'll break bones."

"Yeah, yeah, sure. So ... what it's like with Flynn? I mean who makes the first move? You know, 'permission to come aboard, Captain' that kind of thing?"

Dan merely shook his head, while keeping the grin plastered on his lips. Though he'd have loved to poke his fist into Garner's snout at that moment. The only reason he had pretended that he'd been in an erotic entanglement with Flynn was to explain the bite marks without having to reveal the truth. Though, on reflection, he realized he should have come up with another explanation.

Elsewhere, there was a tumult of activity as people grabbed cups, plates, decks of playing cards, laptops—anything and everything that might turn into flying missiles the moment they were plunged into weightlessness. It's surprising how fast a coffee mug can move in zero-g.

Garner clearly wanted to know more. He followed Dan as he headed toward where a crate of empty bottles sat on a chair.

"Danny. Remember your pals, won't you? Encourage Flynn to give us more TV time. Hey, Dan, did you hear me?"

Dan was pleased when Flynn's voice rang out with powerful authority from the PA. "Garner to the septic tank pumps. Run a manual check that all valves are closed. I repeat, Garner to the septic tank pumps."

No sooner had Garner departed through the frenziedly busy throng of people than Katrina rushed across to Dan to clutch one of his forearms in both her hands. The action of a desperate woman.

"Dan," she hissed. "Do you know about Hassan? Did you hear what they did to him?"

"No. What happened?"

"There was a fucking riot. The mob shoved him into the airlock. Then the bastards opened the outer hatch...."

Flynn's voice thundered: "Zero-g!"

Flynn really didn't need to state the obvious. One moment there was up, and there was down, then 'up' and 'down' vanished with a suddenness that was brutal.

Everyone's feet unstuck from the floor. They were flying. Then chaos …

EIGHTEEN

ZERO-G

The abrupt abolition of gravity gave birth to an entirely new squealing mess of pandemonium.

Someone shouted, "What a fucking shitstorm!"

And it was.

The fifteen people in the lounge resembled clothes swirling around in a tumble dryer. Flashes of feet, hands, faces became a high-speed torrent. Men and women were struggling to grab hold of bolted-down furniture. Others attempted to seize straps that floated from the mattresses that, just minutes ago were (due to the state of 'up' and 'down' conferred by artificial gravity) fixed to the ceiling. Now, people bounced off walls, off windows, off one another. A woman's knee crunched into the side of Dan's head as she made swimming motions, trying to paddle through thin air to reach one of the mattresses. It was vital that they strapped themselves in place before g-force kicked-in. When that happened, the Rib would be decelerating, in order to make a gentle landing—as opposed to smashing into the Jovian moon in a blaze of lethal glory.

A boot was dislodged from a flailing foot—the boot flew away, spinning hard and fast, and it slammed into the face of a guy, bursting his nose in a spray of blood—instantly spheres of red flew through the maelstrom of struggling people—pellets of crimson struck faces, leaving wet dots of blood, but nobody appeared to notice, because everyone was consumed with the desperate need to strap themselves to the mattresses.

Dan began sneezing. Thousands of bread and cake crumbs that had been so carelessly dropped on the floor by the crew now rose up into swirling clouds, which were pushed by air currents from the ventilation system. Everywhere, people began sneezing and coughing as hard specks of baked foodstuff were inhaled into noses and throats. A guy savagely kicked away from the wall, aiming for a mattress where he could buckle himself safely in place.

He misjudged. And slammed headfirst into a TV screen fixed to a wall, then he drifted away, rendered unconscious by the blow. A glistening fissure in his forehead leaked more glistening balls of crimson into the air, adding to the chaos, horror and sheer hell of the situation.

Eggs drifted from the direction of the galley.

Katrina swore loudly as she clung to one of the mattress straps. "Eggs! Fucking eggs! They should have been secured in the food store!" Eggs, one by one, began to explode in spurts of bright yellow yolk as they slammed into tables, walls, and people alike. "What a fucking mess," screamed Katrina—her eyes were still raw with grief from Hassan's murder. "You know what? The Caucus simply shoved a bunch of idiots, with shit-all training, into this fucking Crab, and fired them off into space. These people haven't a clue what they should be doing!"

Dan floated there, still coughing because he'd inhaled crumbs that felt as sharp as gravel in his throat. His vision was blurred and watering from a shitstorm of particles, which were abrading his eyeballs. A hand grabbed hold of his collar and he felt himself being dragged through the air. His legs and arms were making instinctive swimming motions, though a fucking useless activity, considering he tried to swim through air, not water.

Suddenly, a blurred face loomed toward his. It was Katrina. She hauled him to the mattress beside hers.

She yelled so furiously that he felt the tingle of saliva spraying from her mouth against his face—he smelt a raw jag of whisky on her breath, too. She was yelling that they'd been sent on a suicide mission, and that nothing but a painful and lonely death awaited them on some Godforsaken world.

Simultaneously, a video played on TV screens, bolted to the walls. They displayed images of the Crab attached to the Rib. This was followed by an animated sequence depicting stylized crew members methodically securing loose items in the cabins—latching chairs to walls, closing and locking cupboard doors, and so on. The absurdity of the calm, well-ordered procedure (as opposed to the chaotic reality) would have made Dan laugh at any other time, but right now he could hardly breathe due to the fog of crumbs that filled the air with a brownish fog.

A measured voice-over accompanied the video, explaining what would happen next. "Shortly, you will be arriving on Callisto. Callisto is the second largest of Jupiter's moons. Callisto possesses a thin atmosphere of carbon-dioxide. When exiting the habitat pod, a spacesuit must be worn. Always take care to ensure that the suit's power pack is charged, and oxygen tanks have been replenished to their full capacity."

Garner screamed with laughter as he floated by. He used his hands to tug both knees up to his stomach. There was a dangerous-sounding hysteria in that laughter. "Are they fucking joking?" He mimicked the voice on the instruction video: "*When exiting the habitat pod, a spacesuit must be worn.* Do they think we are idiots? Yes, we need fucking spacesuits, otherwise our fucking heads will explode!"

Katrina shrieked, "Just like Hassan's when you opened the airlock hatch!"

"Hassan tried to kill us." Garner somersaulted past, in a slow-motion effect. "He was going to jettison the Crab."

"He tried to save us, you stupid—"

"Katrina, shut your mouth!"

"Murderer!"

Garner swung a vicious punch at Katrina's head—and missed. Newtonian law dictates that with every action there is a reaction. The reaction sent Garner spinning away, colliding with floating men and women—an effect on a par with a pool ball hitting other balls, sending people shooting away in different directions. Increased three-dimensional movement ramped up the intensity of the chaos—objects were colliding with each other, bodies were smacking into other bodies, heads were crunching into walls. Faces were striking tables, chairs. This was nothing less than a vortex of confusion and pain. People were yelping and grunting. Voices got louder as they cursed each bump and graze.

Dan grabbed the straps, then began buckling himself in tight against the mattress. Zero-g was indeed an awful shitstorm. However, when gravity kicked in again, coupled with the extra punch of g-force, then the next shitstorm would be a whole new ballgame of agony.

Actually, restraining himself firmly enough against the mattress was hellishly difficult. Straps would repeatedly float away from his hands. When he grasped a strap, he'd find himself drifting away from the mattress, which would ultimately result in him being swallowed by the whirlpool of men and women who were yelling in panic or cursing fellow crew members who helplessly slammed into them with enough force to blacken eyes and dapple bare arms with bruises.

Katrina was now secured firmly enough for one of the straps to cinch her torso. With one hand, she held Dan securely against the mattress, preventing him from floating into the human whirlpool. Within moments, he'd secured himself against the soft pad of the mattress.

He shot her a smile. "Thanks. You saved me from getting bashed to pieces."

Katrina acknowledged his gratitude with a nod. "Dan, listen. I've been thinking through the sequence of events."

"Oh?" His tongue felt gritty. Undoubtedly, this was due to the stale breadcrumbs that had invaded his mouth.

"Think back to when the Ribs were first discovered. They unstuck themselves from the swamp. Went to Callisto and returned. Right?"

"Yep. We saw it all on the news."

"First of all, they did the journey without crews: all automatic, controlled by whatever alien technology is inside the Ribs. Then scientists attached uncrewed probes to the Ribs. There were onboard cameras filming everything. There must be hours of footage and thousands of still photographs."

"And we've seen photographs and footage on TV and in newspapers, so what's your point?"

"My point is, although we have seen photographs of what appears to be structures on Callisto, they are so blurry they could be of anything."

"Scientists say that the images aren't that clear due to atmospheric conditions."

"Atmospheric conditions." She snorted with derision. "The Caucus faked everything."

"You do love your conspiracy theories, Katrina. Even if they are absurd."

"If you believe me or not, we don't know what we will find on Callisto when we land, because there aren't clear images of the landing site."

"Bullshit. The Caucus must be confident that we will land safely."

"Just you wait and see." Her tone became as ominous as someone predicting his imminent death. "And we're the poor fools that have been sent on a suicide mission ... to find out if we actually return in one piece, or if we end up stranded on that fucking awful planet. Hassan told me—"

What Hassan told her didn't leave her lips. Because the gravity abruptly returned. Along with that savage punch of deceleration. The people who'd been weightlessly floating suddenly got their weight back with a hefty bonus. They slammed against the floor.

That's when Dan heard the dreadful sound that human bones make when they snap.

NINETEEN

THE UNCOMPROMISING POWER OF GRAVITY

The return of gravity dumped all unrestrained crew in the direction of what was now the floor. Accompanying the downward plunge of men and women was the brown fog of crumbs, free-floating eggs from the galley, and a whole mess of footwear that had slipped off feet. There were also pens, dice, dozens of playing cards, and coffee mugs—the mugs, fortunately, were plastic and merely bounced as opposed to shattering.

"What a mess," marvelled Garner with a grin that was as inappropriate as it was wide.

Injured men and women lay groaning on the floor. They clutched broken femurs and tibias. Borman, the guy with the red beard, had grasped hold of a bracket that secured the TV to a wall and was looking out of a window, his eyes bulging with terror.

Borman thundered, "We're going in … we're landing … oh, my God. Do you see what we're going to land on. We're not going to survive this, we're not!"

All this, while the information video onscreen blithely reassured, "The habitat pod will continue to maintain a comfortable temperature and air pressure. Crew members can make use of cabins and service units that auto rotate when the gravity is reversed, prior to landing."

Borman pointed out through the window. "Have you seen where they've sent us?" Terror and amazement were fused into an expression that was shocking to see—his lips quivered, his eyes bulged, purple knots of veins pulsated beneath the skin at his temples. "Those Caucus bastards have sent us to hell!"

Those still physically capable of looking out of the windows did so. There were gasps of shock. One man pulled a crucifix from beneath his sweatshirt and began kissing it, while muttering a prayer to himself.

Dan, figuring that the violent g-force of deceleration was over, unbuckled the straps so he could get up from the mattress. What he saw beyond the window took his breath away. The Crab, still fixed to the Rib, plunged downward through darkness. If he looked upward to his right, he saw Jupiter. A vast globe, patterned with stripes of brown and creamy-white. In mythology, Jupiter was the king of the gods: now here, in the cold grip of reality, Jupiter absolutely did rule the sky. The looming presence was so enormous that he recoiled from the sight of the monster world.

But it wasn't seeing Jupiter that was freaking Borman out. He stared down at the landscape below. A forbidding realm of dead rock—and craters resembling open wounds that appeared to bleed liquid shadow onto the surface. This was surely Callisto.

And then Dan Karlton saw what had terrified everyone. Directly below them—to where they plunged—was their apparent destination. That destination was a huge structure. Horrifically, the structure resembled the ribcage of an enormous creature—one that was a mocking copy of a human being, or, more accurately, a human skeleton. Dan saw blood-red ribs that formed a series of arches, which were adjacent to a domed building that could have been a skull stripped of its flesh. There was even a pair of hollow eye sockets. Yet everything was on a massive scale. Each eye socket must have measured several miles in diameter. The ribs stretched for mile after mile.

Then Dan understood.

"Those ribs," he shouted. "They're spaceships—like the Rib we're riding now."

The crew began to mutter in astonishment.

Borman pointed. "Look, there are gaps where some Ribs are missing. Four gaps. Two must be for the Ribs back on Earth, another is for this one, so that means …"

"One Rib is missing," added Dan. "So, those gaps must be, for all intents and purposes, parking bays for the Ribs when they return."

Katrina wriggled free of the restraining straps and came to the window. She said: "Which means our Rib will slot itself into one of those apertures. If, that is, whatever system is navigating this thing can handle such an intricate manoeuvre."

Borman glanced sharply at her. "We're going in fast. Too fast."

This panicked a good-sized portion of the people there.

Shouts went up of: "We're going to crash!"

"And what about the Crab? What if there isn't enough clearance under the Rib! We'll be crushed flat!"

Some blundered away from the window in terror. They tripped over injured men and women in the process, which triggered more howls of pain.

The Rib dropped like a stone. Directly downward. Instinctively, people grabbed any piece of the structure to hand to hold onto. Not that would help if millions of tons of Rib suddenly bore down onto the Crab. In Dan's mind's eye, he saw the Crab being squashed, just as a bad-tempered drunk squashes an empty beer can under the heel of their boot. There'd be nothing they could do to save themselves if that happened.

Dan's heart pounded. He found himself holding a lungful of air inside his chest so fiercely his own ribs hurt. There was a renewed outburst of screaming. At that moment, it seemed as if his life-force retreated deep inside his head, as if desperate to find some place to shield itself from the bone-shattering force of the Rib. When its massive weight crushed down onto the Crab, mangling metal and bodies together into a single compressed layer of steelwork and bloody flesh.

That horrific mockery of a ribcage appeared to swell and grow as the Rib descended. He could see nothing else now. Directly beneath them was a gap in the sequence of arches that would accommodate their Rib. They plunged downward. There were yells, shouts, cries to be saved, together with curses directed at the people who'd sent them to this blood-red hell—this was a skull-pounding maelstrom of sound as people screamed what they believed would be their final scream.

Then …

No violent impact. No shriek of tearing metal. There was just an all-engulfing sense of stillness.

The screaming stopped and people began looking at one another in surprise.

At last, Borman whispered, "We're here. We've made it. And we're alive."

TWENTY

EXIT

Twenty-four hours later, Dan Karlton stood in the main airlock—one big enough to accommodate the eleven men and women present. All of them clad in spacesuits. Helmets were sealed, and people were anxiously looking out through bulging visors.

The air that Dan breathed smelt of peppermint, an odour added to the mixture of oxygen and nitrogen to mask a distinct undertone of chemical notes, which (it must be said) the peppermint hadn't successfully overwhelmed.

The last twenty-four hours had been hectic. The Comms team had tried to transmit messages to Earth—all their endeavours had come to nothing. Other crew members had a busy time cleaning up the mess after the sudden switch to weightlessness. Plenty of elbow-grease had been used to wipe away smears of egg yolk and human blood from the walls. Dan had helped Spiro treat the casualties—those people who hadn't successfully buckled themselves into restraints before zero-g had created that tumble-drier effect, resulting in panful collisions with floors, walls, ceilings and furniture. More injuries had occurred when the fierce g-force had kicked in. Seven people had suffered broken bones. Eventually, all the bones had been set and the injured wore bright orange casts on arms and legs. Others had required wounds suturing. And Spiro had doled out painkillers to nearly everyone. Fortunately, there'd been no fatalities.

Dan had been relieved to see that the bite marks had quickly faded. What's more, his grim tussle with the dead man, Schwab, now seemed dreamlike and strangely distant. Once again, he wondered if the Rib had the power to reach into the brains of humans and read their thoughts. Whether that was evidence of the aliens' appetite for cruelty or sheer ignorance of human sensibilities he simply did not know. The bottom line, however, was that he knew he must remain vigilant. Bad dreams should remain merely bad dreams, which quickly evaporate after the dreamer awakes. Bad dreams should definitely not become solid, three-dimensional creatures that prowl the real the world. Dan closed off that troubling line of thought and focussed on today's mission.

Captain Flynn had asked—then begged—for volunteers for a reconnaissance party. Now they had assembled here in the airlock. There was little to see beyond the Crab's windows, other than what appeared to be featureless walls of pale grey.

Gen slapped Dan on the back. She was a strong woman and he very much felt that good-natured thump against his spine.

Gen smiled through the visor at him. "Thank you, Dan. Spiro told me that you helped look after me and the other non-AB-plus folk when we were out of commission."

"You're welcome," he told her.

"Who'd have guessed that my rustic O-type blood would function okay as soon as we arrived on Callisto?"

Garner tapped a heavily gloved finger against the side of his helmet. "I've been thinking. The alien guys out there must have been finessing their systems—they're making the place more human-friendly."

Spiro called back from where he stood in line next to the closed hatch. "I ran all the environment checks out there. No particulate contamination, zero trace of bacteria or viruses. Oxygen levels are perfectly A-OK. Harmful radiation levels and toxic gases are entirely absent. The place is as clean as a hospital operating theatre."

Garner called out to the figure at the head of the line. "Hey, Captain. Spiro says the air's good to breathe. Why must we wear these suits? I feel like a dick in a baggy rubber."

Captain Flynn raised her hand to the hatch release lever. "Until we are one hundred percent certain that the air is good and there's nothing out there that can poison us, or corrode us to shit, then my order stands—we wear protective suits. Okay, soldier?"

"Okay, Captain." Then Garner muttered to Dan, "I'm not a soldier. I never have been a soldier. Why does she insist on—"

Dan grabbed Garner's arm while tapping the section of mask that contained the mic stalk. Dan silently mouthed: *Shush. Comms. She can hear you.*

Garner appeared genuinely touched that Dan had cared enough to warn him, because he nodded and patted Dan on the shoulder.

Flynn's voice reached them via the speaker embedded in their helmets. "Just to reiterate, the environment is not harmful to us out there ... at least our instruments indicate that is so. However, keep your suit sealed at all times. If you have a problem, communicate that problem to me straight away." Flynn had segued into professional military mode—her voice all but glowed with a powerful aura of authority. "I'm going to call out everyone's names. Raise your hand when you hear your name. And in recognition that you are civilians, I will be informal and use your preferred names." She began reading from a screen fixed to her forearm. "Spiro. Dan. Margarite. Gen. Garner. Borman. Thomas. Sunil ..." and so on.

After roll call had been completed, Thomas stepped forward. "Captain Flynn. I am actually Professor Thomas Jellsby. With respect to my profession as a whole, rather than I as an individual, I'd prefer that you refer to me as Professor Jellsby."

"As you wish, Professor Jellsby. My apologies."

Jellsby was breathing hard, his exhalation fogging the visor, so only a pair of blue eyes were visible as they peered out. The eyes protruded in a striking way and were distinctly watery.

Garner leaned toward Dan. He was pressing his thumb to a pad at the bottom of the helmet, muting the mic.

Garner's words were muffled, yet sufficiently understandable: "Dan, you do know that Jellsby is a smackhead? He brought a shitload of heroin onto the Crab with him." Garner chuckled. "Danny boy. This crew—all of us—we're just a bunch of crap, aren't we? Our blood group got us this gig. AB-plus types are so rare they just took anyone with the right kind of gravy in their veins."

Gen spoke up. "Captain. Some of us carry weapons, right?"

"No, none of us have weapons."

Borman grunted. "Hey, Gen's got a point. What if the aliens are hostile?"

"Then we don't have a chance in hell of surviving." Flynn pulled the lever down. "After all, even if I did hand out pistols and grenades, do you really think that you'd have the firepower to kill lifeforms who are so technologically brilliant they can build spaceships that can lie in a swamp for a hundred thousand years, then work perfectly?"

Hydraulics hissed, easing the hatchway open.

Garner visibly shuddered. "These aliens ... what do you think they look like?"

"I don't know," said Gen. "But they're bound to be a darn sight more attractive than you, Garner."

Garner looked as if he'd intended to fling back some vulgar response. However, just a glimpse of the open doorway stifled his voice.

Dan thought: *We're going outside. Are we are going to be the first people in the history of humanity to meet creatures from another world?* His heart fluttered in his chest. Though that was a product closer to fear than excitement. He wondered what Shaz would have said if she was still alive. He closed his eyes for a second—instantly, he saw her face again as she fell—that long drop toward the rubble, far below.

A hand closed over his wrist. "You all right, Dan?"

Dan nodded back at Spiro. "Yeah, fine ... just a big moment, isn't it? Going out to meet the guys that ferried us to Callisto."

Captain Flynn led her reconnaissance party through the lagoon of deep shadow beneath the Rib ... and away from what now, in retrospect, seemed the homely and safe environment of the Crab. Dan glanced back. He saw the crew members that had remained behind. They were gazing out through the Crab windows at the line of eleven men and women that moved in a way that was tentative, hesitant—some might even say fearful. The people on the Crab raised their hands to solemnly wave to the people outside.

Garner's voice, carried by the comms, sounded overloud in the confines of Dan's helmet: "Captain, this is like some kind of aircraft hangar, isn't it?"

Flynn glanced back at her team, her brown eyes appearing as luminous orbs behind the glass of her helmet. "We are certainly inside a structure where the atmosphere is regulated."

Dan looked back at the Rib, which had slotted neatly into a curving structure that resembled a monstrous ribcage. The Crab, which was slung beneath the Rib, was just five feet above a floor of smooth rock. If there hadn't been sufficient clearance, then the Crab would have been crushed. Along with its human occupants.

Everyone looked about them, straining their eyes to see their surroundings. But, in truth, there was little to see. They seemed to be moving through a vaporous murk. It had gradually turned a very dark red in color, and it acted as a fog, limiting the view of their surroundings. Soon, both the Rib and the Crab had become hazy outlines. Dan couldn't even make out the Crab's windows now, let alone his travelling companions.

The sense of being vulnerable in this alien place was a powerful one. Gut instinct demanded that he return to the Crab, then climb into its steel shell and curl up in his cabin, where he could close his eyes and shut out this ominous realm, which seemed to pulsate with danger. The sound of his respiration grew louder in his ears—a harsh inward drag of air followed by a throaty exhale, which made a gurgling sound in his throat. Breathing became hard. Not because his suit's air supply was at fault … no, this was fear tightening the muscles in his chest and throat to such a painfully tense degree it felt like his airways were becoming narrower by the second—closing in, restricting airflow. His heart thudded—a dead sounding rhythm as it pushed thick blood through his veins. A blood that seemed viscous to the point it would clog his arteries. Dwindling to a sludgy flow that would spawn clots inside his brain that must …

He suddenly stopped walking because he'd noticed a figure. It was smoothly gliding through the fog. Deep shadows had robbed it of a face. It moved with a long, high-stepping gait. An alien movement.

Everyone else had seen the approach of the thing, which presented itself as a thin silhouette—no other detail was visible. It appeared to have a clear sense of purpose as it walked through a fog that had now deepened into a blood-freezing black, which was flecked with tints of dark red.

Captain Flynn gestured to her team: *stay where you are.*

Dan felt apocalyptic dread. Almost a sense that he stood on top of a high cliff and the ground was crumbling beneath his feet and, at any moment, he would plunge down into an awful abyss.

Gasping voices rustled over the comms as people began to react to what must be the first encounter with an extraterrestrial creature. They were muttering things like: -

"This is it."

"What if it attacks?"

"I've never been so frightened before in my life."

"Stay back."

"Don't let it touch you."

In this murk, the figure remained a ghostly silhouette that could have glided from a tomb. However, the figure was human in shape. Now, Dan could make out two arms, two legs, a narrow torso, a rounded head—yet still no detail beyond that. No features on its face were visible in the dark fog that was stippled a bloody red.

Dan's heart pounded. His breathing accelerated. The cuffs of the suit were uncomfortably tight. Breathing became harder. He felt the urge to rip the helmet from his head—he needed to inhale. And inhale deeply. He wanted fresh air. His windpipe seemed to have narrowed to the point no oxygen was reaching his lungs. Sparks of green light were flashing through his head. *Oxygen starvation. Get that fucking helmet off your head. Something's gone wrong with the suit. You're suffocating!*

Then Flynn raised her right hand. Dan saw an object gripped in her fist. Her thumb moved, pressing a button. Light burst from her outstretched arm, drenching the figure in a blaze of silver.

Everyone there screamed in shock.

The sound was loud enough to thrust a jagged blade of agony through Dan's skull.

The figure, illuminated there by Captain Flynn's flashlight, was a familiar one. And she did not wear a spacesuit.

TWENTY-ONE

WEDDING BAND

Captain Flynn erupted with rage. "Katrina! What the hell are you doing outside?"

"I'm coming with you. I need to learn the truth for myself."

Katrina had spoken with calm dignity, yet Dan thought there were the bright fires of mania in those eyes of hers.

He recalled how Katrina had given a powerful impression of being some alien creature. The sheer tension of the moment, and the eerie fog, must have distorted his perception of the woman before she had revealed herself.

Flynn pointed in the direction of the Crab, which was concealed by the murk. "Return to the quarantine section. That's an order."

"No, Captain."

Spiro stepped forward. "Katrina, where's your suit?"

"If aliens have gone to the trouble of bringing us safely here to Callisto, then they'll be smart enough to create an environment that won't harm us. Therefore, we don't need suits."

Borman began to flip the catches of his helmet.

Flynn shouted, "No one is to remove their helmet! Is that understood? We don't know if there are toxic gases or viruses that could kill us."

Spiro disagreed, "Captain. Our instruments don't reveal any dangerous gases or biological threats. Apart from the oxygen, the environment here is inert."

Flynn growled, "We're not taking any chances. Katrina, return to the Crab, seal yourself in the quarantine area. Stay away from the crew."

"Captain. You don't get to tell me what to do anymore. I'm going to see this place with my own eyes. After all, the Caucus sent us here—us, a bunch of expendables. Yes, expendables on a suicide mission. The Caucus wants to find out if human beings can travel out to Callisto then return alive."

"Nonsense," snapped Flynn. "Our mission is to contact the alien race here. Then do whatever is necessary to restore the gravity generator."

Katrina laughed—it was a grim-sounding one with beggar-all humor. "What? Are you seriously telling me that we are some kind of heroic team of experts that will save Planet Earth? Look at us. Professor Jellsby is a fucking heroin addict. He's the only scientist on our expedition because no other scientist would even willingly come within a mile of one of those fucking Ribs, until they have proof that humans return alive from Callisto."

Jellsby began to protest, saying that his professional stature demanded that Katrina respect him, but she dismissed his protest with an I-don't-give-a-damn-what-you-say gesture of her hand. Then she powered on, her voice becoming more forceful: "We aren't experts with a fucking breathtaking array of qualifications. We're not a squad of fearless soldiers. Just look at us, Flynn. We're a bunch of ordinary Joes. Hardly any of us are qualified for a mission to another planet. Shit. Most of us aren't even qualified to get a nice clean job in an office. Okay, Spiro is a qualified medic, Dan is a structural engineer. But Garner sold lawnmowers before the government told him he was an astronaut. Borman was a truck driver. And me? I was in catering. That is to say, I washed dirty crockery in a diner. Nothing wrong with those jobs, of course. Good honest work ... but astronauts? Us folk? Nah. Never in a million years. We're just like those dogs that the Russians used to shove into the nosecones of rockets before blasting them off on a one-way death-ride into space."

Nobody moved after Katrina's speech. Flynn folded her arms, while staring at the woman in front of her—a woman that was breathing alien air, and sucking who knows what into her lungs.

Flynn threw up her arms. A gesture of surrender, or so it seemed, because she snarled, "Okay, Katrina. You're an adult. You're entitled to decide your own fate." Flynn turned to look at us, her eyes burning through the visor. "If everyone's ready, we'll continue our reconnaissance. Tag along with us, Katrina, if you wish. Or will you strike out on your own?"

"Oh, I'm coming with you, Captain. I need to be certain there's no Caucus trickery. If there are aliens here, I want to see them, too."

The team moved off again, heading into the fog. The vapour formed a smoky body that appeared to mingle a dense mass of shadow with speckles of red. They'd been walking for no more than three minutes when they reached objects scattered on the smooth expanse of rock that formed the floor of the unseen structure that must surround them.

Dan immediately identified the objects; after all, it wasn't difficult to do.

A pencil.

A boot.

A spacesuit helmet, identical to the ones he was wearing.

A tiny object glinted on the floor. Garner picked it up.

"Wedding band," he said. "Who carries a wedding band all the way to another planet, so they can throw it away?"

Dan knew what the man was really saying. The wedding band hadn't been willingly discarded by its owner. And whoever—whatever—had taken the ring had not recognized its monetary or emotional value and had flung it aside.

Dan's instinct for danger told him that there was something hiding out there in the fog—and it was watching that nervous bunch of men and women. Assessing them. Biding its time.

TWENTY-TWO

THE AGE OF RAGE

Down through the canyon of skulls. Limbs brushing against skin that hung in rags of dry tissue from jawbones, cheekbones, and the grey domes of fleshless skulls. Eye sockets deprived of wet spheres that were once eyes had become voids filled with darkness. The creature moved quickly, driven by rage that blazed through its nervous system.

Intruders.

Their monstrous presence violated the air. The intruders were a loathsome stain on the purity of this seraphic realm. Anger quickened the movement of thin limbs. Cardiac muscle spasmed, driving oxygenated liquid through its arterial system. Commands from the creature's brain raised eye-coverings as high as they would go to make the most of the dim light that filtered through black fog. And high above this strange terrain, curving arches spanned a vast cavity.

Down through the canyon of ribcages.

Through the sea of darkness.

Then across a papery rug of skin that had been stripped from living creatures—the arid environment had mummified faces that had been peeled away from skulls. The mask-like things fluttered with the speed of the creature's passing. When the creature reached a mound of thighbones, which reached up as high as its own skull, it paused. Its eyes stared ferociously into the murk.

The enemy approached. Loathsome figures, moving on two legs. Eleven wore protective suits that were topped with a domed helmet. One figure was bare-headed, its eyes glinted in the mist.

The monstrous things sent flashes of terror and fury alike through the creature's nervous system, swamping its brain with dread. The intruders had not noticed they were being watched. They walked in a linear formation. Their pace was slow in the cumbersome suits. They moved their limbs in a way that inspired revulsion in the creature. From time to time, their gloved hands appeared to stroke the air, perhaps indicating that they derived illicit gratification from touching something that wasn't theirs to touch. The creature knew that these repellent lifeforms had disgorged themselves from a silverish vessel. Now they were here—trespassers in a realm that did not belong to them.

They continued to prowl through the murk. Their gloved hands gestured at tall structures that were now becoming slowly visible as the fog began to thin.

The creature hunched down lower behind the pile of bones to avoid being detected by the intruders. As it did so, it happened to catch sight of its own hand. The fingers were hooked into claws. Fingernails were pink, shell-like objects—most of the fingernails were uneven, and splintered at the end. One fingernail had split down the middle and had opened up wide enough to reveal matter that was red and moist. The creature stared at the wound. It understood that beneath its own outer membrane was a vile substance known as 'flesh'. And worming through the raw flesh were blue tubes—they pulsed so grotesquely as thick, red liquid, driven by contractions of the heart, flowed through them.

A yellow tentacle crept up the creature's torso ... up to a bare throat. The tentacle was like a wet tongue licking skin. Just for a moment, memories that were more like ghosts than the recollection of actual events haunted the creature's mind: *Octopus in the fish tank—all those awful tentacles. See how they writhe and squirm over one another, like a man with no bones lacing his fingers together. Awful to look at. Just awful. And then running home after the aquarium visit. Her mother pushing the mower over the front lawn, and her shouting, 'I saw an octopus today. They look revolting. Just imagine one of those slimy things on your head, with its tentacles sliding through your hair…."*

Another tentacle curled around the creature's head—a yellow limb that glistened. It felt as cold as a piece of beefsteak from a refrigerator. Very slimy, too. The tentacle moved, pawing at its forehead. Then that stroking motion again: this time over his eyes, as if the tentacle was a tongue. Licking the creature's eyeballs. And as the tentacle tightened around the skull, the memory of ghosts vanished.

The creature watched the invaders from behind the mound of bones. Rage blazed through its body once more. Its eyes darted to the hand that rested on a thighbone, which was hollowed out by decay until it resembled something like a white pipe.

A chain encircled the creature's wrist. The chain's links were delicate and formed from gold. Another gold object, in the shape of an oblong, was stamped with evil-looking runes. The creature stared at the loathsome symbols, fearful that they could invoke a dangerous curse that might summon entities to rip the creature's flesh away before adding its skeleton to the heap of bones.

With violent speed, the creature snapped the gold chain from its wrist before flinging it back into the canyon of skulls—to a place where its malignant power couldn't reach out and hurt it.

Even so, the symbols, which were punched deep into the gold, now burned a copy of those characters into its brain—creating an evil stigma. The creature had the faint understanding that the symbols spelt a name that had been affixed to its wrist by the chain.

And that name was: *Candice Magnusson.* Just for a moment, the creature had the unsettling suspicion that it had been known as Candice Magnusson long ago. However, the tentacle caressed its forehead again. And all memory of a past life was banished.

TWENTY-THREE

FROM A TOWER, DREADFUL AND FORLORN

Doctor Singh looked out of the window. She was on the top floor of a tower that rose from a floor of dark bedrock. The black fog had shrouded her surroundings for days, not allowing so much as a glimpse of neighbouring buildings, or the spoil heaps of bone, or even a glimpse of the predators that prowled the vast structure, which contained this complex of buildings.

She'd been here for weeks. It was a dreary existence, and one so solitary that sheer loneliness had begun to erase her identity. She had to remind herself of her name by saying it aloud. Constantly, she needed to refresh her memory of what she actually looked like by gazing into a bowl of water so she could see her reflection there (there were no mirrors in the building). Often the sight of a human face triggered such an intense emotional response that she'd release a lungful of air, corrupting the reflection in the water, and ripples would corrugate the image of her face, distorting the brown eyes that gazed back at her. Then tears would drip down her cheeks into the bowl of water, stippling the image once more, mutating her face into something grotesque.

As she gazed out of the window, two hundred feet above that grim expanse of bedrock, she murmured her litany of remembrance: "My name is Priya Singh. Thirty-six years of age. Doctor of medicine. Two beautiful daughters at home with her father … his name is … oh … what is his name? Think. Think." She pressed her bunched fists against her forehead. "This place robs you of your memories. It gets inside your head." She took a deep breath and shuddered as a man appeared in the doorway behind her. He didn't have a face—instead, there was just a blank expanse of smooth skin covering the front of the skull. No mouth, no lips, no eyes. Just a passing resemblance to her husband. A mockery served up by this rotten planet to both tempt her and mock her.

She thought hard. Veins throbbed her temples. "My husband's name is … Ben … Benjamin … no!" She screamed with relief. "Benedict. His name is Benedict!"

Finally, she recalled his face. The way his blue eyes so often had a gleam of pleasure when he looked at her. She remembered the small scar above his right eyebrow—a scar in the shape of a white crescent moon. This blemish was the result of an unfortunate accident with a boomerang, just one month after they'd met. Benedict had bought her a boomerang and they were playfully throwing it in the park. They were laughing and making jokes about their throwing skills (or lack thereof), which told her they were perfectly matched to one another—they were completely on the same frequency emotionally, intellectually, and psychologically. As Priya attempted to throw the boomerang, Benedict told her he loved her. This was the first time he'd directed those words at her. The shock caused her to release the boomerang too soon.

Pop!

The sound the boomerang made as it cut open the skin above his right eye really was a shockingly loud 'pop'. Goodness, how the wound had bled. The right-hand side of his face below the eye was drenched in crimson. Both of them were doctors, but the emotionally charged moment made them all fingers and thumbs as they tried to stanch the flow of blood.

Priya gazed out of the window; the stream of memory was becoming stronger and clearer. She recalled how a passing cyclist—a man with a mohawk of white hair—offered them a pack of unopened tissues.

"Love can do wonderful things to people," Benedict had said, while grinning through his mask of blood.

"Does it hurt?" she'd asked as she pressed a wad of tissue firmly against the cut.

"Does it hurt? Only when I say goodbye to you at night, and then go home alone to my own apartment."

Memory delivered sharper images now. The wedding in a grove of cherry trees—their branches gloriously bedecked with pink blossom. Uncle Max dropping a cream cake onto his four-year-old son's head. She could almost hear the wedding guests' laughter echoing back from the grey walls of the very room she stood in now. The child had cheerfully danced around with the cake on his head, like it was a funny cockeyed hat. When they moved into their new home, Benedict had even put the boomerang in a frame and hung it on the dining room wall. He told her that despite the wound she'd accidentally inflicted on him, it was one of the happiest days of his life. And every morning she'd kiss the C-shaped scar above his right eyebrow.

Priya gazed at the faceless man that stood in the doorway—he, or rather 'it', was a conglomeration of matter that resembled living flesh. As she stared at him, some *thing* scooped the memories from her mind, and painted features on the man's face. Suddenly, the face possessed eyes that sparkled with humor—the bluest of eyes. Blond eyebrows formed—and above one eyebrow a C-shaped scar took flight across its sky of smooth skin. A moment later, flesh bulged from the centre of the face to become a nose. A split above the chin became soft and beautifully sensitive lips.

The figure extended its arms as if wanting to be hugged.

With a sad smile, she shook her head. "Not today, Benedict."

Then she shut her eyes and clenched her fists so tight her fingernails cut into her palms. *Why do I call that monster Benedict? He's not human. He doesn't even have a heart. I won't let myself make love to him ever again.*

Nevertheless, she wanted to be embraced by the creature that resembled Benedict. She wanted to feel his touch so much she ached.

"Go away!" Her yell was so loud it hurt her ears. "Go back down into the vault. Don't ever come up here again ... not unless I ask you." She shuddered as she spoke the words, knowing that nagging ache of temptation would get the better of her. The monster looked like Benedict. But it was not Benedict. Yet she wanted to feel the weight of that body on hers again. She knew her resolve would weaken. Already she imagined the sense of melting release as he made love to her. Her intellect knew that having sex with one hundred and sixty pounds of cold, lifeless matter was repulsive and wrong. However, the emotional underbelly of her mind wanted to feel him inside of her ... she wanted the sensation of him moving into her. Deeper and deeper. The force of his hips pressing down ...

The sound of the breeze snapped her back onto the cold reality of the here and now. Opening her eyes, she looked out through the window of her lonesome tower ... where she lived alone, ate alone, slept alone (when she successfully resisted temptation). The breeze caused the fog to flow—so it seemed as if she gazed down into a fast-flowing river. Streaks of gloom moved from left to right below her. Immediately, her surroundings became clearer. She could make out the arches of the structure overhead, which formed its roof. The complex of buildings extended for dozens of miles. A mile away, a line of towers marched off into the distance. They were massive stone henge-like structures, yet at their base the substance they were made from branched off into something like a root system of a tree, which burrowed deep into bedrock.

What she saw next jolted a scream of shock from her mouth.

"People."

Priya stared in amazement as a line of figures in spacesuits walked in single file toward the pale mounds of bones. She counted the figures with breathless excitement.

"One, two, three ..."

Wait, there's one not wearing a spacesuit. A woman.

Then she noticed movement amongst the bone heaps. Figures scurried down the mounds, their feet triggering small avalanches of skulls, femurs, thigh bones, vertebrae, ribs. Around sixty figures were running toward the people in spacesuits. If she didn't warn them, they would be overwhelmed within seconds.

The monstrous creatures that approached the astronauts moved at furious speed—she sensed their rapacious need to attack. White objects, looking like rounded blisters at this distance, dappled the bodies of those predatory beings.

Doctor Priya Singh raced across the room to a doorway, where a spiral staircase penetrated the centre of the tower, going down through floor after floor, resulting in a dizzying descent. But she couldn't pause for even one second to catch her breath. She had to warn the newcomers out there before they were subjected to the most vicious of assaults. An assault that would have a horrific consequence. She passed the facsimile of her husband, Benedict, as she ran down the steps, her footsteps thumping back at her, creating a fast rhythm that was so desperately urgent.

Meanwhile, storm winds began to blow against the tower, raising mournful cries that rose in pitch to a shriek before falling away to a muffled sobbing.

The Benedict thing continued to slowly descend the stairwell. He'd obeyed her command. He was returning to the vault where the others waited. However, her mind was now fixed on the astronauts who would be attacked within minutes if she failed to warn them in time.

Storm winds rose to a hellish shriek again. A terror symphony of skull-jolting notes that hurt her ears.

Priya helter-skeltered down the steps as fast as she could. She was risking a bone-snapping fall, yet she simply had to save those people outside. She hoped she would make it in time.

TWENTY-FOUR

ONSLAUGHT

The planet had declared war on Dan Karlton and his companions. That's how it seemed as they were plunged into a grim battle to stay on their feet. A hurricane was screaming out of the darkness at them. They were fighting to walk, their fists punching forward through the air, trying to maintain their balance. Fortunately, their helmets protected them from the storm-driven grit.

Katrina, however, was in serious trouble. Blinded by dirt, which shot through the air as savage as bullets, she went down, her body hunching over as she clamped her hands to either side of her head to protect her eardrums from the shriek of the hurricane. The storm was painfully loud when heard through the hard shell of the helmet. Experiencing that sonic assault on naked ears must have been torture. Dan reached down to grasp her arm. Spiro did the same. Together, they lifted the woman to her feet. Splinters of some white material flashed through the air, opening nicks in her skin that allowed beads of red to ooze through. Dan positioned her, so she was on the leeward side of his body, the bulk of his torso and helmet protecting her from the missile-fast deluge of objects that clattered against his helmet.

Spiro shouted, his voice distorting through the speaker in Dan's helmet.

"Dan! Those bits of white stuff! They're bone! Fragments of bone!"

The others were struggling through the maelstrom. Captain Flynn helped those who had fallen, pulling them back onto their feet again.

Dan continued to wrap his arms around Katrina, embracing her head, gently pressing her face to his chest, to avoid the hurtling fragments of bone. Was it human bone, animal bone, fragments of alien skeleton? Who could tell?

Dan shouted, "Captain! We need to find shelter! Otherwise, people are going to get hurt!"

"Agreed, soldier." Flynn pointed to tall structures a quarter of mile away. "We'll head to those."

Flynn had to lean forward into the violent torrent of air as she led the way.

One effect of the winds, Dan realized, was that they stripped away the fog, thus exposing the naked architecture of the place. Above him, was a curving roof, which was formed from a series of vast arches. Were these the underbellies of hundreds of spaceships that had been named 'Ribs' by the media back on Earth? Seemingly, so, because they had a similar shape, even though he was viewing them from underneath.

Katrina shouted some words to Dan as he hugged her close to him. However, seeing as she didn't wear a comms system, he couldn't hear what she said. He pointed toward the buildings and mouthed *We're going there*. She seemed to understand and nodded, then she dipped her head low against his chest, using his body as a shield against the onslaught of debris. The recce party made slow progress toward a building that resembled one of the megalithic slabs that formed the upright structures at Stonehenge. By now, the dark fog had vanished. Yet the air was misted all white with millions of fragments of bone being carried on the raging breath of the hurricane.

Just then, an astonishing sight.

From the bottom of a towering megalith, a figure appeared. The building wasn't the one they headed toward but the next one along in that line of brooding sentinels. The figure gestured with frantic urgency.

Garner stared through his visor, his eyes going wide. "My God. There's a woman."

Dan's unease ramped up to a whole new level of intensity. "She's wanting us to head toward her … and isn't she pointing at something behind us?"

Garner looked back at one of the mounds. "Something's coming this way. Whatever they are, they're moving at a hell of a speed."

Flynn yelled: "As fast you can! Head for the building where the woman is."

The airborne fragments of bone meant that visibility wasn't at all good. Therefore, it was impossible to see the approaching figures in detail—other than they ran on two legs. And that they moved with absolute menace.

Flynn yelled a command that was deeply ominous. "Run! Stop for nothing!"

Dan moved as quickly as he could. He kept his arm around Katrina, hauling her along.

The figures were closer now. Therefore, he could make out more detail. And what he saw was not pleasant. Because whatever bore down on them was strangely scarecrow-like in appearance. The figures advanced on stiff legs; their knees were locked. Those disturbing things were stepping across the terrain like animated scissors.

Dan realized they moved faster than him. And he tried very hard not to imagine what dreadful violence they would inflict on his body if they caught him.

TWENTY-FIVE

RYAN

The hurricane blasted into the group of men and women. Dust devils, conjured by the winds, whirled across the mysterious terrain. Dan's helmet seemed to do little to protect his ears from the demonic scream of the storm. Hard particles struck the visor. A violent tap-tap-tap that sounded like hail striking a tin roof yet amplified to the point of agony.

Though he doubted Katrina could hear him, he repeatedly urged her to keep moving. He had wrapped an arm around her shoulders, and he pressed her face to his chest to protect her from what would be a stinging onslaught of bone splinters that were shot from the gloom by brutal torrents of air.

The storm didn't blunt the aggressive pace of the scarecrow figures that hurried toward them. Their knees remained locked, their legs were straight, producing that uncanny scissoring motion.

Spiro and Flynn helped him haul Katrina toward the building. Flynn had one hand pressed against his back, propelling him forward. Spiro put both hands against Katrina's head, striving to protect her from injury from the never-ending volleys of bone fragments.

The first in the line of megalithic towers was now just one hundred paces away.

Garner blundered toward them. "Make for the nearest one," he shouted. "If we don't, those fucking monsters will catch us."

Flynn thundered back, "No. We're going to the building where the woman is waiting for us!"

"We won't make it!"

"Look at the nearest tower, Garner! There are no doors, no windows— so, how do we get in?"

Garner's eyes blazed behind the visor. "Okay! Okay! But dump that bitch!" He pointed at Katrina. "She's slowing you down."

Spiro pushed Garner away from them. "You fuck off ahead of us, Garner! We don't need your help here!"

Garner laughed—though the sound was more like a shriek of terror. "Okay. But don't blame me if those monsters fuck you all the way to hell."

After that raw-sounding outburst, he lurched off into the mist.

Dan focused on hauling Katrina toward the building. By now, the onslaught of dust and bones were nothing less than shrapnel. They had rendered Katrina semi-conscious; therefore, he had to drag her. Muscles in his shoulders and back blazed with pain. He was panting hard, the exhalations misting the visor. His heart pounded so hard he could hear its drumbeat thudding up through his neck into his head. Purple flashes erupted in his eyes as exhaustion bit deep.

Even though he was worn out, his focus remained nailed to the task of getting Katrina to the building where the stranger gestured frantically at them. The stranger's hands were signaling, *Hurry. Please hurry. Faster. You are in danger. Run!*

Airborne dust caused almost total whiteout. Nevertheless, he could still see the scarecrow figures—they were menacing silhouette shapes, predatory as hell—getting closer and closer. What he couldn't discern was any precise detail of their bodies or faces (if those monsters had faces). What was brutally clear, they were in pursuit of prey.

And the prey is us, thought Dan.

Flynn panted. The mic was capturing the harsh rasping before thrusting it through the speakers in their helmets.

Breathlessly, she yelled, "Those things move fast. They're going to cut us off before we reach the building!"

Spiro shouted, "We've got knives! We'll gut the fuckers!"

Flynn's response was grim. "I like your fighting spirit, soldier, but something tells me that we shouldn't tangle with those things unless we've no other option. Dan, let me take over, you're exhausted."

"No, I've still got some gas in my tank. Besides ... we're nearly there."

Dan knew that what he'd just told Flynn was sheer hope triumphing over reality.

And the reality was this—the scarecrows would intercept them before they reached the building ... and whatever protection it offered.

By this time, the recce party had effectively split into two. Garner and Ryan led the others about fifty paces ahead of Dan and his small group. Dozens of the scarecrows were on a converging route now, which would insert them between the building and the straggling groups of exhausted men and women.

At that moment, however, the scarecrows changed direction, as if some obstacle blocked their route, though Dan couldn't make out any obstruction. His eyes were watering with exertion. He blinked hard, trying to improve his vision, so he could make out what had deflected the scarecrows from their original route that would allow them to intercept the recce party. No, he couldn't see any object that the scarecrows would need to detour around ... and yet ...

... and yet, he did make out holes that resembled the entrances to rabbit burrows—there was a cluster of them, covering an area not much larger than a basketball court.

When the scarecrows adopted a trajectory that detoured them away from the point where they would have converged on the men and women, that's when Ryan and Garner, at the front of the pack, changed course—a course that would take them through the cluster of small holes.

Dan's instinct for danger blazed bright within him: "If those creatures are avoiding the holes, then we should, too,"

Flynn thundered, "Garner! Ryan! Those holes in the ground—keep away from them!"

Garner heard her command and swerved away.

Ryan either didn't hear or was so frightened that he didn't want to delay reaching the building by one solitary second—whatever the reason, he continued to lope through the area pockmarked with holes. Those holes were perhaps just large enough to accommodate a clenched fist.

Ryan quickly reached the openings that pierced the ground. That's when a pinkish object bulged softly from one of the holes. One second, it was merely pink matter filling the hole; the next second it had domed, forming a balloon shape, which was slowly inflating. Rising. Expanding.

Then, with the speed of an airbag explosively inflating when a car crashes, the pink object suddenly erupted outward to form a pink sphere that was the equal to Ryan's height. The pink sphere billowed in the wind—an undulating form that appeared to be made of some soft material. The creature (if that's what it was) reminded Dan of a jellyfish floating in the sea. A lifeform without a skeleton, without a fixed shape.

Ryan merely altered his course a little as he ran. Clearly, he intended to swerve away, so he could bypass the pink sphere without touching it.

Then another movement—so fast, it was just a blur.

Dan had to use memory to process what he'd seen because it happened so quickly. With explosive speed—again as fast as an airbag deploying—brown spines erupted from the pink body. They shot outward—bullet-fast. Dozens of spines began slamming point-first into Ryan's suit and helmet.

The spines remained connected to the pink sphere. And those spines, which were maybe ten feet in length, passed clean through Ryan's body and head. Even the super-tough shell of the helmet didn't stop them. At the end of each spine a hooked barb formed, evidently to stop its prey from sliding off.

Ryan screamed—the scream was a hugely amplified storm of sheer agony ripping through Dan's helmet speaker. Dan watched as Ryan was held upright by the spines. The man punched outward with his fists, while his feet kicked into thin air. The man was fighting for his life.

He was, in reality, dying.

A dozen spines penetrated different parts of his body: chest, belly, head.

Ryan appeared to suddenly grow immensely weary. His arms and legs moved much slower now, his head drooped. Dan could hear a wet gurgling—that was the sound transmitted from Ryan's mic. Dan imagined blood pouring from facial wounds into the dying man's mouth. The red liquid would be flowing over his tongue into the back of his throat. Of course, blood must be running down inside the man's suit, too. Filling his footwear in a sloshing, sucking flush of hot liquid.

Ryan's breath came in quick stuttering gasps. Then he was pleading. "Mother. Help. Mother. I need you … ah! Mama … mamma …"

In that cruel moment of dying, his terror rewound him from man to boy—then to helpless infant, crying for his mother.

Dan heard the gasps and sobs of his companions as they witnessed Ryan's final moments. Then, as quickly as it came, the pink sphere returned to its lair. The barbed spines drew Ryan with it, down through the hole. The hole remained the same size. Barely large enough to admit a fist, so the force the predator used to drag its prey underground was absolutely brutal.

Everyone heard the brittle snap of Ryan's bones as a tremendous strength broke them. There was the squish and squelch of rupturing organs and tearing flesh. The men and women weren't even spared the harsh sigh of air rushing from the dead man's lungs as they were fiercely compressed, when the torso was crushed as the creature pulled the corpse down through the hole before …

Before what?

Before the feeding began?

Flynn yelled. "Keep moving. Those things are coming this way!"

The woman was right. The scarecrows had safely moved around the lair of the sphere and were heading directly toward Flynn's crew.

Now that the scarecrows were closer, Dan could make out white disks covering their torsos, arms, and legs.

Witnessing the dreadful slaughter of Ryan had injected a shot of renewed energy into everyone there. They sprinted toward the building. The woman still beckoned with nothing less than frantic desperation. Her wide eyes revealed she was scared for the newcomers: she was encouraging them to move as fast as they damn well could.

By this time, the scarecrows were just fifty paces behind him. The mist still obscured his view of them. But what he did see increased his unease. The white disks he'd taken as a dappled pattern on their bodies moved. They were jerking from side to side in a way that was revolting to look at. The scarecrows, themselves, possessed heads that were like those of a human. And he thought he saw the cruel glint of eyes that lustfully stared at potential victims.

At that moment, Dan tripped. He fell with Katrina in a sprawling tangle of arms and legs. Straight away, hands grasped him. For one awful moment, he thought the scarecrows had grabbed hold.

But he quickly realized that the hands belonged to Flynn, Spiro, Gen and Borman. With frantic speed, they grabbed hold of him and Katrina. His feet never touched the ground after that as he was carried at dizzying speed.

Five seconds later, he was inside a building. Dust swirled in the yellow light. *Clang* ...

A pair of massive doors slammed shut. The air was instantly still.

The stranger who had beckoned them stood in the hallway—flecks of white matter clung to her black hair. She stared at the closed doors. Her eyes were wide. Clearly, she feared that the doors would be flung open to admit the scarecrows. In Dan's imagination they became snarling monsters, with claws instead of hands. Sharp teeth would be glistening in alien jaws. Faintly, he could hear scraping noises coming through the thick substance of those formidable doors. The scarecrows were trying to claw their way through.

But the doors were holding.

The woman heaved a huge sigh of relief. Her expression was a grave one, though there was a degree of satisfaction there as well. Placing her hands on her hips, she appraised her guests.

Then she spoke loud enough to be heard through the helmets: "You made it ... thankfully, those guys didn't get their hands on you. Believe me, death is something you would love to embrace if they did. Okay, ladies and gentlemen. Follow me. It's a heck of a climb, but we'll get there in the end." She began to ascend a spiral staircase. "By the way, I'm Doctor Priya Singh. Priya works nicely for me, though. You can take off the helmets. You'll find breathing a heck of a lot easier."

Garner had flipped open his visor. "Hey ... Doc. What are those things out there? And what in fuck's name killed Ryan? It was like a giant sea urchin ... all those freaking spines. They fucking skewered him. Hey! Aren't you going to answer me?"

Doctor Singh did not answer him. She continued her long climb up the stairs.

TWENTY-SIX

A TOWER DOES A FORTRESS MAKE

Ryan's spectacularly hideous death plunged everyone into a mood of bleak depression. Understandably so, thought Dan, as he climbed the spiral staircase.

Initially, only he and Captain Flynn had fully removed their helmets, leaving them hanging down their backs by the anchor strapping. However, scaling the steps, floor after floor, became more arduous. The others began to unclip their helmets; after which, they gratefully sucked in the cool air, which smelt of freshly baked bread.

Ascending hundreds of steps became increasingly brutal. Dan's thigh muscles felt like they were on fire. He helped Katrina during the ascent. Thankfully, apart from some bloody scratches on her face, which were inflicted by flying debris, she seemed pretty much okay.

By the time they'd reached the sixth floor, some were beginning to curse loudly.

"Isn't there a fucking elevator?" asked Borman. Drops of perspiration were rolling down his face into his coppery beard.

Priya called back. "I tried to visualise one, but maybe my powers of imagination aren't forceful enough."

"I beg your pardon?" Borman shook his head, puzzled.

"You try picturing an elevator in detail—all the doors, the motors, the control panel where you press buttons that take you up and down. It's not easy."

Borman pulled out his water bottle. "She's fucking crazy."

Jellsby abruptly sat down on a step. "I'm not going any further. I can't. This climb is killing me."

Priya just shrugged. "Take your time."

"Didn't you hear me? Not one more step. My heart … s' going like a jackhammer."

Priya gave a sympathetic smile. "I'm sorry. You either climb up to the twentieth floor or you stay here. There's no food on these levels … you'll go hungry."

"Bitch! Fucking bitch!" Jellsby's voice degenerated into an animal screech of pain.

Everyone turned to stare at him as he hunched up, clutching his stomach.

Garner sneered. "The scientist is getting Cold Turkey for dinner. He needs …"

Without even trying to conceal the gesture from Jellsby, Garner pressed forked fingers against his right arm, miming an injection.

Jellsby awarded him a wounded glance as if to say "Hey, that hurt." Garner didn't care two hoots what hurt Jellsby and what didn't.

Captain Flynn nodded toward an open doorway that led into an empty room. "Professor Jellsby. Do what you need to do, then join us on the twentieth floor."

They continued the hellish climb. Some would, from time to time, curse loudly then sit on the stairs for a while to catch their breath. Nobody else waited with them, and the motley group of figures in spacesuits continued their ascent. The only person there who wasn't out of breath was Captain Flynn—the woman clearly took good care of herself.

Most of the floors didn't even have rooms, they were merely open areas with oblong windows. Artificial light appeared to come from some dim source within the walls, so each floor was a shadowy void.

Gen called out, "Doctor Singh. Any monsters in here that we should be worried about?"

"Just the ones in your own heads. And it's Priya. Scrub the 'doctor'."

When they reached the next floor, Dan saw that along one wall were thirty or so coffins, standing upright. They formed a solemn phalanx of sentinels.

Priya noticed that everyone had paused to stare at those grim objects.

"Yep," she said. "Bone boxes. Actual caskets. I should have warned you. Be careful what you wish for."

Garner frowned. "Priya. What are you trying to tell us?"

"The Factory provides." She gave a grim smile. "I should explain … the Factory is the name we gave to the complex outside."

Captain Flynn raised her hand before asking a question. *School day habits cut deeper into our minds deeper than we suppose,* Dan realized.

Flynn said, "Priya. I recognise your name. You were part of the crew of the first crewed trip to Callisto onboard Rib One?"

"I was."

"You stayed here after Rib One returned to Earth?"

"Yes."

Flynn continued: "Eighteen people had remained on the Rib and were safely delivered back to our planet. That's how we learned that future crews must be AB plus in order to make the journey without slipping into a coma."

"I'm glad to hear that they made it back alive."

Garner still struggled with what he'd heard from Priya's lips earlier. "Hey, Doc. You told us the Factory provides. What do you mean?"

Priya glanced up the stairs and sighed. "We still have a long way to climb. Save your questions for later."

"No, tell us," Borman insisted. "How does this thing you call the Factory provide?"

"Okay." She held up her hands. "I'll answer this one, then you really need to conserve every scrap of your strength for getting to the top of the building." Her calm eyes scanned their faces. "The Factory provides whatever you need. How it accomplishes this, I do not know. Nearest thing to magic I ever did see. The fact of the matter is, somehow the Factory scans your brain, identifying what it is that you need to remain alive, then the Factory supplies it. You understand what I'm telling you?"

Dan noticed how people glanced at one another. Mainly, they were puzzled, though the way he saw some narrowing their eyes suggested that they believed Priya to be insane.

Garner stared at the coffins. "You mean, the Factory looked into your head, and it saw that you wanted lots of coffins, so they suddenly appeared?"

"Yeah, like I said, ladies and gentlemen. Be careful what you wish for." Priya's expression became uneasy. "And the Factory can't differentiate between rational, conscious thought and the dreams you dream at night. Be warned, you're going to see some weird things here in the Tower."

Garner seemed to have difficulty in processing what Priya had told him. "Really? All we have to do is think what we want, and the Factory delivers?"

"Sure. You visualise what you want. If, for example, you wanted a motorcycle, you picture it in your head, though you must picture every mechanical detail. Then, when you wake up in the morning, hey presto, the big shiny motorcycle might be there next to your bed. However, the Factory is capricious; you don't always get what you want. Generally, it scans your mind for fundamental needs—food, drink, etcetera." Her voice became even more serious, like she needed to convey a warning of absolute danger. "So ... beware ... human beings can secretly nurture very unpleasant thoughts. The Factory cannot sift nasty and psychotic wishes from logical requirements for food."

Dan recalled what N'Darbi had told him. That onboard the Rib, your dreams might sometimes come up to you when you're awake and tap you on the shoulder. It appeared the same applied here on Callisto.

Priya began climbing the stairs again.

Borman called out. "One more question. There are rumors that most of the crew of Rib One did not make it back to Earth from Callisto. Is that true?"

"Indeed, that is true."

"What happened to them?"

"Really, sir? You haven't figured that out?"

Borman shook his head. So did most of the people there.

However, Katrina had already figured out the answer, because in a clear voice she said: "The things that chased us—they're the crew, aren't they?"

Priya gave a solemn nod. "Yes. They were the crew. And they were once human beings ... whether they are human beings now, I can't really say."

A barrage of questions flooded the stairwell. Priya, however, held up her hand as if to say *No more*. After that, she resumed climbing the steps, one foot after another. She was determined to reach the top without further delay.

Storm winds blew against the building. They produced mournful cries—the sound of lost souls crying for release from eternal pain.

TWENTY-SEVEN

"YOU WEREN'T CAREFUL ABOUT WHAT YOU WISHED FOR"

They sat at a long table in what served as the lounge on the twentieth floor. The room comprised perhaps a quarter of the entire story. Beyond the window, greyish fragments flew, borne on turbulent currents of air. Pieces of bone clattered against windowpanes, sounding like fingernails tapping—a noise suggestive of a ghostly presence seeking to attract the occupants' attention.

They were at such a height the ground was indistinct, as were other buildings and the pale mounds of bone. There was no sign of scarecrows. Priya had explained that these creatures were once the crew of Rib One. Though she had not described how they had been transformed into things that were nothing less than monsters. As for Priya, she'd tied back her long hair into a ponytail, and was ladling vegetable curry into bowls, which Captain Flynn handed out. The curry smelt pungently spicy. Also, there were piles of pale brown naan bread on plates. Melted butter glistened on the naan. A sight to make Dan's stomach growl with hunger.

Dan thanked Flynn for the bowl of curry she set in front of him. He was the first to be served. Garner and Borman rolled their eyes. Garner silently mouthed the words *Captain's pet* at Borman, and his expression was one of suspicion rather than humor. He'd clearly decided that Dan wasn't in the "us" camp but was firmly in the camp where authority over others resided. The man resented it.

Jellsby rocked up to the lounge. There was a dreamy expression on his smiling face. He'd clearly shot some good gear into his veins—the guy was enjoying his ride on the opiate express. He took his place at the table, tore off a fistful of naan, stuffed it into this mouth, then began chewing with an expression of fuzzy-edged pleasure.

By this time, everyone had removed their space suits. They wore thin sweatshirts and sweatpants—their feet, however, looked cumbersome in the spacesuit boots. They didn't have a change of footwear—so, clumpy boots would have to do.

Priya began speaking briskly as she ladled the curry: "Right. There is a lot to tell you—here are the bullet points. First, though, a question. Are you in contact with your other crewmates on the Crab?"

Flynn answered. "Comms are down. At least they are with regard to speaking to personnel on the Crab. It seems to be a range issue, because I could use comms to speak with colleagues that came with me on the recce."

Priya nodded. "Okay. Don't count on reestablishing radio contact with the Crab. What you're telling me confirms what I suspected. That the environment here chokes radio communication with anyone more than a hundred paces away."

"What a crappy situation," muttered Borman with a shake of his head.

"It's not far back to the Crab," Gen pointed out. "If needs must, we can despatch a runner to deliver a message."

Dan said, "You're forgetting the scarecrows."

"Uh?"

"The things that tried to hunt us down when we came here."

Priya cleared her throat. "Your attention, please, ladies and gentlemen. I need to impart additional information. In the interests of candor, I confirm that the first crewed mission here to Callisto was a big, freaking horror show of a disaster. One hundred and fifty men and women arrived here. A small number remained on the ship as skeleton crew. The others began to explore. And people started to die—there are all kinds of nasties out there. Those that didn't die ended up becoming Scarecrows, as you have termed those creatures. No, don't interrupt. I'll give you the details later. Therefore, soon I was the only human crew member left on Callisto after Rib One returned to Earth. So, I retreated to this building and made it my fortress. We are safe in here from the Scarecrows—yeah, that's a good name you chose. We'll stick with that, eh?" Everyone now had curry, so she filled a bowl for herself and sat down at the head of the table. "Scarecrows won't kill you. However, they will transform you into what they are. Stay away from those monsters—they are horrifying, nasty and downright evil. Remember what I said earlier. The Factory will provide whatever you need. Even as I'm speaking to you, the Factory will be scanning every gooey nook and cranny of your brains. It'll be finding out what you need to live. Be mindful of what you hope for. Because that hoped-for gift from the Factory might turn out to be your worst nightmare." Priya spooned curry into her mouth. "The ingredients it supplies are surprisingly tasty."

Flynn's eyes were bright with anticipation. "So what is the strategy?"

"Strategy?" Priya began eating a piece of naan; the melted butter was making her fingers glisten. "You tell me. I'm just a doctor who became stranded here. I take it you have scientific experts with you, tasked with repairing the gravity generator?"

Captain Flynn gave a sharp nod. "Of course. That is our primary mission. We will locate the mechanism that generates the gravity and assess whatever is necessary for its repair and return to function."

Katrina let out a scream of disbelief as she jumped to her feet. "You are kidding us, Flynn, aren't you?"

"Sit down, soldier."

"No, I'm not a soldier—nobody is, apart from you." Katrina's eyes glittered with rage. "And don't you dare begin by lying to Priya. If she hadn't called us to the building, we'd have been caught by those fucking monsters."

"Katrina. You will obey my orders."

"No, I will not." She pointed a quivering finger at Flynn. "Tell Priya the truth. We, the crew of Rib Two, are expendable. Our mission isn't to repair the gravity gizmo. See? I don't even know the technical term for the thing. No, we were sent here, simply to find out if we returned alive. Then the Caucus would send the genuine scientific team."

Priya actually flinched with shock. "Is this true?"

Garner laughed—a bitter sound. No humor there. "Of course, it's true. We have one scientist—there he is, at the end of the table. Prof Jellsby. He's a drug addict. Our bosses don't have any realistic expectation he's going to get the gravity whirligig firing up on all cylinders again. Believe me, Priya, the people you see here, with a couple of exceptions, are a bunch of misfits. Some of us are ex-jail rats. Some are bankrupts, who are desperate for easy money. Most of us are life's losers who, by the sheer gift of genetics have got AB-positive blood, meaning we can ride the Ribs without turning into a bunch of sleeping beauties. You understand? We've as much chance of fixing the gravity gizmo as a shack full of rats have of inventing time travel. Look at us. We're deadbeats. What we're thinking right now is, how do we get home again so we can get our hands on all that lovely astronaut salary that's been paid into our bank accounts while we've been schlepping across the fucking Solar System." He glared down at the bowl in front of him. Then he raised his head and, with a peculiar smile, murmured, "Lovely curry, by the way."

For a while, nobody spoke. The winds blew against the Tower, conjuring moaning cries that rose and fell. Fragments of bone tapped against the window glass.

Dan looked back when he heard a sound in the doorway. It was distinctly the pitter-patter of claws on the floor. He watched a brown dog enter the room with a swaying walk. Its dark eyes were dull—and they were dry-looking, rather than the shiny moist effect that living dogs' eyes should have. It waddled around the table. Its snout was raised, sniffing the aroma of curry on the air. Dan noticed that one of its paws had been shaved clean of fur.

He thought: *The paw is shaved when a dog has an injection.* In fact, what came to mind was the deeply unhappy day he had to take his mother's golden Labrador to the vet to be put to sleep. The cancer was too advanced for treatment. Dan recalled the veterinary surgeon gently using an electric razor to remove the fur. Then she administered the lethal injection through the bare patch of skin. All painless, of course. But so profoundly sad.

Priya glared at the people around the table. "Who is responsible for this animal?"

Borman raised his hand. He'd glanced at the dog when it arrived, now he looked away from the animal as it came to stand by his chair. The man's heart appeared to be breaking with nothing less than despair.

"Okay, I get what you were trying to do, sir." Priya shook her head. "But didn't I warn you? Always be careful what you wish for."

A tear rolled down the man's right cheek into the red beard. He looked utterly devastated. "I tried to make Bella come back as I remembered her when I was a kid. But when I began picturing her, after you told me what this place could do, all I could remember was how she looked when I took her to be put to sleep. The vet shaved a front paw. Then put the needle in. Bella looked at the needle going in, just watching it like it was really interesting to see, then she looked up at me ... just for a second ... then her eyes went dull looking. Just blank circles ... and I felt so ..." His big shoulders were shaking as he started to weep. "Please," he whispered. "I don't want to see Bella like this. How do I make her go away?"

"You can't." Priya's tone was cooly professional—the consummate medical doctor giving their patient bad news. "Bella is here to stay. All I can add is that she is your problem now. You must take responsibility for what you have brought into existence."

The big man shook his head. "I can't. I can't." His tears fell onto the tabletop, leaving drops of liquid grief.

Bella moved sluggishly forward. Its dead eyes were staring at

Borman. Then it leaned sideways so it could gently press the side of its head against his leg. Borman's sole reaction was to force the palms of his hands against his eyes. He did not want to see the grotesque thing that he had created. But it wasn't going to leave his side.

TWENTY-EIGHT

THE ROTTEN TRUTH

After the meal, Priya Singh invited everyone to follow her down to the basement.

Nobody wanted to go with her. Not all the way down hundreds of stairs.

When she explained why she wanted everyone to see what was in the basement, they all nodded. They began the long descent.

"Borman," she said. "Bring the dog."

"No. I don't want to even see Bella ever again."

"Bring her. Or you will be seeing her all the time."

Borman brought the dog.

Dan walked beside Katrina as they began their descent from the twentieth floor.

Katrina shot him a sideways glance. "Dan. I'm right, aren't I?"

"About what?"

"Pretty much everything. That we've been sent on a suicide mission. Our only purpose is to see if people with the AB soup in their veins can make it back to Earth alive. Then they will send the real scientific team here to repair the gravity generator."

Dan sighed. "Yup. The mission bosses lied to us, didn't they?"

"They lied to the entire world. Remember when all those live TV pictures went out of astronauts arriving back on Rib One? They certainly hadn't been to Callisto. At least, not all of them. Because Priya told us that most of the crew turned into those scarecrow things."

Those words of Katrina's would take some time to digest. They walked in silence after that. The only sound was the clump of feet. That and the slow click of the dog's claws. The dog—or, rather, something that resembled a dog—walked beside Borman. Dan knew that the man had used the mysterious powers the Factory possessed to conjure the animal into existence. But he'd failed to conjure an exact replica. All he'd succeeded in doing was creating the abomination with the dull eyes. Admittedly, Borman's face was the essence of misery. He regretted his attempt to bring back his beloved pet from childhood. He'd got a monster. Now he was stuck with it.

The hurricane still blew around the Tower. The winds morphed into vicious roars of sound that could have been the hunting calls of dinosaurs. Dan knew that the terrain outside the Tower was still inside some vast building, but that didn't stop the massive space from being the venue for storms that were frightening enough to make the bravest person's blood run cold. Dan glimpsed Priya at the head of this sombre procession as it trudged downward. Every so often, Flynn would glance at him. Once, she gave him a secret smile that only served to trouble him even more. What did the woman expect from him?

Well … he could guess. But even if he was hot to trot regarding a romance with the captain, that would only be a source of aggravation amongst the crew. He decided to remain polite but emotionally cold with Flynn. Even standoffish. After all, a commanding officer's authority didn't extend to ordering a guy to strip naked and climb into bed with them. Did it?

Flynn glanced at him. He pretended to find something interesting on the back of his hand and gazed at that instead of allowing her to catch his eye.

The stairwell was gloomy. Dim light oozed from walls that appeared to possess some quality of luminescence. Shadows pooled in the open doorways of rooms that led off from the landings. If anything, those dark chambers had all the chilling appearance of tombs. All too easy to imagine that creatures lurked in there. And were there open windows where the Scarecrows could climb in? And were there other horrors prowling around outside the building as they searched for an entrance?

Walking down the stairs was nowhere as difficult as climbing them. Even so, by the time they reached that set of formidable doors, which sealed off the outside world, Dan's legs were shaking with the effort of the descent. He stared down at the floor.

Priya evidently deduced what he was thinking. "Self-cleaning. Debris blown into the building, when I opened the doors, has been absorbed into the floor. Don't ask me how it happens. I simply do not know. Then again, you will encounter lots of strange things while you are here. Okay. Follow me down the ladder. The basement will be even gloomier than this part of the building. Borman. You will have to carry the dog down with you."

He shook his head. The man looked so miserable that Dan thought he'd begin weeping again.

Borman muttered, "I can't … I'm not touching that thing. It's not Bella. It's not."

Dan stepped forward. "I'll do it."

Priya frowned. "Dan. It is Dan, isn't it? Bella is Borman's responsibility."

Dan glared back at Priya. "I'll do it."

Katrina stepped forward, too. "Priya. Don't you have a heart? You can see what it's done to Borman. He's suffering."

Priya slid back a door. "I do have a heart. And I'm going to show you what happens if you get too sentimental and do the dreadful thing of turning your sentimental wishes into flesh and bone. Follow me."

Priya climbed down the ladder set in the wall of the shaft. Flynn followed her. Then went Jellsby. The others followed.

Borman put his hand on Dan's shoulder. "You don't have to do this for me. I can carry Bella down there."

"I'll do it. If you ask me, you've suffered enough."

"Thanks, bud."

With that, Borman quickly climbed down the ladder. He was clearly relieved that he didn't have to touch the dog.

TWENTY-NINE

RAWBACK

Carrying the dog down into the basement was difficult. Not just the weight of the thing, which was considerable. Dan found it hard to touch the furry body. This close contact with a living replica of a creature that had died years ago was emotionally tough to handle.

He had to climb down using one hand. The other was under the dog's belly. He felt the bristle of its hard fur against the bare skin of his palm and his fingers. Although his hand was under its chest, he could not feel a heartbeat. *Then does it possess a heart?* The Factory had molded the dog from images in Borman's memory. The dog had a brown nose. There were no open nostrils, however. Just a soft lump of flesh that vaguely resembled a canine snout. As Dan carried the dog down the ladder, it stared up at him. The eyes were dry. They were also completely dull. Dan sensed the dog gazed at him while asking itself, *Why does this man carry me? Why doesn't my owner carry me?* Thankfully, the dog did not protest at being carried by a stranger. It remained a passive lump of flesh in Dan's grasp. Soft flesh at that. He couldn't feel a ribcage. Unpleasantly, the dog had a stale odour. A bit like going into a room that hadn't been aired in a long time.

At the bottom of the ladder, there was Katrina. She helped him put the dog down onto the floor.

"Thanks, Katrina."

"You're welcome."

As they both released their grip on the dog, when it was safely down, Katrina lightly ran her fingers over the back of Dan's hand and smiled at him.

Priya's voice echoed from the walls. "This is what I brought you to see. Consider it a method of driving home the lesson that you conjure up people and pets at your peril."

The basement appeared to be vast. It was so gloomy that Dan couldn't see more than twenty feet in either direction.

Priya raised a flashlight and switched it on. Instantly, a blaze of dazzling light sprang out, which destroyed the shadows that veiled their surroundings.

"This is what I brought you here to see." Priya's voice became a shout. "The Rawbacks!"

The light revealed dozens of men and women standing in a line along a blank expanse of grey wall. The figures were off all different ages. Dan noticed that there were even children. The ages of the boys and girls must have ranged from five years of age upward. Nearly everyone gasped with shock. Dan saw Katrina shiver. Goosebumps rose on her bare arms. She glanced back at him. Her eyes were filled with horror.

Garner let out a shout. "What the hell? Why have you locked people in a cellar?"

Flynn stared at the figures. "There are children. Just little children."

The mood was turning from shock to anger. Dan suspected that Priya wasn't far away from being attacked. Not just a verbal attack, either.

Gen clenched her fists. "Priya? You fucking monster!"

Priya played the light over the figures. "These are the Rawbacks. Look closer. They aren't what they first seem."

Dan did look closer. The light revealed men, women, children—yes. But then he realized why Priya had chosen the name Rawback. Those peoples were 'raw'. That is to say, they weren't fully formed. Most were missing features from their faces. This, in some instances, included a lack of eyes, nostrils, mouths. They wore clothes, yes. But the clothes were shapeless garments. Fabrics lacked any coherent color scheme. Just a smudge of green here. A streak of blue there. Generally, they were shades of grey.

Professor Jellsby appraised what he saw with a scientific eye. "These are products of the Factory?" he asked. "You used the power of your thought to form these creatures?"

"Just one of them. The rest were wished into existence by my crewmates when they realized that they could bring a loved one back, just by wanting it to be so. That was before they understood that it's more difficult than you first think to picture a loved one down to the last detail. They succeeded in getting the general appearance right, but it's very hard to sustain an accurate visualisation of a boyfriend, say, from long ago. Or the dog that you loved so much." She glanced at Bella who'd gone to stand close to Borman.

Flynn stepped closer to the aptly named Rawbacks. "They're alive?"

"Yes." Priya moved toward the figure of a young man. He had no face. "This is my husband. Imagine how happy I was when I realized I could make him appear in this building, so I wouldn't be alone. You can see how badly it turned out for me."

The man without a face took slow steps toward Priya. Then, in a way that was utterly zombie-like, he raised his hands.

Priya shuddered. "He wants to embrace me … in fact, he wants to make love to me … draw your own conclusions, guys." She held up her hand. "Benedict. Go stand against the wall. You are not to move. Unless I call you."

It had taken a while for the understanding to filter through the Rawbacks' brains to realize that they were in the presence of human beings.

Benedict obediently remained against the wall. However, the others began to shuffle forward. They all moved slowly. Most were clumsy. Again, they resembled zombies.

A boy of around ten moved away from the wall. "Daddy. Have you come to take me to the park?" The voice was hoarse and deep and anything but childlike. "Daddy. Will you buy me an ice cream? Daddy. Give me a hug."

The boy moved toward Katrina. His eyes were tightly closed.

"Daddy."

Katrina backed away. "Please. Don't come any closer."

"Daddy."

"I'm not your daddy."

Priya shone the flashlight at the boy. The oval face that was as white as milk appeared to gleam with dazzling brightness. The boy lunged forward. He grasped Katrina's hand in his.

Katrina did not shout or pull away. Clearly, she was distressed, though.

"My name is Katrina. I'm not your Daddy."

Priya's expression was one of deep sadness. "The boy doesn't understand. Their brains don't function properly. But then could anyone here fully understand how a brain works, never mind conveying that in an image to the Factory, so it could build an intelligent mind."

"Daddy. Let's go for a walk." He began pulling Katrina by the hand.

"No."

"We'll go for a walk to the park."

"No!"

The boy suddenly froze. His eyes were still tightly shut. Then, with a sudden movement that was incredibly fast, he spun around and tilted his face upward toward Katrina's. The eyelids opened. And dozens of red spiders ran out from the sockets. They poured down the boy's cheeks, then down his chest.

Katrina jerked her hand free from the boy's hand, then took several steps backward. Her expression was one of utter horror as she stared at the boy, and at the spiders gushing from his otherwise empty eye sockets. There were gasps of shock from the people around her.

Gen looked as if she might vomit. "Uh ... spiders. All those horrible, disgusting spiders."

Garner snarled at Priya. "You trying to freak us out?"

"I'm trying to demonstrate to you why you must not repeat our mistakes."

Everyone stared at the boy. He'd opened his mouth—yet more spiders ran down his face. They flooded over his lips and onto his tongue.

Flynn grimaced. "Whoever created this thing must have been evil."

"Remember what I told you. The Factory cannot differentiate between a wish we make when we are awake, and a dream when we're sleeping. The Factory has a habit of making our dream come true."

Borman's expression was one of disgust. "I'm never going to go to sleep again."

The dog shuffled closer. It leaned a bristly side against his leg. Borman groaned with despair.

Priya said, "I think you've had enough of this horror show down here."

Garner's eyes flashed with anger. "These Rawbacks are just copies. Why not kill them?"

Jellsby agreed. "If these aren't real people, just slaughter them."

Priya shrugged. "Go ahead. Some of my colleagues tried. You'll find that they aren't easy to kill. Also, you must deal with the emotion of becoming a murderer." She led the way back to the ladder. "Oh … Borman. Leave Bella here. She can join the rest of the Rawbacks. She won't be lonely."

"Is that a joke?" Borman was the one to look angry now.

Priya shook her head. "We're human beings, aren't we? We have empathy. It's only natural for us to worry about the wellbeing of these Rawbacks. Yes, logically, we know they don't have brains like we do. They don't have feelings. But we are emotional creatures—on an instinctive level we continue to believe that the Rawbacks might be suffering. So, why not pretend that Bella will happily play with these children when you're back upstairs?"

Borman was emotionally crushed. Nevertheless, he nodded. "Yeah. I get it. Why not?"

"Indeed." Jellsby smirked. "It's like pretending that dead people go to heaven."

Nobody answered him. One by one, they scaled the ladder back to the hallway. Then they plodded upstairs. Everyone was exhausted by the traumatic events of the day.

When they reached the seventeenth floor, Priya shone the flashlight through an open doorway.

"The Factory has been busy," she told everyone. "You'll find what you need."

The light revealed lines of beds that hadn't been there before. Everything looked clean and in good order. There were sheets on the beds. Pillows. Blankets. Bedside tables. Jugs of water. Glasses.

"Utilitarian," said Gen.

"Like my old barracks," added Flynn.

Katrina yawned. "I don't care if it's not a thing of beauty. I'm going to bed and I'm going to sleep for twenty hours straight."

Jellsby chuckled: "Make sure all your dreams are sweet ones."

THIRTY

THE UNWANTED CONSEQUENCES OF DREAMING

Dan Karlton woke to discover that the dormitory was different to the one he went to sleep in. His bed was in the middle of a long line of beds where fellow crew members slept. Some were still asleep. Most, however, sat up in bed and looked around at how the room had changed. From the wall above Spiro's bed, vines had grown. They tumbled in long, flowing strands of green that held bunches of black grapes. Elsewhere in the room, pink ribbons crisscrossed the ceiling. And in the corner, next to Katrina's bed was what appeared to be something that resembled a film studio set. That is to say, two freestanding walls had been erected. The structure formed a rough approximation of a bedroom. There was a small child's bed against one of the walls. The bed had a grey comforter and an oversize pillow. There was a little table with dolls sitting on top of it. However, the dolls were formed from shapes that rose out of the table itself and weren't separate from the substance that the table was made from. On the walls were posters of horses. The images of the horses were blurry smudges, merely suggestive of actual horses. The clearest part of the image were overlarge eyes that bulged from the horse's skulls.

Spiro reached up to cup a bunch of grapes in his open palm. He marvelled at the sight of the grapes, which were glossy and plump with juice.

"Last night," he said, "I dreamt I was back at my grandparents' farm in Kefalonia. Vines grew up against the outside of the house. They always seemed to be heavy with grapes, just like this."

Garner scowled as he climbed out of bed. "If our dreams come to life in this damn spook house, God help us if we have nightmares."

Katrina darted out of bed to the faux bedroom. "This is my room from when I was a child, but I don't remember dreaming about it last night."

Jellsby cleared his throat. "There is indubitably some exotic technology that is scanning our minds. It's sifting through our memories. And turning what we remember from our past into reality."

Another crew member laughed and said cruelly, "Why didn't you wake up surrounded by oversized syringes full of junk, then?"

"Nobody takes addicts seriously, do they? We're just figures of fun to most people." Jellsby rubbed his bare forearm. Track marks left by years of heroin injections were clearly visible. He coughed in a throaty way and Dan thought he looked shivery, as if he was feeling the early symptoms of the heroin leaving his system. The guy would have to shoot up again soon or start to suffer from withdrawal.

Katrina walked into the rough-as-they come recreation of her childhood bedroom. Spiro reached up and pulled a grape from a bunch.

"The posters of horses are almost identical," Katrina said, "though the images are blurry. And those are my dolls. The big one is Sue-Sue. That's Running Star with the basket." She gave an embarrassed smile. "I gave names to all my dolls." She looked closer at the dolls. "But they're part of the tabletop. It's like it's molded from one piece of plastic."

Katrina lightly touched one of the walls. "No attempt was made to replicate the flowered wallpaper."

As she ran her finger over the wall, it crumbled into tiny pieces, which cascaded down onto the floor with a pattering sound.

"Uh." She wrinkled her nose. "It's like the wall is made from the kind of crackers you put cheese on. It's not even properly solid. She touched the child's bed. With a soft whispery sound, it dissolved into a mound of dust.

Spiro bit into a plump grape. "Ack! Damn thing's like rubber. There's no juice inside. Fucking bitter as hell, too."

Spiro pulled a face as he wiped his mouth on the bedsheet.

Borman stood with his hands on his hips as he looked around. "What a place? It's going to send us crazy, isn't it?"

Gen nodded. "We won't dare go to sleep at night in case we wake up and the place is full of monsters from our dreams."

Another crew member voiced some troubling questions. "And what about those things in the cellar? Those things that the Doc calls Rawbacks? What if they get out and come up here in the middle of the night?"

"The Rawbacks won't hurt you."

Nobody had noticed Priya standing in the doorway.

She continued: "Rawbacks are, on the whole, obedient to our commands. They do want to be with human beings. Therefore, they will sometimes leave the basement and come up the staircase to these levels. Don't be afraid of them. Yes, being in their presence does have a distressing effect on us, but they won't attack you."

Spiro pulled off another grape. "I bit into one of these. They aren't real grapes."

"Just as the people in the basement aren't real."

Dan said, "What do we do about the vines and the bedroom? Is there a way to get rid of them?"

Priya shook her head. "No need. These aren't like Rawbacks. I term them 'phantom extrusions'. The building will gradually reabsorb them back into itself."

Garner poked a finger into one of the fake bedroom walls. Again, it crumbled into tiny fragments.

He eyed the mound with contempt. "In all the time you've been here, you haven't seen the aliens who do this shit? You know, making our dreams into something we can touch?"

Priya shook her head. "No, I haven't seen any intelligent extraterrestrials. Not to my knowledge, anyway. In truth, I think the creators of the Factory vanished millions of years ago. The machines they built still work—but only just. That's why the gravity generator failed. There's nobody to maintain it anymore."

Borman was all fired-up and ready to act. "So, it's up to us to fix the gravity generator. We're the only ones who can save our planet."

Jellsby gave a scornful laugh. "How do we repair a sophisticated mechanism devised by extraterrestrials? Their intellect must have been vastly superior to ours."

"We gotta try."

"Sure ... you try, Borman. But you won't have a chance in hell."

Borman lunged at Jellsby and grabbed the man by the throat. "Hey! Instead of talking fucking garbage, you should be coming up with ideas to fix the thing! You're the scientist."

Garner bunched his fists. "Yeah, Jelly-belly. Start thinking or I'll start punching some clarity into your fucking head."

Violence crackled in the air. An electric feeling that, to Dan, was potently dangerous. Come to that, the entire situation was stressful. He knew that it wouldn't take much for fistfights to erupt. Right now, Jellsby was the focus of everyone's anger.

Captain Flynn walked into the dormitory. Dan glanced at the bed she'd occupied last night. In fact, the one next to his. And he guessed that was a deliberate choice of hers. The bed was neatly made, and he concluded she'd woken early before going on some errand of her own. Flynn stared at Borman as he shook Jellsby by the throat.

Briskly, she clapped her hands together. "Borman. Leave him alone."

Borman rounded on Flynn. "It's up to you to turn this piece of shit into something like a functioning scientist. It's his job to fix that machine so it stops asteroids from smashing the Earth to crap. I've got kids. What if the next chunk of sky rock wipes them out?"

Flynn spoke coldly. "Professor Jellsby will play his part."

"The only part he can play is a fucking doormat. And I'd happily use him to wipe the shit off my boots." Borman shoved Jellsby back onto the bed.

Jellsby jumped back to his feet. "Okay. I'm an addict. You know what did it? Seeing my wife and my kids die in a house fire. Her ex-husband poured gasoline through an open window and set it alight. I got out. They didn't." He was screaming now. Tears rolled down gnarly cheeks into black stubble. "I tried to save my family, but my neighbours held me back. So, yes … I inject myself and, for a few hours, it's like a merciful death. Okay, you all know the truth now. But, sure as poop sticks to a blanket, what I've said won't stop Garner and Borman punching me in the face as soon as Captain Flynn leaves."

Flynn spoke firmly. "There will be no physical violence while I'm in command. Though Borman is right. It's our responsibility to save every man, woman, and child on Earth. Somehow, we've got to repair the machine. When we accomplish that, it will draw the asteroids back from our planet and so prevent further collisions."

Jellsby dragged his rucksack out from under his bed. Then he pulled an ampoule of golden liquid from a side pocket. He was going to inject his dose of blessed forgetfulness again. Everyone there noticed what he was doing. They said nothing. Even Garner and Borman, the two hotheads who were as unpredictable as a forest fire, said nothing. Their eyes were expressive enough, nonetheless. Anger flared there, together with a barely repressed urge to commit violence.

Flynn took a deep breath. Dan realized that the woman's heart must have been pounding, as she expected Borman to do his utmost to murder Jellsby. However, the moment of real danger appeared to have passed—for now. Jellsby tied a strap around his upper arm to force the arteries up against the underside of the skin. Nearly everyone looked away; they didn't want to see him inject. Dan wondered why the guy hadn't gone off somewhere to shoot up in private. Maybe he wanted to demonstrate to everyone that this wasn't really about getting out of his skull on narcotics.

That, instead, this was really about medicating the painful grief away for a spell.

Dan spoke up. To break the silence as much as anything, which was starting to become fraught with tension again: "Okay. We do everything in our power to fix the machine. Where do we begin?"

Flynn smiled at him—the same kind of smile a teacher awards to their favorite pupil who asks the perfect question. "Good point, Dan. And it's something we can't postpone, because as soon as we get word from the crew back on the Rib that the Bleeds have started, we'll have to return to the Crab or there's a danger the ship will leave without us, and we'll be stranded here."

Priya sighed. "I do know where the machine is located. But getting the thing fixed might be the least of our problems. You see, if you step outside the Tower, you will be attacked."

Katrina shuddered. "You mean by those scarecrow things?"

"Yes. Outside, you will find a fate much worse than Death waiting for you."

THIRTY-ONE

MANIFEST

Dan ate a chicken sandwich. The Factory had provided the bread, the chicken, and a highly-salted butter. A little while ago, the notion of putting something into his mouth that had been extruded by a mechanism built by alien creatures had seemed strange—even disgusting. However, the bread tasted like ordinary wholegrain bread, the chicken tasted like roast chicken. The butter was very salty, just how Dan liked it. OK, there was a slight peppery aftertaste to the sandwich. It had a pleasant enough flavor, though.

"Given time, you get used to anything."

He glanced back to see who had spoken. It was Captain Flynn, and she was smiling.

"I've got apple pie." She sat beside him on the sofa (also fabricated by whatever alien mechanism worked its magic here). "It tastes like apple pie. The apple is crunchy. There's a crispness to the pastry. This proves, in my opinion, that the alien species who made all this ..." She waved her spoon, indicating both the food and the structures visible through the window. "... are benevolent."

"*Were* benevolent," said Dan. "Priya thinks that the species is now extinct, and all the machines are automatic. Though the machines are quite shy about the extrusion process. The food appears in cupboards when we're asleep. Nobody sees it being manifested. And nobody sees the machines that make it."

With an odd change in the topic of conversation, Flynn declared, "Despite what is happening to us, we need to live a life. We must find happiness here."

What is she driving at, thought Dan. And then guessed exactly what she was driving at. Blandly, he murmured something along the lines that she was right, and everyone should find ways to relax and not allow the stress of a decidedly strange environment get to them.

"I've had an idea." Flynn locked her gaze onto his face "We could explore this building. Just the two of us. You never know, we might discover something interesting."

At that moment, Garner ambled up with a glass of beer clutched in that massive paw of his. "I've had eight of these." He held up the glass. "Tastes like beer. But I haven't felt even the tiniest glow. There's no alcohol in here, I'm sure."

Dan smiled. "Maybe we can all get together and imagine what a real brewery is like, then maybe the Factory will build one for us."

Garner chuckled. "Yeah, as long as we give it enough information about how yeast, hops and water and stuff all ferment to make alcohol." Garner had other things on his mind, too. "Hey, Captain Flynn. Shouldn't we send someone back to the Crab to tell the others what's happening, seeing as our comms aren't up to getting a message through?"

Dan grabbed the opportunity to make his excuses and leave, just in case Flynn invited him on an expedition to explore whatever nether regions the woman had in mind.

Dan headed down the steps to the floor below where the dormitory was located. He wanted to be alone for a while. Also, he'd been preoccupied with an idea—one that alarmed him yet was becoming irresistibly attractive. He sat down on one of the steps. And from there he gazed down the gloomy stairwell that spiralled down and down through the Tower's core.

"Shaz." Dan spoke his dead friend's name aloud.

A day hadn't gone by when he hadn't thought how she'd died, when the meteor strike that had ripped away half the building that housed their workplace. He recalled how she'd slipped from his grasp. The long, terrifying fall.

"Shaz Chandler." Dan's voice echoed softly.

His heart began to beat faster as he pictured Shaz. He forced himself to recall details of her face. The freckle on her cheek. The dark arches of her eyebrows. The little upward tug of the lip before her face broke into such a pleasant smile. And her eyes, of course. How they twinkled with delight. It always warmed his heart when he saw her in a happy mood. He'd decided to ask her on a date. But several tons of rock barrelling down from the sky had prevented him from ever uttering the words: 'Would you like to go out for a meal with me?'

"Shaz, I miss you." He closed his eyes. "Okay, Factory. You know what I want."

Dan concentrated on picturing Shaz. The upward tug of the lips as she smiled when she saw him entering the office. The freckle on her cheek. The expression of concentration on her face when she studied architectural drawings on the big table in the plan room.

Dan opened his eyes. He sensed a change in the atmosphere. Cool air swirled around him. Cold fingers, it seemed, stroked his neck. *Surely imagination,* he told himself. Even so he swiftly raised his hands to his neck. There were no fingers touching him, just the breath of cold air flowing through the stairwell.

And now there was now a sense of tension in the air. As if lightning was getting ready to strike. And with that sense of the air being charged with electricity his heart began to pound. His chest became tighter, making it difficult to breathe. He stared down the stairwell into the gloom. Something appeared to be sucking the light out of the place. His surroundings were becoming darker.

And there, just a few steps below him, was a swirl of shadow. Almost like a black liquid being poured into water. A dark cloudiness that moved and billowed and rippled. Instantly, he felt a trickle of shivers down his back. Was this the Factory at work? Was it making a duplicate of a woman, right in front of his eyes?

Apparently so, because now he could make out the shape of a head. A pair of arms extended out at either side of a torso: this was the pose of someone who was being crucified. He saw glints from a pair of eyes. These were glints of menace and blood-freezing danger.

Dan jumped to his feet. Terror burst inside of him—purple flames of absolute fear ripped through his chest. They detonated inside his head. Pains bit deep into his skull. His heart lurched with such force he grimaced.

"Stop ... Factory, I want you to stop. Don't bring her back. I don't want to see her!"

He gulped air down his throat, trying to ease the convulsions of terror he felt inside of him. Then he fled upstairs. Right now, he wanted company. It didn't matter who. He needed to be with other people. Already, he was praying that he had not succeeded in turning the image he had formed inside his head into a chunk of living flesh that would resemble the woman he watched die all those months ago.

THIRTY-TWO

"OH, MY FATHER ..."

The crew members were secretly trying to create individuals they had loved and lost. They knew they shouldn't. They each remembered that Doctor Priya Singh had warned them not to even attempt such a thing. They'd seen what happened when it went wrong. Borman's dog, for example, with the dull eyes. Everyone had seen the creatures that Priya's colleagues had Rawbacked into life—or at least a ghastly, part-formed version of life. Those men, women and children in the basement shuffled like zombies. They were little more than fleshy robots that aped being alive. Everyone knew that. But when given the power to become a god or, at very least, a Frankenstein, then who could resist such temptation?

Professor Jellsby snuck down to the fifteenth floor. He was getting jittery as heroin levels became depleted in his bloodstream. His eyes flashed in the gloom. He was scared—yet knowing that the Factory gave him a miraculous power drove him along the road to a destination as incredible as it was terrible.

The shadowy corner of a chamber, high above the grim landscape outside, suited his purposes. He squatted down in the darkness, his hands were on his knees, and he began to mutter: "I am picturing my wife. Her name was Ruth. I am picturing my children. Philip, age nine, and Sonia, age seven. My mind visualises my family. They died in the fire. My ability to picture their faces in every detail is perfect. Factory, make them live again. Factory, resurrect my wife and children." He closed his eyes and began to chant. "Make them live again. Make them live again...."

Merrick Lee wanted his first love back. He lay on the bed in the dormitory with the sheet over his face, pretending to sleep. And there he pictured Vicky. They had spent three happy years together when they were students at university. Then Vicky met Wayne, who was a professional dancer, and who had somehow cast a spell over Vicky and took her away from Merrick. As far as Merrick knew, Vicki was still alive and teaching high school kids in Nebraska. But Merrick had a raw, bloody wound in his heart—which was brutally inflicted when Vicki said, "I'm sorry, it's over. I'm leaving you. I love someone else."

Vicki had gone to Nebraska with Wayne, but she had never left Merrick's soul. And, today, Merrick Lee had the power to bring Vicki back, and they could be together forever and ever.... Storm winds moaned against the Tower's windows. Heart-wrenchingly sad music for the dead. Or so it sounded. Merrick scrunched his eyes tight shut, and he concentrated as fiercely as he could. He pictured Vicki standing there in the dormitory. Then he imagined the beautiful love of his life slipping under the bedsheet to curl up alongside him. And his arms would hold her tight before his eager lips found hers.

Gen had noticed Professor Thomas Jellsby furtively creeping downstairs. The man looked like a thief in search of loot. Gen had been searching for a secret place of her own. Moments later, she saw Jellsby go through a doorway on the fifteenth floor. Gen didn't want her own mission to be disrupted so she went down to the fourteenth floor. Instead of there being just one big room that took up the entire story, this one consisted of dozens of small chambers that resembled prison cells. Goodness knows what their purpose was, so she tried not to imagine what type of creatures previously had the tenancy of this chunk of real-estate.

The air was cool. Winds blew hard against the walls, conjuring eerie cries. They sounded so forlorn that Gen shivered to the roots of her bones. She didn't even ask herself if what she was doing was wrong. Or if it could end in disaster. No. She had the opportunity to perform a miracle now. Who could blame her for not seizing the opportunity to bring happiness back into her life?

Gen tiptoed into one of the windowless cells. Only the dimmest of light oozed from the walls. Yes, they did possess a certain degree of luminosity, but it was so feeble that shadows pooled there, as if they were a dark liquid that was slowly drowning the building. Gen clasped her hands together, like she was going to say a prayer. The air smelt stale, which reminded her of the dusty attic back home, with its cobwebs and bits of furniture and old Christmas decorations that nobody wanted anymore.

"Oh, my father …" The formality of her words sounded strange to her ears. But what words do you use to bring a parent back from the dead? She took a deep breath. And tried again. "Dad. I want you here." The breeze swirled around the Tower. It sounded like the respiration of a gigantic creature. "Dad, I want you here." She pictured his face. The image that came to mind shocked her. Revolted her. "No, I don't want to remember that."

Because she recalled the awful moment when she walked into the room in the funeral home. There he lay in the open coffin. He was dressed in a pale blue suit, with a white shirt and orange necktie. His face looked as if it had been molded from plastic. Sort of shiny. Artificial. His lips were grey. His eyes were closed. Though she expected that, at any moment, his eyes would snap open. She'd seen so many horror films that she expected such a ghastly scenario. The room smelt powerfully of lavender. "That's to mask the smell of the corpse." That's what Rory had told her. Then her brother's mouth always had been a blunt instrument, better suited to cursing problems in his own life then gently murmuring reassurances to his grief-blighted sister. "Lavender." He'd grunted. "I hate the stink of lavender."

Gen endeavoured to picture her father when he was alive. She tried to push her mind back through time, when Dad was happy in the carefree years before the bankruptcy of his limo hire business, and the start of the all-day, everyday drinking.

"Dad. I want you here." She tried to picture him smiling a happy smile. "Dad, I want you here with me."

The winds became a violent shriek that hurt her ears.

"Dad. I want you here."

Gen took a deep breath. And she smelt …

Lavender.

Awful lavender.

THIRTY-THREE

"BE READY. YOU'RE GOING TO HAVE TO FIGHT FOR YOUR LIVES."

Katrina grabbed hold of Dan's fist.

It was as sudden as it was unexpected.

Dan had been standing next to Katrina as they watched the storm arriving. Winds had whipped up grey particles (probably bone fragments, he guessed) and already the view had become murky. He could still make out the other towers nearby, and the mounds of bone that rose up in macabre pyramids here and there. And he could just make out the curving rib structures that formed the roof of this complex that was the Factory.

As they watched the dust forming into eerie ghost shapes, Dan had felt her fingers close around his. It was only then that he'd realized he'd bunched his hands into fists as the view from the window made him increasingly uneasy. He opened up his hand. Katrina immediately moved her fingers so that they now stood hand in hand. For a moment, they said nothing. Dan sensed that Katrina needed the reassurance of being in physical contact with another human being. Her fingers were soft against his skin. She felt warm—the sensation was so pleasant that he had no intention of pulling away from her. Besides, after his thankfully failed attempt to bring Shaz Chandler back to life, he needed the reassurance of human contact, too.

They stood there, saying nothing. Dan felt a shiver run through Katrina's fingers. A fluttering sensation, not unlike a frightened heartbeat.

At last, she spoke. "Dan. This place terrifies me."

"I feel the same."

She leaned sideways a little until their arms touched. Then she shivered again and murmured, "This isn't how I imagined Callisto. It's a place of absolute horror. I keep thinking about the scarecrow things we saw out there, and how they chased us. They were human once, weren't they? They were the crew from the Rib that brought Priya here."

"That's what she told us."

"And Rawbacks? They are utterly terrifying. I know they don't try and hurt us. But they are revolting copies of people who have died. Who, in their right mind, would attempt to bring back to life someone who has died? It's not natural."

Now it was Dan's turn to shiver as he remembered how he'd sat in the stairwell and tried to do exactly that. He recalled the shadows twisting and turning as they began to solidify into Shaz Chandler. Thank goodness his nerve had failed him, and the shadows that were becoming Shaz had dissipated. Dan steadfastly kept his gaze locked on the storm outside. He knew if he made eye contact with Katrina, he'd give his decidedly unwholesome secret away. Thank goodness, he wasn't cut out to be a necromancer.

Katrina moved slightly, so that her body was now pressed more firmly in a tell-tale way against his arm.

"Dan, I don't even want to be alone at night. I'm scared that whatever I dream about will be there in real life in the morning. You know? Like the bedroom I had when I was a little girl." Her shivers now became shudders of dread. "Sometimes I dream about monsters chasing me. Big red demon things. They have huge mouths full of sharp teeth. I'm running and running but I only move really slowly. And I know they're catching up. What if I dream those things into real creatures?"

"Priya told us that Rawbacks can't hurt us."

"If I saw one of those demons, I'd die of fright. I know I would."

Dan squeezed her hand tighter and tried to reassure her with a smile. "You'll be fine. I'm only a couple of beds away from yours."

"I like you, Dan." She smiled at him. "There's no rule about sleeping alone."

His own emotions were churning within him now. His throat felt tight. Suddenly, his mouth had become dry as dust. And, in truth, he didn't know what to make of this. Was it the terrors of nightmares potentially driving Katrina into his bed? Or did she genuinely like him? He even wondered what Captain Flynn's reaction would be if she saw him in the same bed as Katrina. After all, there was no privacy in the dormitory. Not that he'd even contemplate making love to Katina in such close proximity to the other people in their beds.

Dan just didn't know how to verbally respond to Katrina at that moment. Instead, he slipped his hand out of hers and put his arm around her shoulders. His heart was pounding.

What now?

Kiss her?

They were alone in the room. Everyone had sloped off earlier, like they had something important to do. Yet their faces were oddly stony. They seemed to be afraid that their expressions would give away some secret plan they had been cultivating.

Dan took a deep breath. "Katrina."

That was the moment a loud wail began to scream through the building. He felt Katrina's body suddenly become tense.

"What the hell is that sound?" she asked.

"If you ask me, it means just one thing. Danger."

Priya appeared at the doorway. Her words came out in a yell of panic: "Where is everybody?"

"We don't know."

Priya's eyes flashed with terror. "The main doors have been breached! That's what the alarm is signalling." Priya beckoned them. "Come on.

You've got to help me. We can't let them get in." Then she said the words that turned Dan's blood to ice. "Be ready. You're going to have to fight for your lives."

THIRTY-FOUR

DREADZONE

Dan was running down the stairs, taking three at a time. Priya was out in front. Katrina was just behind him. The siren was nothing less than a screaming animal, shrieking out its warning of danger. Dan hoped he wouldn't fall. Just one slip would, likely as not, leave him with shattered bones.

The way down through the building was choked with shadow. He could barely see the stairs ahead. What he did see clearly enough, however, was Professor Jellsby. He stood with his arm around a stranger—a woman with short curly hair. A pair of children stood at either side of them. The dull eyes of the children and the woman revealed their nature.

Priya released a loud shriek of rage. Even though she didn't stop running down the stairwell, she yelled furiously at Jellsby. "Damn it! You couldn't stop yourself, could you? You fool! You'll regret bringing them back!"

Then Priya vanished around the next twist of the stairwell. Dan continued running, leaving Jellsby, and his "family" staring impassively after him.

Dan's boots clattered against the steps. He was gasping for air. His heart smashed blood through the arteries in his body. The pulse in his neck thudded. The muscles in his legs burned. *Don't slip. Whatever you do, don't slip.* The thought of fracturing bones scared him. But what terrified him even more was visualizing the horror that would inevitably greet them when they reached the open door to the Tower.

Katrina's eyes flashed as she ran. Yes, there was fear there. And there was also total determination. She was ready for the fight.

But what will we be fighting?

From down below, cold gusts of air rose to blast into their faces. That was evidence enough the doors were open, allowing the storm to rampage into the building.

The entrance hallway to the Tower appeared in front of them. Indeed, the doors were wide open. Fragments of old bone, accompanied by a grey-colored dust, were blowing in. Priya raced across the hallway to the doors, clearly intending to slam them shut. However, the storm winds were having none of it. The sheer brutal force of those torrents of air defeated her attempt to push the doors shut.

Dan yelled, "Wait! We'll help you!"

He ran to one of the doors and began to push the massive slab of steel. Katrina appeared at his side, and soon all three put their shoulders to the doors. The winds, nevertheless, pushed the doors back. Hard particles stung Dan's face. Grit got into his right eye. The grit was so abrasive it felt as if tiny teeth were furiously biting his eyeball. He grimaced as pain shot through his eye and snapped along his nerves to his brain.

Then ... success. They succeeded in shutting one of the doors. Priya swung a lever down that was fixed to the slab of metal, locking the door in place. *Now for the second door ...*

Priya shouted. "We've got to close it before they get here!"

But even as she finished shouting those ominous words a hand appeared from around the far side of the door. The fingernails were torn. Some were completely absent, revealing fleshy nailbeds that were covered in scabs and dried blood. The thumbnail had turned blue and there was a suggestion of necrosis in the flesh around the nail. The hand gripped the edge of the door, and it began pushing with the heel of the palm.

Then a sight that made Dan flinch.

Tentacles appeared.

They were tentacles that could have belonged to an octopus. They were grey. They were wet. They probed around the door, and they were absolutely sickening to see. Dan had the awful feeling that the tentacles were trying to find whoever was on the far side of the door. Namely, Priya, Katrina and himself.

Then something of huge strength pushed at the other side of the door. The metal slab began to slowly move inward.

Priya shrieked. "Don't let it in!"

A tentacle touched Dan's forehead. It felt like a cold tongue had licked his skin. The shudder it produced in him was nothing like he had experienced before. It went beyond physical. Or even mental. The reaction was so intense that it seemed as if every cell of his body had cringed back from the coldness of the wet tentacle that lapped at his forehead.

He swung his right hand to knock the boneless limb away from him.

Priya's eyes flashed. They were nothing less than explosions of terror. "There's a Scarecrow at the other side of the door. If the Blisters detach, avoid them at all costs. Don't let them climb onto you."

Dan didn't even know what that meant. The tone in the woman's voice was compelling enough, though. Whatever the 'Blisters' were, they must be formidable.

At that moment, it seemed as if they fought a life-and-death battle with the door. Whatever was behind the door was pushing. But they couldn't see it, so the door itself had become the vicious enemy that they fought. All three pushed at the slab. Yet they could not close it. If anything, the door was inching forward, gradually opening wider and wider. And, all the time, tentacles danced through the air with a sinuous motion, like venomous serpents getting ready to strike and sink fangs into flesh. Katrina grunted at the visceral touch of a tentacle as it wiped its slimy tip across the bare skin of her throat.

Nevertheless, Katrina didn't retreat. She panted the same mantra: "Get the door shut. Get it shut ... get it shut."

Dan tried to uncurl the ugly fingers that gripped the edge of the door. Just touching that noxious hand rammed a jet of bile up into his throat. He wanted to vomit but held it down. His throat was burning. His arms were tortured by the agony of trying to force the door shut against what was a powerful adversary. He punched the hand that possessed the ruined fingernails. The creature appeared to feel no pain.

The creature pushed again. Then the door abruptly swung in by two feet or more. Now they had a clear view of their enemy. The creature was, in fact, a tall woman with tangles of blond hair that cascaded down over her shoulders, and as far as her waist. She wore the uniform of a Rib crew member, though the material was torn open in places to reveal bare skin that was pale blue in color—a deathly blue. The same palette of blue if she'd been a corpse.

Her eyes locked onto his with such a hard stare that the eyes seemed to possess a biting quality, such was the woman's hatred. But worse than her savage appearance, which was more corpse than living woman, were the abominations that clung to her.

Dan fought to push the door shut. Pains ripped through his shoulders as tendons neared snapping point. He stared at those abominations. His mind scrambled to interpret what he saw, even though he found himself in a world of struggle and pain and exhaustion. He was thoroughly deafened by the scream of the siren. And he was nauseated by the explorative touch of the tentacles that, again and again, skated wetly across his bare face and throat.

There, in front of him, was a woman. Clearly, she had been a crew member from the first Rib to arrive on this world with people on board. Yet her body had been colonised by what surely must be some form of parasite.

They were ugly things. No, they went beyond ugly. Just seeing them was like having a vile finger reach into your head to stir your thoughts into a cocktail of disgust and absolute horror.

The woman had six blister-shaped things fastened on her hips, chest, belly, right thigh, and her throat. Dan's mind laboured to find a comparison that would have a counterpart found on Earth. But these were truly alien. They resembled a vile fusion of a giant white spider and an octopus. The blister shape was like the spider body. The tentacles that grew out from the football-sized monstrosity resembled octopus tentacles, which extended to the length of ten feet. And the spider bodies each possessed a face that hideously resembled the oddly compressed face of a newborn human baby. Each face had a snub nose. The two eyes were puckered shut. There was a tiny mouth with a soft pair of lips.

Some of the tentacles roved out through the air toward Katrina, Priya, and Dan. They also seemed to be sensory organs that were exploring their surroundings. Maybe even searching for fresh prey. The other tentacles were wrapped python-like around the woman, apparently holding on tight, and so clamping the loathsome spider-things to her body.

At that moment, one of the Blisters loosened its body from hers, so that the rounded shape slopped wetly against her. The tentacles were releasing, one by one.

Priya grunted. "Careful. One's beginning to detach. It will attempt to climb onto you."

Katrina still tried to push the door shut. "Is this what happened to your crew? Did they all become these things?"

"Some died." She panted hard. "But, yes, the others were taken by those blister creatures."

Dan shouted. "There are more Scarecrows coming this way!"

"Got to get this door shut and locked, guys. If they get inside, we join their gang."

Beyond the doorway, a white mist swirled as the breeze blew. From the murk, ten figures approached. They moved on stiff legs. A kind of scissor gait because they did not bend their legs at the knees. Dan could make out that each figure carried their parasitic cargo. There were five or six of the rounded blister shapes on each man and woman.

The Scarecrow that pushed from the other side simply did not weaken. And though they tried their hardest they couldn't even begin to close the door.

Katrina warned, "They'll be here soon."

Dan gritted his teeth with the effort of pushing. Nevertheless, he managed to pant out, "What's her name? Can we reason with her?"

Priya's expression was a grim one. "That's First Officer Franco. I've tried speaking to her in the past, but the Blisters control her. Franco doesn't have a human mind now."

Dan, however, tried. "Franco. Stop pushing the door open. We're human like you. Whatever's got a hold over you, fight it. Don't let them win."

Franco merely glared at Dan with renewed hatred.

Meanwhile, a Blister had lowered itself to the ground, using its slimy tentacles. Only two tentacles remained gripping its host now, and they began to slowly uncurl.

Dan glanced back into the hallway. His eyes hungrily devoured the space there. He was looking for something he could use as a weapon. Almost straight away, he saw what appeared to be a discarded water pipe made from metal. It was perhaps eight feet long and leaned against one wall. The pipe's diameter was perhaps the thickness of his wrist.

"Keep holding the door!" he shouted, then he ran to the pipe and grabbed hold.

The pipe was reassuringly heavy. Without hesitation, he positioned his hands at a distance of perhaps two feet apart at one end of the pipe. Then, gripping it as tightly as he could, he ran back toward the doorway. Almost as if he were a medieval knight wielding a lance, he charged toward Franco. He aimed his makeshift lance in the center of her face.

The end of the pipe struck her, exploding her nose into shards of bone and flaps of skin. The pipe penetrated her face to a depth of two inches or so. Blood shot from the wound in a flash of crimson. A red slick soon covered Franco's chest. More blood rained down onto the ground—red splotches forming craters in the dust that were sticky-looking. The blow knocked the woman off balance for a moment. Even so, she didn't fall down. With a viciously powerful downward swing of the pipe, he smashed it against her forearms as she held her arms out to push the door. One forearm snapped. It actually looked as if it had become hinged at a point halfway between her wrist and her elbow.

Even so, she continued to push with the other hand.

"Dan! Look out!"

He saw the Blister squirming rapidly across the ground. It was propelling itself with its tentacles, almost like a rowing motion that was nauseating to watch. Dan swung the pole down onto the creature. It was like clubbing a mound of wet flesh, from which a baby-like face bulged. He didn't know if he had harmed it. But at that moment the other Blisters that clung to the woman suddenly contracted. They puckered up to half their usual size. The moment this happened, Franco moaned with pain. She touched the bloody ruin where her nose had been and muttered, "What da fuck?"

Her eyes changed, too. Suddenly, they were the eyes of a woman that was confused and in pain.

Katrina yelled, "Now! Push the door!"

Even as they pushed the door, the expression changed on the woman's face again, reverting to a hating scowl, with hard eyes that all but screamed out to this Godawful planet that she wanted to cause hurt and destruction.

The trio of humans had, however, snatched the slimmest of chances to save themselves. Dan pushed the hinged slab as hard he could. Beside him, Katrina and Priya were grunting. The veins in their necks stood from the skin as they sank every atom of their strength into closing the door. Abruptly, it swung shut. There was a massive clang. The door was closed tight against the outside world. And against the monsters that roamed there. Priya pulled down a second lever and that was that. The door was locked.

For a moment, they leaned back against the door. Drops of sweat fell from Dan's face onto the floor as he doubled over clutching his aching belly. Goodness knows how many muscles he'd pulled to the point of agony as he'd fought the creature. For a while, the three of them panted as they sucked oxygen back into their lungs.

Then Katrina voiced a question that she must have been burning to ask. "Who opened the door?"

THIRTY-FIVE

COLD CUTS

Priya didn't hold back.

"I know what you idiots have been doing. Today, you crept off into other parts of the building—and you did what I told you *not* to do!"

Everyone was there. Most stood with their arms folded. Their attitude was sullen and defensive. Merrick stood hand-in-hand with a woman that lacked a nose. She had an overlong neck that merged with narrow, sloping shoulders. Jellsby sat on his bed with two children that had their arms around his waist, giving their father a loving hug. At least, that's how it looked at first glance. But the "children," though they were accurate representations of a boy and a girl, had dead eyes that looked like they should belong to a fish in a container on a supermarket shelf. A woman with curly hair stood next to where Jellsby sat. She stared in a mindless way at the real men and women in the dormitory. Dan realized that Jellsby would keep his family with him at all times. They were his new drug of choice. Already they were the crutch he leant on, though they supported his mind rather than his body.

Priya strode back and forth, panting with absolute rage. In fact, so angry she could barely form the words to speak.

Though speak she did. "While Katrina and Dan and I were fighting to save your lives, you were cooking up copies of people that you selfishly wanted to be with you. But they aren't real. Don't you actually remember when I showed you those things in the cellar? Now, you foolish people have created more Rawbacks." Priya wagged her finger at the individuals gathered there. "I will tell you this. Those things you have created are your responsibility now. You take care of them. And you deal with all the misery that they're going to inflict on you. Do you hear me?"

Nobody answered. Outside, the storm began to howl as the winds assumed an even more ferocious power. And the atmosphere inside the room became colder. Dan could not help but feel that they were facing disaster. And disaster, in whatever form it would take, was inching closer by the second.

Gen faced her father. He stood in the corner of one of the small cell-like chambers.

He wore a blue suit and a white shirt, together with an orange necktie. He smelt of lavender. And he was dead. At least, that's how he appeared to her. Gen had tried to recreate Dad as she'd remembered him when he was happy. But her strongest memory of her father was when he lay dead in his coffin. Now he stood there without moving. The face looked like it had been made from plastic. The skin was glossy and pale and as cold as ice. His eyelids were closed. He didn't even appear to be breathing.

Then he opened his mouth. "Love you, Spud."

Borman stood in the doorway to the cell. "Spud?" he echoed.

"Spud was his nickname for me," Gen told him.

Her father spoke again. The voice was flat. Loveless. "Love you, Spud."

Borman grimaced. "Is that all he says?"

She nodded.

"And that smell of lavender." Borman swallowed. "It clings to the back of your throat, doesn't it? If I stay here much longer, I'll puke."

"You go if you want," said Gen. "I can do this myself."

"I promised to help you … Spud."

"Don't!" She had to stop herself from lashing out at Borman. "It's not funny."

"Okay." Borman held up an electric saw that they'd found in a store area on the top floor. Why it was there was anyone's guess because it was the same kind of electric-powered chainsaw that people used to shape topiary and cut logs. Maybe someone had wished it into existence and then the Factory had made it happen.

Borman said: "Go back out onto the landing. You shouldn't see me do this."

"It's my father, Borman. I'll do it."

She held out her hands.

"As you wish."

Borman handed her the saw.

Her father kept his eyes shut. His pale lips parted with a clicking sound, as if the lips, themselves, were sticky.

"Love you, Spud." Her father's voice was still utterly colorless. A dead man talking. "Love you, Spud."

Gen groaned with despair. "I'm sorry, Dad. I shouldn't have brought you back. You won't feel this … I know you won't."

She thumbed the switch on the saw. The teeth began to rotate. The whine of the electric motor was painfully loud in this grim tomb of a place. Borman put his right hand over his mouth, looking like he'd vomit. Then he took a step back.

Gen applied the saw's cutting edge to the top of her father's shoulder. Sharp teeth bit deep. Pieces of flesh spat from the blade. They struck her in the face. They were cold and moist.

Borman groaned loud enough to be heard above the saw. "Oh, God … oh, my God. This is awful."

The blade sliced down through the torso until it reached the midpoint, roughly where the heart should be. No blood flowed from the wound—so proving, if proof were needed, that this wasn't a human body. Moreover, the density of the flesh eventually defeated the chainsaw's motor, and the blade stopped cutting. Borman had to help Gen free the embedded blade. And this was only achieved after tugging as hard as they could.

Borman was close to weeping. "Gen. Why not just put him in the basement with the others?"

"You heard Priya. Dad's my responsibility. I made him. Now, I'm going to unmake him. I can't bear to think he'll be wandering around down there. What if he does have feelings?"

Her father whispered. "Love you, Spud."

Gen switched on the saw. This time she succeeded in cutting off his left arm above the elbow. The severed limb dropped to the floor with a *thump*. There was no blood.

"The brain," she muttered. "If I destroy the brain, that will make him die, won't it?"

Borman, however, had tottered away. He held both hands over his mouth as he backstepped through the doorway. A moment later, she heard his footsteps as he ran upstairs.

"The brain," she repeated—this time to herself. "If I cut into the brain …"

She switched on the saw again. Then she angled the blade so she could cut sideways through the skull just above the line of the eyes.

Her father mouthed the words: "Love you, Spud."

The blade hacked into flesh above the right ear.

"Love you, Spud."

Gen wept. "I love you, Dad."

Then she applied force. And the blade cut deeper than she could have ever imagined.

THIRTY-SIX

WE ACCUSE YOU

Trouble started as everyone was getting ready for bed. Katrina had already pulled the comforter over herself. She glanced at Dan, then wriggled sideways, making room for him. He went to his own bed to collect an extra pillow. He fully intended to join her. Despite everything, his skin tingled with excitement and his heartbeat quickened.

Spiro touched the vines that had sprouted from the wall above his own bed. Leaves were still green, but the grapes had wrinkled as they began to shrivel. Leaves crumbled under Spirio's touch. The Factory was beginning to reabsorb what it had created back into itself. The most disturbing sight was Professor Jellsby. He lay on the mattress with the grotesque copies of his children and his wife. Softly, he was singing them a lullaby. Merrick Lee, meanwhile, curled up under the bedsheets with the girlfriend he'd managed to conjure up. Dan could hear Merrick whispering tenderly to his companion.

Garner suddenly yelled out a question that must have been preying on his mind.

"So ..." his shout echoed back from the walls. "So who opened the fucking doors?"

Garner and Borman were buddies, which meant Borman immediately played the loyal sidekick. "You heard Garner. Which one of you lot opened the doors to let the Scarecrows in?"

Dan stood there with the pillow in his hand. "The Scarecrows didn't get into the Tower. We kept them out."

Katrina sat up in bed. Her eyes had a nervous glint as she glanced from face to face. Dan guessed she knew what was coming next. Already, the air crackled with the frightening promise of violence.

Garner persisted. "Someone deliberately opened the doors." He was cocky and arrogant. "That 'someone' is trying to sabotage our mission."

"And get us killed," added Borman.

Spiro shook his head. "Mission? Mission? All you have done is play at being Frankenstein and bringing the dead back to life."

Merrick's head appeared over the sheets. Beside him, lay the dull-eyed creature that he lovingly referred to as Vicki.

"My girlfriend is still alive," Merrick insisted. "Though if I can have a copy of her here with me, that will bring me comfort." He spoke with sudden defiance. "Who can complain about that?"

Dan felt himself becoming angry, too, for a different reason. "What we need to do is concentrate on our real mission. And that is stopping the Earth from being smashed to fucking bits by asteroids."

"Yeah." Garner gave an exaggerated nod. "Gotcha, buddy. That's our mission. We repair the gravity machine. We save Planet Earth … but the fact of the matter is, there is a traitor who is trying to stop us."

Borman added a chorus of his own. "Yeah, a traitor who is going to get us all killed or turned into fucking Scarecrows."

Katrina climbed out of bed to join the argument. "Garner. Borman. You're just happy to shoot your mouths off. You never think through what you're doing."

"Don't we, Katrina? Oh? But where were you when the doors got opened?"

"Garner! This is exactly what you did when you attacked Hassan, back on the ship. You did not allow him to explain."

"Hassan tried to murder us."

"No." Katrina's eyes flashed with rage. "He believed he was doing the right thing. He was going to detonate explosive bolts that fixed the Crab to the Rib."

"Then we'd all die."

"You never listen to what people tell you, do you? There is an automatic propulsion and navigation system on the Crab. As soon as it separates from the Rib, the autopilot takes over and the Crab is returned to Earth."

Dan added in grim tones. "So, you, Garner, and your baying mob, pushed Hassan into the airlock and dumped him out in space."

Katrina nodded. "You are murderers."

Gen clearly wasn't sure who to believe when she asked, "Hassan wanted to abort the mission, then. That means we wouldn't have been able to repair the gravity engine."

Katrina said: "There never was any chance we could repair it. The Caucus merely used us as lab rats. They wanted to see if we came back from Callisto alive. That's when they send out the qualified scientists and engineers to fix whatever the hell it is that creates the gravitational field that holds the asteroids back from swatting our planet."

Garner sneered. "Katrina makes a good speech, doesn't she?"

The other crew members began muttering amongst themselves as they shot angry glances at Katrina.

Garner continued. "Doesn't it sound like she's trying to divert attention from my very important question: who opened the fucking doors?"

Katrina shook her head. "I did not open them."

"Where were you earlier today?"

"Up on the top floor."

"Got a witness to back you up?"

"Have you, Garner? Where were you when the doors were opened?"

Borman snarled, "Katrina did it. Everyone knows she's been stirring up trouble ever since day one."

"I've simply been trying to discover the truth. And I found it. We've been sent on a suicide mission." Katrina pointed around the room. "Look at us all. Junkies. Bankrupts. Life's losers. Our sole qualification is that we've got the right sort of blood, which means we don't go into a coma as soon as the Rib lifts off."

Merrick leapt out of bed. He was bunching his fists, ready to fight. "Katrina is a liar! She and Hassan were in it together, trying to destroy the ship before we even got here."

Talking was over. Fists not words were going to settle this argument. Dan knew that was the route events were taking right now. Merrick ran across the room toward Katrina. The Vicki-shaped Rawback climbed out of bed and slowly followed. Meanwhile, Jellsby's family sat up in bed. They watched events unfurl with dead eyes that lacked curiosity and even the tiniest spark of what could be termed genuine vitality.

Dan moved forward to put himself between Katrina and Merrick. Even so, Merrick began swinging his fists—trying to punch Katrina. He missed by a yard. Nevertheless, one of his punches accidentally connected with Dan's skull with painful force.

Dan grunted as a jag of pain ripped through his head. "Stop it. Merrick. Cut it out!"

Borman, Garner and other crew members ran forward.

Borman shouted, "Dan's on her side. The fucking traitor!"

Within five seconds, there was a chaotic mass of swinging fists, angry faces, shouts.

Spiro tried pushing Borman, Garner and the others back.

Spiro was shouting: "Leave them alone! You've no proof that Katrina did it! Merrick! Back off!"

Garner landed a bruising punch on Spiro's face. He went flying back over a bed before tumbling onto the floor. He lay there in a daze. Blood was trickling from his nose.

Dan yelled at the mob, "Have you gone crazy?! Stop attacking us!"

Borman swung his fist at Dan. The punch missed Dan's face but still caught his shoulder, which sent a fresh blast of pain through him.

Garner had grabbed Katrina by the hair, and he began pulling her toward the swinging fists of the mob. Dan tried to drag her back—the tearing pain that she must have felt in her scalp almost overwhelmed her. She let out a tremendously loud scream of agony.

"Let her go," thundered Dan. "You'll kill her!"

"It's only what she deserves." This came from Merrick as he slammed his fists down like hammer blows against her arms that she was using to defend her head.

By now, the mob was hauling her away. No doubt they intended to commit sheer bloody murder.

Then another voice cut through the air. "Enough! I said: Enough!"

Captain Flynn waded into the tangle of bodies that fought and yelled death threats.

"I order you to stop!" Flynn waved her arms above her head. "I am your commanding officer—you will do as I tell you!"

Borman tried to shove Flynn aside. Flynn was faster, and immensely strong. Her knee came up and she slammed the hard kneecap straight into Borman's testicles. He gave a howl of pain. For a moment, sheer bloodlust burnt like the fires of hell in his eyes. But the blow to his groin must have been utterly fierce, because the fight very quickly went out of him. He shuffled to the nearest bed where he sat down. He began shaking his head, trying to dislodge the pain from his body. But a pain as savage as that doesn't quit for a while.

Flynn's presence began to have an effect on the mob. They started backing off. They still shouted death threats. There was plenty of fist-shaking. However, their anger was at last easing to a degree.

Flynn spoke with a powerful air of command: "If you have a suspicion that the doors were opened deliberately, then we will discuss it in the morning—when you have all calmed down. Do you hear me, Garner? Well?"

Garner nodded, albeit with a surly expression.

Flynn nodded, too. "Good. Then we understand one another. If there is a saboteur, they will be identified. And dealt with." Flynn turned to Dan and Katrina. "You two had better come with me. You can sleep on the sofas in the lounge tonight. You too, Spiro."

Dan followed Katrina and Spiro out of the dormitory. He felt eyes burning into his back. The other crew members still wanted their own form of justice—a justice that would be as swift as it was violent.

Flynn remained for a moment. Her steely gaze dissuaded anyone from following to cause more trouble.

A moment later, Dan and his companions climbed the stairs to the upper floor. Outside, the winds were dropping. They left an eerie silence as they began to ease. Dan realized that the first battle with his crewmates had ended in a stalemate. Yet, he knew full well that there would be more battles to come. And maybe, next time, Lady Luck would desert them. And blood, lots of blood, would flow.

THIRTY-SEVEN

RETURN OF THE CORPSE DRIVER

The dream returned. The old one that had recurred throughout his teenage years—when he would dream about a street in the utter blackness of night. A car would be parked next to the sidewalk. The car's driver was a rotting corpse. Its claw-hands revealed grey bone through wide-open cracks in the skin. The corpse's face would always slowly turn toward Dan, and it would sit there, patiently waiting for him to reach a decision. As always—though Dan was both revolted and absolutely terrified by the corpse behind the steering wheel—the result was the same.

Dan would open the car's passenger door, then slide into the seat beside the driver.

A moment later, the corpse turned the key. The engine started. The car would then move off, picking up speed through the dark streets. There'd be no streetlights. The car lights weren't switched on. And there'd be a sense of speed, and of them hurtling through the black fog of darkness. The engine roared. The car tore through the night, tires drumming against the road. Then, straight ahead, a figure with a screaming face. It held up its hands begging him to stop. He recognised the figure as his dead colleague, Shaz Chandler.

The car struck the woman. She exploded into a spray of dark liquid. Yet her screaming continued to fill the car. A yell of terror. Identical to the one that was torn from her mouth when she was dragged down by murderous gravity, screaming all the while … until her body smashed into the rubble at the foot of the office building that had been partially destroyed by the meteor-strike all those months ago.…

Dan woke to find himself sitting up on the sofa where he'd been sleeping. Captain Flynn occupied a sofa across the far side of the room. The sofa opposite his wasn't empty, either. Katrina lay there under a blanket. She remained fast asleep.

His heart was thudding painfully hard. The nightmare had been a frightening one. Okay, he'd dreamt the same dream—or as near as damn it—many times before, yet it still hadn't lost its power to drive torrents of ice-cold terror through his veins. There was no doubt about it: Old Billy Dead Bones was as frightening as he ever was.

The same glow oozed from the walls. Just bright enough to reveal the interior of the room.

Oh, evil Factory … look what you've done now. The words slithered as ominously as grave worms through his brain. Because a fresh horror had been drawn from what should be the tomb of his mind … where long-dead memories should remain—never to surface again. Even so, he thought: *But unpleasant memories have that evil habit of coming back, don't they? Persistent ghosts, they are. Hell bent on haunting us forever more.*

Because there in the center of the lounge stood a car. For the first time, it had a color. And that color was the blackest of blacks. As if it had been painted using shadow found in the deepest of ancient tombs. The corpse driver sat behind the wheel. The corpse looked at him with plump eyes that bulged from the sockets, all wet and glistening. The eyes reminded him of the disgusting gloop of frogspawn that he'd sometimes scoop from a pond on the end of a stick.

"You're not real," he murmured. "You are a Rawback. The factory made you."

The car's motor throbbed—as ominous as a growl in the throat of a rabid wolf.

Dan moved slowly toward the car, the driver watching his every move. When he was close enough to the car, he did as he always did in the dream, he reached down to open the door.

The Factory had created a flimsy version of the nightmare car. As if little more substantial than a dream, both the car and its corpse driver crumbled to dust. Immediately, the floor began to absorb the tiny fragments that his dream had made into a three-dimensional reality.

"Good riddance," murmured Dan with relief.

However, the worst was yet to come.

A figure stood in the doorway. It had dark hair. An oval face. When it turned its head slightly, he immediately saw the single freckle on the right cheek.

"Shaz."

His heart actually convulsed as he stared at the creature that the Factory had brought back from the dead.

Dan shuddered from head to toe. His fear caused blooms of purple to manifest in the air before his eyes—or so it seemed to him. He wondered if this was emotional overload. Would an artery break inside his head? He pictured himself clutching his skull as the Satan of all headaches erupted behind his eyes … and then he'd be collapsing to the floor as the bleed on his brain destroyed motor functions, rendering him paralysed until the day of his death.

"Shaz."

What drove him, he didn't know. But he must go to her. He had Rawbacked the woman from the grave. She was his responsibility. Shaz, or the thing that resembled Shaz, turned, and walked away. Her face had been almost hidden by gloom. All he had clearly made out was the freckle on her cheek.

By the time he'd left the room, she was already descending the stairs. Dan followed. She was perhaps twenty feet below him, moving quickly, silently, her hair fluttering out.

Dan moved faster, too. At one turn of the stairs, he saw another figure in the gloom. For a split second he thought it was a Scarecrow. However, the figure intoned, "Love you, Spud." Another Rawback.

He continued after Shaz, just catching uncertain glimpses of her, because she was now rendered as little more than a swiftly moving shadow. Five floors down, and there were more figures. These were slowly climbing the stairs. He recognised them as the Rawbacks from the basement. Perhaps they were going to the higher levels in search of company? Or did some instinct drive them to find the sorry bunch of folk that had created them? He saw the boy that had grasped hold of Katrina's hand and called her "Daddy."

He must have passed thirty figures in the stairwell. None appeared to understand that he, a real human, had walked past them. They simply continued their zombie-like plod upward. Dan saw the dog padding up the stairs. No doubt Bella was in search of its owner. Borman would be in bed. In a few moments, Borman would feel a cold nose against his face as he lay there. The faithful dog was going to find its master.

Dan moved faster. He was now within ten feet of the woman. Her dark hair fluttered as she walked. Her arms hung down by her side. Seemingly, she had no need to steady herself with a hand upon the stair rail.

"Shaz. Stop. It's me, Dan."

Shaz did stop.

He really wished she hadn't, though. Because this was sickening. He was ashamed of himself. Even if she had come into existence as a result of a dream.

When Shaz looked up at him, there was no beautiful face. The front of her head was blank. There was a slight bulge where the nose would be. There were no eyes, no eyebrows, and not even a suggestion of a mouth. There was only the single black freckle on her cheek.

His blood ran cold. The pulse in his neck thudded. This had all the demented horror of opening the grave of someone you loved and discovering, too late, they'd been buried alive.

For a moment, he stood there, dry-mouthed, not sure what to say. More young children climbed the stairs. One brushed against his arm, then paused to look up at him with eyes that belonged to a dead fish.

The little boy moved its lips, and something that combined the hiss of a snake with a tubercular gurgle came out of its mouth: "Mr, Gerrard. Please may we pick apples from your tree?"

Dan couldn't even bring himself to correct the boy—nor was there any point, really—because the boy didn't wait for an answer and continued plodding up the stairs. Besides, even if he had explained the truth to the mock-child it wouldn't have understood.

When he looked for Shaz, she had vanished into the gloom.

Even though he couldn't see her, he called out, "Shaz. Go down into the basement. Stay there. Never come out."

Dan had no way of knowing if she'd heard. Or if she would obey. He waited for ten minutes to see if Shaz returned. When she didn't, he climbed back upstairs. He passed Gen who stood on a landing with a man that lacked an arm. He was also missing the entire top section of his skull, just above his eyes. There was no brain that Dan could see. The skull was filled with something that resembled dark granules. They were tightly packed into the cavity. More evidence that the biology of a Rawback wasn't even remotely human.

Gen glanced at Dan with eyes that glittered with sorrow.

"My father," she whispered by way of explanation, then she clamped her lips together tightly, as if not trusting herself to say anything more.

The man's voice was as cold as it was dead-sounding. "Love you, Spud."

Dan continued up the stairs. There was nothing he could do to help Gen. Like everyone else, they must confront their own personal nightmares in this nightmare world. Just for a second, however, he did pause as he sniffed the air. He could smell lavender.

Dan continued to the top floor. There he climbed onto the sofa that served as his bed for the night, and he pulled the blanket up over his head. Closed his eyes. He hoped with all his heart that he would not dream.

THIRTY-EIGHT

IT BLEEDS …

The sound woke Dan Karlton the next morning. That sound would make everyone forget about the previous evening's fight, and accusations that Katrina had opened the doors.

It was the doors again. This time, there was a thunderous pounding that echoed up the stairwell. Someone—perhaps some *thing*—was hammering at the door. It sounded like a desperate attempt to attract their attention. It succeeded because this time everyone ran down the stairwell, determined to find out who, or what, sought entry into the Tower.

Borman yelled, "Scarecrows—it's got to be."

Garner was in a vicious mood. "I'll rip their fucking heads off! Just you watch me!"

Priya called out, "Don't do anything rash!"

Flynn added her own order. "And do not open the doors!"

Gravity helped their descent. Soon everyone was gathered in the hallway. They were panting. But they were ready. Their eyes were bright. They were alert. Game faces on. And most of them had armed themselves with sections of metal pipe that leaned against one of the walls—this was the same place that Dan had equipped himself with the pipe, which he'd used to launch his assault on Franco.

Bang ... bang ... bang. The pounding sounded desperate rather than indicating hostile intent. Flynn moved to one of the pair of doors. Her hands reached up to the lever that would release the lock mechanism—yet she didn't actually touch it. *Bang ... bang ... bang.*

Flynn called out: "Hello. Who is it?"

There was a pause.

Flynn shouted again. "Hello. Identify yourselves!"

Then a very muffled voice came back that absolutely pulsated with fear. "Captain Flynn ... It's Navigation Officer Bexton."

"Yes?" Flynn sounded unsure whether to believe that it was Bexton or not.

"Ma'am. Please open the door." The voice paused—a sense that Bexton needed to take a deep breath before revealing very bad news. "Ma'am ... Captain Flynn. It's the Rib. The bleeds have started. Our ship could lift off at any moment."

THIRTY-NINE

ADVANCE OR RETREAT

Bexton all but exploded through the doorway.

Bang! Garner crashed the door shut behind him. Flynn pulled the locking lever down—*clunk!*—sealing the door shut against any attackers that might home in on the open doorway. The onslaught of yells and screams was immense. It seemed everyone was bombarding Bexton with questions as he stood there in the spacesuit. The helmet visor was flipped up. His face was pouring with sweat. The man's eyes seemed to be all white—just as if the eyeballs had been replaced with fleshy balls of white. That was sheer terror. The color had shrunk to almost nothing. The pupils were tiny black dots.

Bexton whirled through the lobby; he was waving his arms. He seemed to think his fellow crew members were attacking him, such was his panic—his mind appeared to be on the point of disintegrating into a million fragments of utter psychosis.

And everyone was yelling.

"The ship! When did the Bleeds start?"

"Why didn't you use the radio?"

"Why didn't you tell us earlier?"

Borman grabbed hold of the man, then shook him so violently

the helmet visor snapped back down over his face as his head whipped backward and forward.

"You little shit," screamed Borman. "Why didn't you use comms? You should have warned us the second the fucking Rib started to Bleed! You lazy fucker!"

The accusations were as irrational as they were viciously cruel.

Dan erupted with fury. "Leave him alone! He's here, isn't he?"

Dan shoulder-charged Borman to one side. He was risking a fistfight with the big guy, but he wasn't going to stand by and watch Bexton being pushed around and yelled at.

Garner waded into the melee. "Bexton. Hey! When did the Bleeds start?"

Bexton was panting as he lifted the helmet from his head. His hair was matted against his skull. His skin glistened—absolutely soaked wet. The guy had been running for his life.

Borman thundered, "Why didn't you use comms?"

"Where are the others? Did you come alone?" This was Captain Flynn, trying to speak calmly above the shouting.

Bexton held up both hands as if afraid he'd be attacked. "Comms don't work," he panted. "Bleeds started five hours ago. We tried to get here as fast as we could."

"We?"

"Me ... Khalid and Sophie. We were attacked. These weird things came down out of a mountain of bones and—and they had maggot things on their bodies, and the maggot things had babies' faces."

"Scarecrows," barked Garner. "Those were Scarecrows!"

Bexton looked like he needed to throw up. His lips were silvery-bright with saliva. "They chased us. Khalid and Sophie were taken. And those maggot things are alive. They climbed onto their bodies. Stuck there ... oh, God. Oh, my God."

That's when he turned to the wall and vomited.

Merrick shouted, "We must return to the Crab!" When he spoke next, it was with utter defiance, as if daring anyone to challenge what he said. "And I'm taking Vicki with me."

Jellsby sang out: "My family is coming with me."

Borman's expression was furious. "Nobody is taking Rawbacks on the ship. Got it?"

Garner nodded. "If you want to live with Rawbacks, then stay here. And if you disagree with that, I'll bust your fucking faces."

Flynn held up her hands. "Listen. Please listen."

The din subsided.

Flynn took a deep breath. "We have a mission, remember?"

Gen snarled, "Mission? What? To fix the gravity machine? Forget it. We haven't a chance in hell of making that thing work again."

Flynn remained calm, yet there was real force in her words. "We must try."

"Crap."

Spiro stepped forward. "I agree with Flynn. I will go with her."

"Count me in," said Dan. "There's nobody else here, but us. So, it's down to us to fix that thing."

Jellsby shook his head. "You're crazy." He gave a sudden laugh— one shot through with hysteria. "Look at yourselves. A sorry gaggle of bankrupts, supermarket shelf-stackers, truck-drivers, pen-pushers. You will never repair what must be a mechanism of near infinite complexity."

"For once, I agree with Jellsby." Merrick nodded in the direction of the doors. "I'm going out through there. I'm taking Vicki with me. And I'm going back to the ship."

Dan pointed out what should have been obvious to him. "What about Scarecrows? They'll be all over you in a heartbeat."

Katrina added, "You'll turn Scarecrow, too."

These comments about Scarecrows took some of the heat out of the burning compulsion to get back to the Crab. Even so, some crew members began to mutter about what would happen if the Rib hauled the Crab back to Earth without them. *Marooned here … no possible chance of returning home.* That was the gist of what they were saying.

Flynn spoke in a clear voice: "Okay. Ladies and gentlemen. We know the situation. The Bleeds have started on the Rib. That means it will launch soon. We also know that there are hostile creatures outside. Especially the Scarecrows. However, if anyone wants to return to our ship now, then you are free to go. But my personal decision is that I will go to where the gravity engine is located. Then I will endeavour to repair it. Or die trying. Therefore, my question is: who will join me?"

FORTY

TERROR-ZONE

Dan Karlton would be the first to admit the truth of his feelings. He was amazed.

Every single person there fell silent after Captain Flynn's extraordinary question: *Who will join me?*

Garner bunched his fists. The man wanted to start punching faces. Then he turned that sour face of his to Flynn and he growled, "Fixing the machine? That's a suicide mission." He shook his head. "But I've got kids back on Earth. If there's a chance to save them then ... I'm in."

"Me, too," declared Borman. "My family deserves a chance to live."

Borman and Garner, loyal friends to the last, exchanged grim smiles and slapped each other on the back. They were two warriors ready for the suicide mission.

What did continue to surprise Dan was how the others began nodding. This was a Road to Damascus revelation. They'd all seen the shining light of Flynn's vision of saving the world.

That is, if the Earth isn't already a smoking ruin, thought Dan with such bleak intensity that shivers tingled down his spine. *There's no way of communicating with mission control. For all we know, an asteroid might have smashed the living shit out of everything. We'll only know the truth when we get home—if we get home. For all we know, the Rib might have already unstuck itself from Callisto and be heading back to Earth.* Dan forced himself to stop the pessimistic train of thought, besides people were pepping up. Some were actually excited by the prospect of continuing the mission, come what may.

Priya emerged from the shadows, where she'd been quietly observing events.

"If you're going to do this," she told them, "… it must be now. And you're going to have to somehow evade the Scarecrows."

Garner looked upbeat. "We could Rawback some weapons. The Factory will cook up some machine guns for us."

"That's already been tried by people from my crew. It didn't work. There must be inbuilt safeguards that prevent the Factory from producing military hardware."

Dan nodded in the direction of sections of metal piping leaning against the walls.

"Then we arm ourselves with those," he said. "I used one to ruin the fuck out of a Scarecrow's face." His choice of savage language was deliberate. He wanted to instil a sense of the weaponry's power. "What's more, they won't run out of bullets."

Borman was satisfied by the answer. "Good thinking, Dan. That metalwork will smash any damn Scarecrow to pulp."

Priya's expression wasn't particularly confident, however. "We're better off avoiding Scarecrows, rather than fighting them."

Gen said, "Priya. You do know where to find the gravity machine?"

"Yep. About an hour's walk from here."

Flynn nodded. "Very well. Grab what supplies you need. And pick your weapons. We move out in twenty minutes."

Merrick said, "Do we need spacesuits? Because Vicki hasn't got one."

"You're crazy." Garner sneered. "Leave the Rawback here."

"No."

Priya spoke up: "Listen. This isn't going to be a stroll in the park. The

Scarecrows will attack. And I don't know if arming yourself with bits of water pipe will be as effective as you hope."

Flynn sighed with frustration. "So? What do you suggest?"

Priya's tone was firm: "You need an army to help defend you."

Borman actually laughed, like this was the most ridiculous suggestion he'd ever heard. "Where do we get an army from?"

There was silence as everyone puzzled over what Priya had just told them.

Then, finally, Gen understood. "Absolutely no way."

Priya stood her ground. "It's our only chance. We've got to bring them with us."

FORTY-ONE

WE ARE LEGION

"**B**army army ... that's what we've got, haven't we? Our very own barmy army."

Borman had made the observation with no humor whatsoever.

Dan Karlton could hardly fail to disagree as he watched the strange group filing out through the doorway at the base of the Tower. There was Priya, and his fellow crew members. And there were the Rawbacks. The Rawbacks were an assortment of grotesque figures that resembled men, women and children. There was Borman's dog, too. Bella plodded across the dusty ground to where Borman stood. The animal was loyal to him in a way that seemed purely automatic. Its eyes were dull. The ears drooped down. Dan watched a Rawback take Merrick's hand in hers. Merrick loudly insisted that the Rawback was Vicki, his girlfriend. Vicki, in truth, was one of the most perfectly formed of the creatures, which, in most cases, were very raw representations of the human beings that they copied. Some lacked mouths, or necks, or eyes.

The Rawback that Dan had seen on the stairs last night emerged from the Tower: the creature that lacked an arm and pretty much the entire top half of its skull. There was a gaping crater in the top of the head. There was no brain there, only charcoal-colored granules. And in this brighter light he now saw that a vertical cut ran down from the top of its shoulder to the bottom of where the ribs would be, if it was a genuine human being.

The creature ambled up to Gen and, in a monotone, uttered, "Love you, Spud."

Gen gulped as a powerful sadness engulfed her. "Love you, too, Dad."

Rawbacks were being reunited with the people that had wished them into existence. There were other Rawbacks that had been created by Priya's colleagues, who were either dead or had transformed into Scarecrows. Nevertheless, the older Rawbacks tagged along, perhaps driven by a dim yearning for human company. When a tall Rawback stepped through the doorway, Dan hoped that was the last one. However, fate would twist the knife of grief in him, and it would show no mercy, because the last Rawback to leave the Tower was Shaz Chandler. Yes, he had deliberately tried to create her and had failed. He was certain that this version of Shaz came into being because he'd dreamed her into existence as he slept. He hoped she wouldn't be viable and, like the car with the corpse, would simply crumble away. But, no, here she was. As large as life. Yet, perversely dead-looking. A zombie thing that lacked a face. The abomination, which barely resembled Shaz, moved away from the Tower to join her fellow Rawbacks that stood in a group. They showed no interest in their surroundings. Some drew on their meagre stock of phrases.

The man with one arm. "Love you, Spud."

The boy without eyes. "Can we go to the park, Dad?"

Vicki: "Merrick. We'll be together forever and ever."

Most of the real human beings—those men and women with hearts, and feelings, and fears for the future—stared in the direction of the piles of bone. Clearly, they were alert to any sign of the Scarecrows. So far, there were none in sight amongst those grey mounds of ribs, femurs, vertebrae, skulls, and other morbid relics of the human anatomy.

Above their heads, they could make out the roof of the Factory, through the mist.

Dan could smell nothing, other than a stale odour of dust. The temperature was neither hot nor cold. He wondered if some alien mechanism regulated environmental conditions to suit their human guests.

Flynn strode across to them. "Ladies and gentlemen, it will take us an hour to walk to the Engine Room—that is the name the crew of Rib One gave to the zone where the gravity device is located. Keep your weapons close. Keep your wits about you. And keep encouraging the Rawbacks to stay with us. Don't let them drop behind."

Jellsby was his with his "family." "You don't expect my wife and children to fight, do you?"

Garner barked, "They're not your wife and children. They ain't nuthin'. Got it? They are just a bunch of stuff that moves."

Jellsby spoke stiffly: "I will keep them close to me. I will not order them to fight."

Priya said, "They won't fight anyway. Their purpose is to serve as a distraction. With luck, the Scarecrows will get busy with the Rawbacks while we keep moving."

Borman shook his head. "We have got ourselves a Barmy Army, haven't we? They're not living humans. They're not functional soldiers, either." He reached down and patted his dog on the head. It must have been an action born of habit because he suddenly realized he'd patted a creature that wasn't genuinely "living." He pulled his hand back fast. And he looked ashamed of what he'd done.

Dan glanced around at the crew. They all carried pieces of pipe of various lengths. He'd reclaimed the pipe he'd used earlier to attack the Scarecrow that had once been a woman by the name of Franco.

A breeze stirred dust on the ground, raising a grey mist that reached up to their knees.

Flynn called out, "I don't need to remind you that Priya is vital to our mission. She's the only one who can lead us to the engine. If we're attacked, make sure that you protect her."

Jellsby spoke up in a tone that suggested he was sulking. "I'm important, too. I'm the only scientist here. If anyone can repair and restart the engine, it is I."

Garner spat on the floor with disgust. "Jellsby, you're a damn botanist. If we see a bonsai tree, you can prune it ... but fixing engines? God help us."

Flynn scowled at Garner. "Professor Jellsby has scientific training. That intellectual discipline just might help us pull off the miracle we're all hoping for."

Spiro quickly added, "Dan, here, is a structural engineer. We need him, too."

Flynn nodded. "Therefore, we need to move in strict formation. The ones that require special protection should be in the center. Everyone else, form a loose ring around them. Encourage the Rawbacks to be part of that protective ring."

Borman and Garner each gave Dan a dirty look. Dan knew what they were thinking.

Dan shook his head. "I'll be part of the ring. Yes, I have engineering qualifications, but I don't think that actually qualifies me to repair alien technology."

Dan took his place in the protective ring around Priya and Jellsby. Meanwhile, Jellsby muttered instructions to his 'wife' and 'children'. They joined hands and moved up close to him. The creatures were pitiful. Dan had to look away.

Flynn patted Priya on the shoulder. "We're in your hands, Priya. Get us there—we'll do the rest."

Priya appeared to be struggling with some inner conflict. For a moment, she froze there. She was repeatedly clenching and unclenching her hands. Then she took a deep breath and ... "Before we start walking, I have a confession."

The breeze quickened. Small pieces of bone rolled across the flat ground, making a faint clicking sound.

Priya's face was grim. "It was me," she said. "I opened the doors to the Tower."

Everywhere, the expressions on faces yelled, *WHAT THE FUCK?*

Garner raised the five-foot length of pipe he carried. He was so angry he looked like he wanted to smash out her brains there and then. "Why?" he bellowed.

Merrick pulled Vicki closer, ready to protect her, should violence erupt.

One of the crew members shouted, "She must be a Scarecrow herself. She wanted to let them in so they could turn us into fucking monsters!"

Men and women shouted angrily as they closed in on Priya. The pipes had become dangerous weapons in their hands. Those people wanted to spill blood.

Priya's voice rang out with absolute clarity. "Listen. I opened the doors. Yes. I admit it. But I needed to shake you all up. You were becoming obsessed with the idea of bringing dead family and dead lovers back to life."

Garner shouted. "I did no such thing. I fucking hate Rawbacks!"

"Granted, you didn't! But most of the others did. See the guy that's missing an arm and part of his head. That's Gen's father. Borman Rawbacked his dog into existence. Merrick conjured up Vicki. The woman without a face? That's Dan's sorry excuse for a resurrection."

Dan's fists tightened around the heavy pipe. "Priya! Take that back. The woman was a colleague. She was killed by the meteor that hit Manchester eighteen months ago. I didn't deliberately bring her back." He felt his cheeks burn with an embarrassment he couldn't adequately explain. "I dreamt about her. That's all."

Spiro patted Dan on his forearm. Human contact being the best form of reassurance. "That creature isn't Dan's fault. Those grapevines appeared on the wall because I dreamt about the vines at my grandparents' house."

Katrina went to stand beside Dan—another gesture of solidarity. "And I somehow made my old bedroom appear in the dormitory. That was due to a dream. And one thing we can't do is control our dreams. That woman isn't Dan's responsibility."

Borman's voice suddenly rang out. "I don't give a fuck about who's

responsibility she is. I only hope she's going to be of use to us. Because …"
He pointed. "Scarecrows! Incoming!"

From the mounds of bone, they were streaming.

Dan saw dozens of figures moving on legs that did not bend at the knee. He could see the Blisters that wore something resembling babies' faces on their vile flesh. And he glimpsed the sinuous undulations of tentacles. The Scarecrows were running down the sides of the grey hills of bone. They were fast. And they were coming this way.

And he sensed their naked menace.

FORTY-TWO

SCARECROWS

Dan thought: *If there is such a thing as a miracle, we need one now.*

They were outnumbered. He guessed that perhaps close to a hundred Scarecrows were loping through the mist of wind-driven dust. Dan's group comprised a dozen or so, together with perhaps thirty Rawbacks. He suspected that the mock-humans were more a liability than an asset. However, if the plan worked, they would serve as cannon-fodder. The Rawbacks would be sacrificed to keep the Scarecrows busy while the humans forged ahead.

Scarecrows were getting closer by the second. The blister-like parasites bulged from their bodies. Grey tentacles, which extended from the Blisters, moved with a cobra motion above the Scarecrows' heads. What was most revolting of all, the faces embedded in the Blisters. By sheer chance, they resembled the puckered faces of newborn human infants. They had tiny mouths. While their eyes were little more than shriveled-up pellets of gristle set into grey flesh.

Flynn urged everyone to move faster. "Don't stop," she shouted. "Keep together in a tight group—as close together as you can. Keep the Rawbacks moving."

The Rawbacks, however, ambled along. They were like a herd of cattle.

They kept grouped together, but nothing like human thought illuminated their brains with intelligence. They were bovine creatures, with dull as dirt eyes.

Dan shuddered as he glanced at Shaz. She traipsed through dust that was ankle-deep, her feet splashing up gouts of grey powder that were then carried away in the breeze.

Priya repeatedly pointed ahead. "The Engine Room is over there. You've must move faster. Don't let the Scarecrows catch you."

Dan realized that the Scarecrows would inevitably catch up. They moved much faster than this wretched platoon of frightened human beings, which were accompanied by a bunch of part-formed shambling freaks that had neither blood nor functioning minds in their bodies.

Professor Jellsby was at the center of the group. He held hands with his wife and children, so they formed a strung-out daisy chain. The son was the slowest and plodded in a zombie-like way—his mouth hung open, the bottom jaw completely slack.

Jellsby continued to play his role as the scientist. "Priya. What formed the heaps of bone?"

"Who knows," she replied. "At one point, in Callisto's history, I suspect the Ribs became fishing boats. They went to Earth to net human beings and bring them back here—maybe thousands of them. For what purpose, though?" She shrugged. Then she glanced back at the Scarecrows. Her eyes flashed with anxiety as she called to the forlorn gaggle of human beings that formed a ring around her: "Can't you move faster? We're still forty minutes away from the Engine."

Of course, they couldn't move faster. Dan experienced a pang of fear that was so powerful it felt like a painful jolt of electricity running through his body.

He muttered to Spiro and Katrina, who walked beside him: "It's all going wrong, isn't it? We're outnumbered. Are we really going to kill all those fucking monsters with bits of plumbing hardware?"

Spiro grimaced. "We're going to have to try, Dan."

Katrina agreed: "Absolutely. We all have family on Earth. We've got to stop it from being smashed to bits."

For some reason, considering that Katrina had been so skeptical about their mission, she seemed to have fully bought into this quest to repair the gravity machine. Despite the situation, Dan found himself staring at her, and wondering what was really going on inside her mind.

Dan glanced back. The Scarecrows were perhaps two hundred yards away. He could see that two of them wore spacesuits. Those must be Khalid and Sophie. The spacesuits hadn't saved them from the Blisters climbing onto them and … then what? Piercing their skin with something like a mosquito proboscis, which then injected a mind-control venom into their bloodstream? It had to be something like that, he reasoned.

"Love you, Spud."

He glanced at Gen who pulled her father along by the hand attached to his remaining arm. The man, if you can call him a man, lurched along. The fact that he lacked an arm, and the top of his skull, exposing dull matter where a brain should be, didn't appear to affect his ability to move. Or to utter that same refrain. "Love you, Spud."

Everyone was panting now. Bone dust dried their throats. People were coughing. Lots now reached for water bottles, attached to their belts. Though they didn't pause, they began taking long pulls on the bottles, gulping water down their painfully dry throats. Dan licked his lips. He immediately wished he hadn't. His lips were gritty with bone dust. The dust transferred itself to his tongue. His stomach heaved. He spat the vile filth out onto the ground, then reached for his own water bottle.

The breeze stirred up enough dust to fill the complex with mist. Even so, Dan could make out the roof that arched above his head. If anything, the roof here appeared to be a series of domes. He found himself recalling his engineering lecturers at university speaking in tones of absolute admiration about the Pantheon in Rome, and Hagia Sophia in Istanbul, where their long-dead engineering colleagues of Rome and Constantinople had built colossal domes that were still wonders of structural engineering. Those innovators had circumvented gravity to create enormous spaces that were protected from the elements by elegant inwardly curving walls of concrete or brick or stone. The alien creatures had adopted the same engineering solutions in order to create their own vast enclosed spaces on Callisto. The other structures that rose from the Factory floor had become indistinct. And the place seemed to exist in a permanent state of dusk, so it was hard to see more than a few hundred yards into the deathly gloom.

Spiro glanced back. "Scarecrows haven't tried attacking yet. Maybe they're frightened of us."

Katrina stared at the monstrous legion of figures that kicked up fountains of dust as they marched. Suddenly, she gasped as she realized an important fact.

"They aren't trying to catch up." Her voice was tight with fear. "They are herding us. They want us to keep moving in this direction."

Spiro stared back at the figures. "Katrina's right. But what are they planning to do?"

There was no answer to that question. Not yet, anyhow. Though the question, alone, was enough to pour a cascade of icy shivers through Dan's body.

And he'd seen something else. Dan nodded in the direction of the Rawbacks. "Have you noticed?" The shivers returned. "The Rawbacks are starting to change."

FORTY-THREE

NOT SO MUCH RAWBACK

"Love you, Spud." The man who lacked the roof of his skull blinked. Suddenly a flash of pain illuminated his eyes. "Gen? What happened to me?"

Gen stared at her father in horror. The man's eyes were no longer dull. They were coming alive. They flashed with intelligence. That and an awareness that something was deeply wrong.

Dan turned to look at Shaz. Her face had consisted of smooth skin. There had been a swelling in its center that suggested a mere hint of a nose. But what Dan saw next delivered a punch of shock to his belly. Two dome shapes formed in the mid part of the face. Then the domes split and, bulging out, all wet and round, were a pair of brown eyes.

And suddenly she possessed a mouth where there had only been tightly stretched flesh.

The once featureless face wore an expression of alarm. "Dan! Where are we? The last thing I remember was that we were in the office when it began to collapse."

Dan didn't answer.

Couldn't answer.

Jellsby's children began to cry. They were scared by their alien surroundings.

Garner yelled, "Shut those things up!"

"Don't you see?" Katrina stared in astonishment. "The Rawbacks … they're becoming human … they're alive. Properly alive!"

Flynn clearly ignored what was happening. She waved her arm. "Come on! Hurry!"

Merrick stared at Vicki. Her face was becoming a truly living face. Her eyes were bright. They soon began to intelligently assess her surroundings.

"This can't even be Earth," Vicki said. "Merrick. Did you bring me here?"

Dan called out, "Priya. You're a doctor. Why are the Rawbacks changing?"

Priya stared in horror as her once part-formed husband appeared to wake from his sleep-walker state to regard her with shining eyes. There was an expression of astonishment on his face.

Priya shook her head—her expression was fraught with worry. "I'm not sure. I can only imagine that everyone here—we humans, that is—are in a heightened emotional state. This will be due to the danger we're facing. Our minds are functioning at a higher-level. In turn, that amplifies our capacity to imagine the people we want back in our lives in a far more detailed way. I guess … I-I …" She began to stammer as she struggled to understand what was happening. "My belief is … that this is happening at an unconscious level. And we, whether we intend it or not, are feeding the Factory with much more sophisticated data about the loved ones that we conjured here in the first place."

Spiro marveled at the Rawbacks. "Therefore," he said, "these things are getting an upgrade. They are becoming real men and women—with minds and memories."

Borman's cheeks glistened with tears as he saw Bella scamper toward him. Her tail was wagging, and her dark eyes were bright as glass. She was fully alive. And she was loving being back with her master.

Shaz rushed across to Dan and hugged him. Her eyes were glittering and vibrant. Her embrace felt soft and wonderful … and then he realized the immensity of the horror to come.

They had brought the Rawbacks with them to fling at the Scarecrows as a grotesque form of obstacle to slow them down. But now the Rawbacks were real people—they had emotions, feelings. A fact verified by Gen's father who groaned in pain.

"How did I get injured?" He flinched at the hurt. "My arm? Gen, sweetheart, what happened to my arm?"

Shaz, meanwhile, hugged Dan. The woman was so happy to be there.

You're dead, he thought. *How do I explain that you died eighteen months ago? When you fell all that way ... after I failed to grab hold of your hand.*

Jellsby screeched, "I'm taking my family back to the Crab. They'll be safe there."

"The mission," cried Flynn. "We must complete the mission!"

"No!" Merrick's grip tightened on the pipe he carried. He looked ready to fight anyone that disagreed with him. "I'm leaving. Vicki's coming back home with me."

Vicki looked repulsed. "Merrick, don't you ever take 'no' for an answer? Our relationship is over. I don't love you anymore."

Merrick was appalled. "You can't say that! I made you! You only exist because I wanted you to exist!"

Merrick lunged at Vicki and grabbed her by the wrist.

Vicki tried to pull away. "I warned you—that I'd tell the cops if you didn't leave me alone. Let go of me!"

"I love you!"

Dan had seen plenty of shit storms of emotion when love affairs turned bad. But he'd seen nothing like this. Vicki was trying to pull away in disgust. Merrick was screaming that he loved her. That she had no choice. She had to be with him. Had to love him. Because he had created her.

Spiro's eyes bulged from his head as he tried to make sense of it all. "How do we solve this?"

The question hung on the air, never answered. Because that was when the Scarecrows attacked.

FORTY-FOUR

BATTLE ONE

Dan realized that a dozen Scarecrows had outflanked them. They rushed on stiff legs toward Dan's group. The legs still did not bend at the knees. Their feet came down in hard, flat-footed stomps that sent up eruptions of dust.

Flynn yelled, *"Here they come!* Gather closer. Don't try and hit them with the pipes—push them back. Just keep pushing them back!"

When the Rawbacks were dull, half-dead things without minds, that was bad enough. Now that they could feel, think and experience terror—that was worse. A helluva lot worse. Because the Rawbacks that had undergone the mental upgrade began shrieking in panic. Merrick grabbed hold of Vicki's hand, but she tried to pull away. She was screaming to Merrick to let go. Jellsby attempted to put his arms around his entire family in the center of the cluster. The children were sobbing.

Shaz looked around her in shock and kept repeating, "Dan? What are those things? Are those parasites clinging to their bodies? Tentacles? Look, tentacles!"

"And Godawful baby faces," muttered Garner.

Borman shouted, "Here they come! Don't let them get inside the circle!"

The protective circle was very much likely to be that in name only. Their defensive perimeter consisted of a dozen or so men and women armed with metal pipes.

Scarecrows lunged toward the group. Dan stabbed outward with the long hunk of pipe. It slammed into the face of a white-haired man. The end of the pipe ripped open the eye socket. The eyeball burst in a snotty cascade of gel.

Borman and Garner viciously used their improvised weapons as clubs. They hacked downward, splitting open scalps, discharging torrents of crimson that were wet and thick.

Despite their wounds, none of the Scarecrows backed off, nor did any fall to the ground.

Priya shouted a warning. "Watch out, the Blisters will start to detach. They'll try to climb onto you. Strike at the tentacles if they get close!"

Spiro slashed the metal pipe at a guy with a beard. The blow ripped away the guy's bottom jaw. The red tongue flapped out, like a red necktie dangling down the outside of his throat as far as his chest.

"We're not hurting them," bellowed Garner.

A pair of Scarecrows darted forward. They grabbed Bexton. In seconds, they'd hauled him away from the group. Immediately, three Blisters detached themselves from nearby Scarecrows and slithered their tentacles forward over his body. When he dropped to the ground, he was screaming and convulsing. Then, suddenly, he stopped shouting. He sat up, bolt upright. He stared at the humans with absolute fury. Then he was on his feet and, with his new comrades, began to attack.

Dan caught sight of a Rawback moving slowly toward the Scarecrows. This was a Rawback in the form of the boy that Dan had seen earlier in the basement. It had remained one of those dismal part-formed creatures. Seemingly, the upgrade only benefited the Rawbacks that had been created by the men and women here. The old Rawbacks still continued to be zombie-like—they only possessed a superficial resemblance of life.

The boy walked toward the Scarecrows.

"Dad. Will you take me to the park? Will you buy me ice-cream?"

The Scarecrows launched themselves on the Rawback that mockingly copied the shape of a human boy, albeit one without eyes. It was just a grim piece of matter that the Factory had crudely carved into something vaguely human.

The Scarecrows caught hold of the little figure. They flung it back and forth between them, as if wanting it one moment, then rejecting it the next. Because no Blisters migrated to the boy-thing—they knew that this wasn't a human being that could successfully play host to their parasitic biology. The boy-thing's head whipped loosely backward and forward as hands seized hold of the body then flung it aside again in disgust.

Finally, the creatures launched their savage assault.

Dan saw the Scarecrows' hands seize the child-shaped horror. They brutally ripped at the flesh. Before Dan turned away, sickened, he saw limbs detach. Arms and legs fell to the ground where they lay twitching in the dust. There was no blood.

For one last heart-wrenching time, the dismembered Rawback sang out: "Dad. Will you take me to the park?"

Then there was the abrupt crunch of a skull being crushed.

After that, the Rawback (which wasn't a child and never could be a child) was silent.

Another Rawback experienced a similar fate. A woman-thing with silver hair blundered into a snarling pack of Scarecrows. She was torn apart.

Jellsby screeched. "Protect my family!"

Those who held metal pipes ferociously stabbed them into the faces of their attackers. Though they weren't trying to protect Jellsby's wife and children, they were fighting to save themselves. Garner was clearly frustrated by their inability to even knock a Scarecrow down. He lunged toward a male that had long blond hair. Garner caught hold of the hair in his fist. That done, he dragged the Scarecrow toward him before hurling it to the ground. He was bellowing all the time. At that moment, he'd become a ferocious beast in his own right. He stomped down with absolute fury onto the creature's head. The nose burst—blood was a red flash that spurted across the ground. Then Borman and Garner wielded the pipes like axes. They viciously chopped at the figure as it writhed in the dust. Frantically, the Blisters tried to fend off the weapons with their tentacles.

But Garner and Borman were blazing with utter bloodlust. The urge to kill was like a nuclear-powered motor inside of them. They slammed the metalwork down onto the Scarecrow. Blows were fierce enough to rupture the Blisters that were fixed to the body. Pink liquid spurted from the vile things. The once tight skin of the sacs deflated. That in turn made the little goblin faces shrink. The faces even scrunched up as if in pain.

Garner was shouting over and over: "You can kill them … you can kill them!"

Katrina panted, "You've only killed one. There are eleven more. And here come another ninety."

She was right. The other phalanx of Scarecrows was moving quickly. And they were no more than a hundred yards away.

Flynn beckoned everyone to follow. "Keep moving. We've got to reach the Engine.

By this time, the nearest Scarecrows, which now included Bexton amongst their number, had begun to slowly retreat, though Dan knew that this was only a tactical withdrawal. The monstrosities would join their comrades before renewing the attack on the humans. Everyone was panting hard, trying to get enough oxygen back into their lungs. The pipes they held were red and dripping.

The Rawbacks that hadn't been upgraded continued their zombie shuffle alongside the humans. However, the Rawbacks that had been elevated to something very close to real people were beginning to run. Most were sobbing. They didn't know where they were. They didn't know what was happening. What they did know was that they were in mortal danger.

Priya shouted, "We're nearly there. Keep moving. If I don't make it, go through the archway between those two buildings. That's where you'll find the Engine."

Vicki broke free of Merrick's grasp. Her mind was so crushed by terror that it seemed as if she couldn't make a rational decision. She ran toward the Scarecrows.

Merrick yelled, "Vicki! Come back! I can change!"

The Scarecrows still identified Vicki as a Rawback. Therefore, due to her synthetic biology, there was zero chance of her turning Scarecrow. Nevertheless, they still rushed at her.

And then they tore her apart.

FORTY-FIVE

THE BREEDING POOL

Katrina rounded on Merrick as they ran toward the archway. "Merrick! You should have let me talk to Vicki."

Before Merrick could respond, Garner delivered his own observation in a manner that was as cold as it was cruel: "She's gone now. Case closed."

Merrick let out a cackle of laughter that glittered with nothing less than mania. "It doesn't matter about *that* Vicki. She was a shit!" He laughed again. "I can make another. Look … *look!*"

Dan noticed a shadow figure that was maybe ten feet away from him. When he looked closer, he saw what appeared to be a woman, yet she had no eyes or nose or mouth. But, as he watched, human features began to smoothly extrude from the blank matter of the face.

"See!" Merrick pointed. "I made another Vicki."

They were now twenty paces from the archway. Everyone was running faster, and they were leaving the old zombie-like Rawbacks behind. Nevertheless, the sorry creatures shuffled faster as they tried to catch up.

Shaz caught Dan's arm. "Can't you tell me what's happening? Or am I dreaming?" Then she laughed. But it was such a morbid laugh that it chilled his blood. "Or am I dead?"

"Shaz. Don't worry. I'll look after you."

Katrina shot him a grave look. A look that said: *I take it all back. Shaz really is your responsibility now. You made her. You damn well keep her safe.*

☮

What they saw, after they ran through the archway, took their breath away.

Dan found himself in a huge room—one that was perhaps a mile long, with a ceiling five hundred feet above his head. Bone dust, along with fragments of skeleton, covered the floor here, ankle-deep. Entire skulls littered the place, too—they were dome-shaped things. This was like gazing at a field of grey mushrooms.

Everyone had now spilled in through the archway, and there they stopped dead. Merrick gripped Vicki Mark Two by the hand. She appeared dazed. Yet she seemed to be more fully human than her first duplicate. Perhaps Merrick was getting the hang of Rawbacking his ex-girlfriend into something that was very nearly identical to an actual living human being. Shaz kept close to Dan. Spiro stood at the back of the group with Borman. They were the rearguard. They gripped the steel piping in their fists, ready to face the onslaught from the Scarecrows.

Priya began speaking. "There's the Engine. See, that structure with all the discs? They all interlink like cogs in a clockwork watch mechanism. My colleagues, while they were still human, ran tests and discovered this was the source of immensely powerful gravitational forces."

The structure she pointed at was the size of a three-story building. However, it might have been even larger, because the lower parts were submerged in pinkish fluid. And that pinkish fluid formed a vast lagoon, which was veined with lines of purple. These lines, which radiated outward from the Engine, lay flat on the liquid's surface. The lagoon appeared to be a reservoir of some sort, because a wall contained it. This resulted in the Engine becoming an island in the middle of the pink stuff.

A young woman brushed against Dan. He glanced at her, thinking she was one of the old Rawbacks, then he looked again, realizing he hadn't seen her before. She had short dark hair and wore a white blouse and a denim skirt. Her face was perfectly formed. The eyes, however, were shut.

Dan said, "There are new Rawbacks appearing." He paused in surprise, then glanced at Katrina. "She looks like you."

"That's my sister. She's called Tambara." Katrina's expression was one of utter misery. "I didn't make her. I swear that I didn't."

There were more and more new figures moving toward the group. Initially, they were shadowy and blurred. However, they swiftly resolved themselves into solid beings that looked absolutely human.

Priya had noticed them, too. "We are *in extremis*. That has led to our anxiety heightening the power of our imagination. The Factory is acting on our fear and is producing people that are important to us. Possibly the Factory believes that it is creating defensive measures to protect us."

Garner called out, "If they give the Scarecrows something to do by ripping them to shit, then that's okay by me. It gives us breathing space."

Jellsby shouted, "My family have become real people. They must be protected."

Garner yelled back, "Shut your fucking mouth, Jelly Belly. They are Rawbacks. They're expendable."

"Say that again … and I'll hit you!"

By this time, there were upward of thirty brand-new Rawbacks milling around the *bona fide* humans. The creatures all looked as if they'd woken into a new reality, which they found shocking—almost overwhelmingly so.

They were saying things like,

"Where are we?"

"Is that you, Garner?"

"Katrina? Katrina. Are you there?"

Katrina took her sister's hand. "Tambara, it's all right. I'm here."

"Thank goodness I found you."

Katrina appeared to be embarrassed by the manifestation of her own flesh and blood. In a stammering way, she explained to the others.

"Tambara was born blind. I was her eyes. I loved her so much, but … when she was nineteen, she died."

"Katrina. Why are you saying such awful things? I'm alive. I haven't died. Where are we? It smells strange. Like there's dust everywhere."

"Tambara, I'll explain when I can. We must go somewhere now."

"All right. Hold on tight to my hand."

"I will."

A tear rolled down Katrina's cheek.

Spiro called out a warning. "I'm going to have to hurry you, guys. The Scarecrow army will be here in less than five minutes."

Flynn had been moving closer to the wall of the dam. However, she abruptly stepped back—she'd seen something that disgusted her.

Flynn pointed at the grey expanse that formed the dam wall. "Those are Blisters. See? They've interlinked their tentacles then pulled each other tight. Millions of Blisters have become the blocks of the wall. They're holding the water back."

Priya's expression was grim. "I've not been here myself, but members of my team explored this place."

"So, what is this lake?"

"It's the Breeding Pool. That's what Professor Longstrom believed. She was a biologist. It's a lagoon of plasma—similar to the plasma that forms a substantial part of our blood. This is where the Blisters are born—in all that pink gloop. Then they leave the lagoon to find people like us to fasten their parasitic bodies to."

"Exactly what are these Blisters?" Katrina regarded the wall with complete disgust. Because the mass of Blisters had begun, ever so slightly, to pulsate.

Priya's voice became sour. "Professor Longstrom theorised that the Blisters, or more accurately their antecedents, built the Ribs and the Factory. However, the wonderful lifeforms that created those technological marvels gradually evolved into vile parasites. Or, rather, degenerated into parasites. They don't appear to have intelligent minds. In fact, they have been reduced to creatures of pure instinct."

Spiro sang out: "Here's your two-minute warning. Scarecrows are getting pretty close."

Professor Jellsby turned his own scientific eye toward the lagoon of pink horror that engulfed the Engine. "The first question I have is: how do we even reach the Engine without drowning in that stuff? Question two: how on Earth do we fix such an exotic mechanism?"

A grey-haired couple stared at Spiro.

Spiro grimaced. "Grandma. Grandpops. I'm sorry. I didn't mean to bring you back."

Tambara touched the side of Katrina's face. "Katrina. Can we go home now? This place frightens me."

"Frightens the fuck out of me, too." That was Garner—the guy as brutal as ever with his words.

"Garner," said Dan. "Have you ever shown a shred of empathy in your life? These people are …"

Dan Karlton's voice had faded away, because he had just seen a new edition to the Rawback Clan.

The car was back. The one he knew so well. And so was its driver.

FORTY-SIX

"DEATH DRIVES THE CAR OF YOUR DREAMS ... YOUR BAD DREAMS, THAT IS"

Ten Scarecrows attacked.

They must have already been lurking in the shadows of the Engine Room when the sad assortment of Rawbacks and humans arrived. Meanwhile, the rest of the Scarecrows, comprising a deadly squad of possibly a hundred or more, were steadily approaching. Dan hadn't been paying attention, however. Instead, his focus had been locked onto the dream car of old that had haunted his hours of sleep since his youth. A car as black as midnight shadow. And there was the corpse driver. Claws of white bone gripped the steering wheel. A pair of bulging eyes that glistened brightly, as if a light burned inside the skull. The eyes stared at Dan. He didn't want to climb into the passenger seat. He didn't want to at all. But-

Garner yelled, "Here they come!"

The battle erupted. Dan immediately swung the pipe at the nearest Scarecrow. A guy with dreads that hung down his back. The pipe clunked against skull. The Scarecrow didn't even flinch. He felt no pain. Garner kicked out—his boot connecting with the creature's leg, knocking it off its feet. It struck the floor, which raised a splash of bone dust.

The more human of the Rawbacks began to scream in terror. The

Scarecrow that Priya had identified as Franco lunged at Dan. He saw the circular wound in her face, where the end of the pipe had cut into the flesh when she'd tried to get through the doorway and into the Tower. The broken arm hung limply down. Yet the other arm lashed out, trying to grab hold of the humans there.

Suddenly, Dan found himself in a vortex of movement. Scarecrows lunged at him. Blisters jiggled on Scarecrow bodies. Sometimes, a Blister would extend a tentacle, attempting to lasso a human with that slimy limb that was wet from root to tip. People slashed at the tentacles with the metal pipes.

Dan's blood roared inside his head. His heart had become a pounding motor in his chest. His throat burned from the dust he was inhaling. Flashes of agony blasted through his shoulders as he repeatedly slammed the heavy pipe down onto the heads of the Scarecrows. Blood gushed from huge wounds in their faces and in their scalps. But they showed neither fear nor an indication that they were tiring.

Behind him, the car and its corpse driver trundled closer.

He wants me to get into the car. The thought blazed with such a powerful aura of terror that it threatened to tear Dan's mind apart. *The corpse wants me to go with him. Maybe he's here to drive me to hell.*

Franco lunged at Dan. Her face was so close that all he could see were her eyes that screamed pure rage at him. He felt her breath on his face—it stank of beefsteak that had been left to rot in a trashcan. His belly convulsed so fiercely that the pain made him yell.

Everywhere, people were fighting the Scarecrows. And these creatures were just the advance shock troops. There was a real danger that they would succeed in overwhelming the men and women that desperately fought for their lives. When the full legion of monsters arrived, there'd be nothing that Flynn and her crew could do to stop them from transferring the Blisters to new victims.

Thunder cracked through the air. The sound was immense.

And though Dan was using every atom of his strength to push Franco back, lest the parasites detach and scramble onto his body, his eyes were drawn to the purple lightning, which blazed overhead. Was this a natural storm? Natural for the interior of this massive building, that is? Or was the Factory reacting to the humans' battle for survival?

Apparently so. Because when Spiro's Rawback grandparents were torn apart by Scarecrows, more lightning tore through the gloom overhead, as if in response to the slaughter. The lightning darted in straight lines of purple fire—travelling across the massive void from one side to the other. Thunder became a screaming sound. The volume was immense. Dan's teeth shook. The bones in his head felt like they were clattering together: his entire skull throbbed with nerve-shredding agony. Purple lines flashed faster. A repeated sequence over and over. If one of those lines of hard light should strike a human being … what then?

His elbow made a loud cracking sound as a sinew overstretched and the pistol-shot of pain that sped through his arm forced him to drop the pipe.

Garner appeared to be utterly in love with this insane outburst of violence. He had a demonic grin on his face as he smashed one of the Scarecrows into the ground, then stomped so hard on the skull that the bone structure collapsed—something that caused the face to deflate. Blood sprayed from the mangled head. Drops of crimson flashed through the air to speckle the white dust.

A Scarecrow lunged at Bella. Its claw-like fingers sank into the dog's back. Bella's head whipped upward as sheer agony tore through it. Borman howled with fury. Lightning cast its blazing light onto the man's face—turning it into a mask of purple fire.

By this time, the dog was dead—or rather its synthetic appearance of life had gone.

Borman grasped the Scarecrow's head with his bare hands. Then, with an immense surge of muscular power, he tore the head away from the neck. There was just a bloody stump of neck where the head had been. A severed nub of spine poked up through an upswelling of flesh that was as red as raw sirloin.

Blisters immediately quit dead flesh. They detached and scrambled up Borman's legs to his chest. There, they looped tentacles around Borman's torso and head. Borman attempted to pull the tentacles away.

But it was over so fast.

Borman was a Scarecrow now. He immediately attacked Garner.

Garner had seen what had happened, and with a battle cry erupting from his lips, he slashed at Borman with the steel pipe.

Thunder cascaded explosions of sound down onto the heads of everyone there. Lines of purple darted through the gloom. The Factory was either applauding the battle taking place. Or it was convulsed by the horror of it all.

Dan felt an object bump against the back of his leg.

It was the car.

It was nudging him. The corpse driver glared out through the windshield.

Climb in beside me, Dan. We've got somewhere to go.

Katrina ran toward Dan. "You made the car, didn't you?"

He nodded. "It wants me to get in."

He didn't have the chance to say more. Because, at that moment, Franco grabbed Katrina and started pulling her away—toward the shadows at the edge of that grim nightmare of a place.

FORTY-SEVEN

BATTLE TWO

The car nudged Dan Karlton again. Like a dog wanting attention will softly push its nose into the owner's leg.

Dan had enough on his plate. He needed to figure out a way to save Katrina. Even so, some other part of his mind paid close attention to what was behind the windshield of the car. After all, the dream had haunted him from years. In some way, he felt genetically bonded to the imagery of the dead man and the car that relentlessly cruised through his sleeping brain. Despite the danger that Katrina faced, some part of him absolutely needed to observe the corpse driver that sat behind the wheel ... but now the rotted assembly of bones and flesh was changing. Purple veins wormed over bare ribs to connect with a chunk of red meat in its chest. Even as Dan watched, the bloody chunk began to pulsate.

Billy Dead Bones had grown a heart. The heart pushed blood through a cat's cradle of arteries in the chest. The bulging eyes shone with a renewed lifeforce.

The car nudged forward again, the fender thumping into the back of Dan's leg. This time he gritted his teeth and ignored both the car and its macabre driver. Katrina needed him.

Katrina screamed as Franco hauled her away from the crew, who still battled the Scarecrows. Thankfully, the Scarecrows were much reduced in number. Garner had used the pipe to break the legs of one of the creatures. It tried to continue its attack by pulling itself forward by its hands. One of the new Rawbacks (a silver-haired woman) appeared to understand what was required of them, and she picked up one of the skulls that littered the floor and began to pound it down onto the head of the Scarecrow with the ruined legs.

Dan raced across the rug of dust, his feet kicking up explosions of white. Katrina's eyes were huge with terror. She flailed her fists at Franco. Meanwhile, one of the Blisters began to unstick itself from Franco's shoulder. Its tentacles reached out to slither around Katrina's throat.

"Katrina!" Dan yelled. "Don't let it fasten on to you!"

He would be too late. He realized that Katrina would become one of those wretched Scarecrows. She would become one of the damned. And she would find herself dwelling amongst the heaps of bone and dried human flesh. Exhaustion had ripped the strength out of him. He was too slow.

"Dan!" Katrina's voice rose to a screech. "It's too strong! I can't stop it!"

Just then, a figure sprinted by. Dan stared in astonishment. Shaz was running much faster than him.

Purple lightning etched lines against the roof. The flashes revealed the structure of interlocking ribs above his head. The roof was dark red—the color of thickening blood.

Shaz kept running. She slammed into Franco, almost knocking her off balance. Franco glared at Shaz. Meanwhile, the old wound that Dan had inflicted with the pipe on the woman's face re-opened. The wound's red lips pulled slowly apart, releasing crimson beads, which rolled down her face.

The Blister, meanwhile, had begun migrating from Franco's shoulder to Katrina's back. Yellow tentacles were entwining around her neck. The flesh of the tentacles was thoroughly wet enough to drip onto the ground. Shaz grabbed the Blister in both hands and tugged it away from Katrina's shoulder before the loathsome thing could fasten tightly on.

Franco's eyes blazed with fury. That's when she launched a savage attack on Shaz. Powerful hands detached Shaz's arms—and then her head.

Dan experienced such an eruption of horror within him that he couldn't even breathe.

He'd seen Shaz die when the building collapsed. Now she had died in front of him all over again. Horror morphed into nothing less than rage. Dan moved faster. He didn't stop when he reached Franco. He clenched both fists and, with his elbows locked, he double punched Franco in the throat. The woman crashed backward to the floor. There she lay. Her hands were clutching her throat and she was making a gurgling sound. He kicked aside the Blister that had lost its host.

He then grabbed Katrina by the hand. His intention, to run back to the others. As he turned, he saw that the car had followed him. Now its fender almost touched the backs of his legs once more.

Katrina panted, "Who's that in the driver's seat?"

"I call him Billy Dead Bones. But he seems to be changing."

The front of the skull now had a partial covering of sorts. It resembled one of those anatomical paintings of a human face, where the skin had been peeled away to reveal areas of exposed bone and straps of muscle. The eyes were more like living eyes. Yet they still lacked eyelids. The eyes were the size of eggs and protruded from the sockets.

Dan knew that the eyes were fixed on him. The corpse driver was wanting him to do what he'd always done.

Behind them, Franco was slowly rising to her feet. The creature was seemingly indestructible.

Flynn continued to battle with the Scarecrows, some fifty yards away. The humans and Rawbacks had clustered together to form a defensive group. Steel pipes flashed as they were swung at the heads of the Scarecrows. Flynn saw Dan and Katrina.

"Get back here," Flynn yelled. "We need to cluster tight together!"

Garner bellowed. "The other Scarecrows are coming!"

Dan saw that the hundred or so Scarecrows were headed this way, using that stiff-legged scissoring walk. They weren't in a hurry now. They understood that their enemy was weak. They would soon overpower the humans in order to allow the Blisters to scramble onto them. Then the only human-like creatures left in this Godforsaken hell would be Scarecrows and Rawbacks.

The car moved forward. Its hard nose bumped Dan's legs.

Katrina warned, "Franco's getting closer."

The corpse driver had lips to hem the mouth now. And skin covered what had once been skeleton claws. The corpse driver slid sideways from behind the wheel and across to the passenger seat. That was the moment that the driver's door swung open.

Dan shouted, "Katrina! Get in the back!"

She didn't wait to be invited a second time. Grabbing the door handle, she swung the door open, dived into the back seat, then slammed the door shut. Dan slid into the driver's seat. He glanced at the corpse beside him. Ears were budding from the side of its head, which had a covering of flesh in parts, and nude bone elsewhere.

Dan spoke to the Rawback that had been conjured from his dreams. "Okay. You were always the one that drove me. But now you want me to drive you."

The corpse merely stared forward through the windshield as Franco lurched toward the car.

Dan slammed his foot down onto the gas pedal. Tires let out a banshee howl of a scream. Purple lightning tore vivid lines through the gloom. Thunder pounded the roof of the car.

The car pounced with all the fierce aggression of a panther. The fender crunched into Franco. She went down in front of the car. Briefly, she clung onto the hood and was dragged along, the bottom half of her body and her legs were beneath the chassis. Then the hands slipped away. Thereafter, the rear wheels bounced over a hard object. When Dan glanced in the rearview mirror, he had the satisfaction of seeing Franco lying there—she was a mutilated mess of nothing now. Blisters had burst.

They had squirted their gel innards onto the dust. All the tentacles lay limp on the Factory floor.

Dan flashed such a leering grin of triumph at the corpse sitting beside him that he knew he must have looked deranged.

"You gave me a weapon, didn't you?" Dan felt a dangerous exultation surging through his body. "Who needs a gun, when I've got a death machine as devastating as this?"

He drove the car hard, aiming the vehicle like it was a missile at the Scarecrows that attacked Flynn and Garner and the others. By this time, the car had reached a screaming velocity that didn't merely knock the Scarecrows down. Such was the vehicle's speed that the Scarecrows exploded when they were struck by two tons of nightmare steel. The Scarecrows' bellies ruptured. Intestines vented outward. Their heads whipped down onto the hood—skulls popped like balloons. Blood and brains struck the windshield. The contents of the creatures' heads left streaks of red and slimy grey. Dan hit the wiper lever, and the Rawbacked rubber blades scraped away the morbid gunk, allowing him to see clearly.

The corpse gazed cooly across at Dan. He sensed approval in its bright eyes.

"Last one," yelled Dan.

A Scarecrow had, at last, decided to flee. For the first time, he sensed fear in one of these creatures. And although it moved quickly—it was not fast enough.

A moment later, the car slammed into the running figure. The impact drove its bones out through the flesh. The sheer muscular punch of the car travelling at eighty miles an hour generated a whiplash effect of such power that it ripped the head clean off the shoulders. The severed head smacked back into the windshield, its mouth leaving a streak of saliva on the glass. An eye had ruptured. The convulsive snap of its dead jaws bit off the tongue. Then the head was gone. No doubt it would bounce along the floor for some time before coming to a rest, all bloody and dusty ... and utterly lifeless.

Katrina pounded a fist against his shoulder. "You marvellous man, you! You did it! You did it!" She yelled into his ear. "Get the rest of the bastards! You can kill them all! I know you can!"

Dan aimed the car at the legion of Scarecrows that goose-stepped toward the humans in the Engine Room. And just behind the beleaguered humans rose the wall of the dam. Above that was the vast array of discs that formed the engine that had, for millions of years, prevented killer asteroids from striking the Earth.

Dan drove the car toward the Scarecrows. Meanwhile, lightning still cut purple lines through the grim-as-death darkness above their heads.

Dan crushed the pedal to the metal. The engine howled—the machine sounded like the battle cry of the God of War.

Then his beautiful plan collapsed. And it collapsed into ugly failure.

FORTY-EIGHT

CATASTROPHE, THE DESPISED CHILD OF FAILURE

Dan drove the car at the Scarecrow legion as they headed toward the crew and the Rawbacks.

The car slammed into a Scarecrow—the machine's sheer speed caused the creature to explode into nothing bigger than fist-sized lumps of flesh. Blisters popped and then immediately deflated. The tentacles became lifeless strands of matter that lay in the dust.

Lightning bolts tore through the gloom above their heads. Purple flashes illuminated the vast room that was fully a mile in length.

The corpse in the passenger seat gazed at Dan. Though, in truth, it wasn't all that corpse-like now. Bones were clad in muscle, and the muscle was gaining a full covering of skin. The eyes had acquired eyelids, and those fleshy eyelids were slowly blinking.

Dan drove at another Scarecrow. This time, the side of the car caught it a glancing blow and the figure went spinning fully twenty feet before landing flat on its back.

Katrina's fist thumped down onto Dan's shoulder again. "You're doing it! You're killing them."

Dan glanced sideways at the corpse. The corpse stared back at him … then it slowly shook its head.

"I'm killing Scarecrows," he shouted at Billy Dead Bones. "It's working!"

The corpse, once again, slowly shook its head.

That thing that sat in the passenger seat was clearly shrewder than Dan because Dan was now missing his targets—or, rather, his targets quickly side-stepped, so avoiding being smashed to hell by the car.

"Damn it," howled Dan. "They know how to keep out of the way."

He drove in big loops. Tires flung up a living spume of dust. The same tires crushed ancient skulls lying on the floor to splinters.

Again and again, Dan hurled the car at the Scarecrows. Deftly, they stepped out of the way. The Scarecrow legion was, finally, closing in on Flynn and her crew. Dan saw his fellow crew members prepare for the final battle. They were gripping the steel pipes in both hands like they were battle-axes. Priya's Rawback lover sprinted out of the clump of figures there. He launched himself into the midst of the Scarecrows and attacked them with his fists.

The fight was a brutally short one. The Scarecrows pounced. They ripped off his face. Then they tore away his limbs.

Katrina yelled, "Dan! Do something! The Scarecrows will overwhelm them!"

"I'm trying. But I can't kill them. They're too fast."

Again and again, he launched the car at the creatures, like it was a missile. Its motor was screaming. Tires ripped up clouds of dust. Yet every time he approached a Scarecrow it simply stepped to one side, then the car hurtled past without even touching the creature, and he had to make another huge looping turn, the rear end fishtailing as he fought for control.

"Okay, Mister Bones," Dan said. "What do you suggest?"

The corpse merely stared out of the passenger window. Even the creature that Dan had conjured from his dreams appeared to want no part in this now. He was just a passenger along for the ride.

"Well, then?" Dan shouted. "Are you going to give me a fucking clue? What's the plan? How do I kill these Godawful monsters?"

No reply.

Dan powered the car onward. He aimed it at a Scarecrow with a froth of white hair. The Scarecrow ducked to the right.

Missed again.

Dan glared at the figure in the passenger seat. "I thought some last-ditch instinct had created you to help us. I was wrong. So, what's so interesting out there? What are you staring at?" Dan gripped the steering wheel so tightly his hands ached. "Okay! You're no use to me. And if you're no use to me, then you might as well get out and walk!"

Dan braked hard. The car came to a shrieking stop.

Katrina leaned forward from the back until her face was almost level with Dan's.

"Dan! He is looking at something in particular. He's trying to help you."

Dan shifted his gaze in the direction that his unearthly passenger was looking. Then he understood. Dan took a deep breath. Nothing less than a fiery revelation raced through his body.

Lines of purple incandescence blasted through the air above them. After the lightning came the thunder—louder than ever.

Dan, if anything, gripped the wheel even more tightly—his knuckles pushed up against the underside of the skin, raising the veins in the backs of his hands. "Katrina. He's looking at the dam." He took a deep breath. "Now's your chance, Katrina. If you want to get out?"

"I'm staying with you."

"Okay. Lie down on the seat, and hang on tight to whatever's back there that's bolted on."

He glanced sideways at the thing that had once been the corpse driver. Now, it had become a man of his own age. A Rawback, yes. But it did resemble a living, breathing human being, albeit one that a was total stranger to him.

Dan said, "You're free to get out, too."

The Rawback simply smiled. A moment later, it opened the side window, then rested its elbow on the doorframe, like they were doing nothing more dangerous than going for a pleasant drive in the countryside.

Dan slammed his foot down on the gas pedal. By this time, the Scarecrows were attacking the crew. Garner and the others were using the pipes to push them back. But they couldn't repel the attackers forever. It was only a matter of time before they were overwhelmed and became Scarecrows, too.

Dan accelerated. Thunder rumbled. Lightning flashed. And the car moved faster and faster. This felt like the kind of speed a jet achieves just before take-off. The engine howled. The car flung up a V-shaped plume of dust behind it.

A voice that transcended sound erupted inside the car: "I'll kill you! I'll slaughter you! I'll rip you apart!" He realized that the voice belonged to him. Then a transformation occurred.

Dan's heart even seemed to stop inside his chest. He held his breath.

The car had embarked upon a lethal trajectory. The wall formed from Blisters rose in front of them. This was the loathsome barrier that held back millions of gallons of pink fluid.

Dan spoke quite softly now. "Hold on tight, Katrina. Hold on tight. And … if we make it out of this … I think…"

"Yes, you think what, Dan?"

"I think we should be more than friends."

The needle of the old-style speedometer was flickering over one hundred. Purple lightning poured such a dazzling light into the car that Dan could see through the flesh of his hands… and he could pick out individual bones connected to knuckles, and knuckles connected to finger bones.

The car struck the wall. Blisters exploded in showers of glistening gel.

The car kept going. It penetrated deeper and deeper into what must have been a structure that was astonishingly soft. Tentacles streamed out as Blisters experienced the agony of death.

The car then crunched to an absolute stop.

Dan's forehead slammed into the steering wheel. The windshield disintegrated into a blizzard of white crystals that sped back into the car to sting his face. He felt the bones in his right forearm snap. The vicious pain was an axe blade cutting his brain into two distinct halves. That's how it felt to Dan.

A moment later, his savage injuries drew a dark blanket over his face. And he felt nothing more.

FORTY-NINE

FLOOD ZONE

There was silence. And utter darkness …
It did not last.

Spurts of pain flashed through his arm. He opened his mouth and screamed so loud and so hard that it felt as if the lining of his throat had ignited. This was like swallowing flaming napalm. He was howling himself back to consciousness. His eyelids lifted, and immediately his eyes locked onto precise details.

Arm broken.

Thumb of left hand dislocated. Thumb hanging back flat against the side of his wrist.

Car gliding backward.

No … *sweeping* backward. Fast!

Gloom shredded by purple fire. Lightning moving in brutally sharp lines. Thunder, always thunder. Bellowing nonstop.

And another roar. This was as deep as the bass notes of an entire universe as it finally died in the abyss of eternal night.

Dan's mind was creating a maelstrom of surreal imagery. Was this due to a bleed on the brain? Was he dying? Was he already dead?

Then … a hand was repeatedly punching his shoulder.

"Dan … Dan!"

"Katrina?"

"I thought you were dead."

Dan glanced at the passenger seat. The corpse driver that had haunted his dreams for longer than he cared to remember was no longer riding shotgun.

"Mr Bones," Dan muttered. "Where is he?"

"Gone! Vanished! Probably been sucked back into your damn skull! Dan. Look at me … uh, your mouth is all cut. Are you functional? Do you know who I am?"

"Katrina."

"Okay. That's a good start. But look … we're floating."

Dan gazed out through the opening where the windshield had once been. He took it all in. He absorbed the astonishing transformation of the Engine Room. Pink fluid gushed through the breach in the dam that he had created. The force of the flow pushed the car backward. And Katrina was right, the car was floating.

A gigantic lagoon was spreading out across the floor of the Engine Room. It must have stretched out for half a mile in every direction. Floating in the pink lake were thousands of Blisters. Their tentacles feebly moved, like they were trying to swim. Yet the Blisters, themselves, were deflating—turning as wrinkly as party balloons leaking air.

Katrina slid through the gap in the front seats and moved forward to sit in the passenger seat.

"We are actually floating." Dan knew his voice sounded dazed. And there was a note of astonishment, too. "I did it. I broke the dam."

Katrina leaned over and kissed the side of his face. "Yes, you did it. And look at the Blisters. They're not at all well, are they?" She grinned. "In fact, they are dying."

Even though there must have been a vast quantity of fluid, which had once formed the lagoon, it was dissipating in this colossal space. Levels were dropping quickly. The car had been floating smoothly, but now it juddered as its tires scraped against the floor. A moment later, the vehicle came to a rest as the flood level dropped to no more than knee-deep.

Dan turned in the seat and managed to shoulder the door open. Liquid slopped over the edge of the door sill to pool in the footwell. Katrina had opened the passenger door, too. She climbed out, then waded through the goo to the driver's side of the vehicle and helped him out. His forearm between wrist and elbow now appeared to have acquired another joint, because his forearm was bent at the midpoint. The enormity of what had just happened pushed even the agony of a broken arm so deep down into his brain he barely felt it.

Pink figures were rising from the lagoon all around him. Fingers scraped away the fluid to reveal faces he knew.

"Flynn ... Priya."

Katrina slopped toward them.

Dan called out, "Where are the Scarecrows?"

Flynn pointed at figures that slowly writhed in the shallow lake. "They're all around us. Something's happened to them, though. They can't climb to their feet."

The familiar voice of Professor Jellsby cut through the air. "The Blisters must have some fundamental link with the embryonic fluid, if indeed that is what it is. Possibly, there is even a form of wireless connectivity between the nervous system of the parasites and the fluid. And now that connectivity has been disrupted by the catastrophic release of the fluid that is essential to their well-being."

"Which means they are fucked." Garner spat out a mouthful of pink stuff. "Gah! Tastes like bad cheese."

The fluid had been contaminated with bone dust that had covered the floor. Streaks of grey now veined the pink. And a frothy scum floated on its surface.

The crew were helping each other to stand up. The Rawbacks seemed to be more human than ever and spoke in human tones. Gen grasped hold of her father's hand. Despite lacking an arm and part of his skull, he appeared to be fully functional.

"Love you, Spud."

This time his tone revealed that he meant it.

Professor Jellsby was gathering his family around him. He hugged them each in turn. He kissed their faces. They kissed him back. Katrina soon found her sister. There was a sense of happy family reunions after a time of crisis.

Meanwhile, thunder still rumbled, though it was much softer now. Lightning continued to draw lines of purple through the air, yet those lines were becoming dim.

Garner said, "You think the Scarecrows will become human again?"

Jellsby shrugged. "I don't have enough data to draw any conclusions."

Priya added, "For the sake of our safety, I suggest we don't linger here to find out."

Borman now sat up in the pink fluid. It came up to his chest. The Blister that was fixed to his shoulder had a sickly, deflated look. Even though it might have been dying, Borman's expression didn't appear human. He stared blankly at the breach in the dam where a sluggish flow of pink emerged. He appeared to be mourning the loss of some vital necessity.

"Look!" Gen pointed.

Everyone turned to see what she pointed at. For one terrifying moment, Dan expected to see an entire army of Scarecrows marching this way. However, Gen was pointing at the huge structure that Priya had identified as the gravity generator. When Dan had first seen the machine, it had been inert, even dead-looking. And it appeared as if it hadn't functioned for years. The cogs and disks had been dull-looking. He surmised that the disks interlocked with a complexity that defied human intelligence to calculate how it all fitted together.

However.... The discs glittered now. They were bright and clean.

Even more striking was the fact that the discs had begun to make twitching movements, as if some motive power was attempting to make them revolve. The hundreds of discs turned a little, then stopped. A sense of hesitancy.

Flynn stared at the machine. "It's trying to restart itself, isn't it?"

Garner's expression was sour. "It's kaput. It's too far gone to start working again."

He was right. The ripple of movement through the discs had stopped. They were all motionless once more.

"That's that, then," Merrick declared. "It's a total failure." He spoke these words as he stared at Vicki Mark Two. She glared back at him with pure hatred.

The flashes cast by the lightning flickered against the metal discs. Spurts of vivid purple sped across the machine.

And then ...

A sighing sound ... that morphed into a faint grating noise. Dry metal on metal.

Slowly, gradually ... there was movement.

Dan found himself holding his breath as he willed the machine to return to life.

And, gradually, it was happening.

Discs began to turn. Slowly and jerkily at first. Then the rotation became smoother—faster—soon every disc had begun to rotate. And the grating sound faded out and was replaced by a pleasant-sounding purr.

Priya gaped in astonishment. "Did we just the fix the machine?"

Dan shrugged. He was pleased and bewildered in equal measure. "The only way we can know for sure is if the asteroids stop colliding with the Earth."

Katrina rested a hand on his shoulder. "We need to get that arm into a sling," she told him.

Dan Karlton shook his head. "Thanks, Katrina. But there's something else we need to do first." Then he called out to everyone there. "Listen. We're done here. Therefore, what we need to do now is get back to the Rib. It's time we went home."

FIFTY

THE HOMEWARD WAY…

Impact with the dam had wrecked the car. It was no longer driveable.
There was no sign of the corpse driver, either. Dan wondered if that was
the last he'd see of Billy Dead Bones. Perhaps so. Maybe Mr Bones had
been some manifestation of unresolved childhood trauma—a psychologist
might venture such a theory. Not that Dan intended to worry himself un-
duly about that anymore. The corpse driver had gone. And Dan knew that
he would not fear Mr Bones anymore.

Priya had put her medical training to good use (along with a first-aid
kit) and she had made a sling from bandages in which Dan now cradled
his broken arm.

"I'll set the bone when we're back on the Rib," she told him.

After that, the group of humans and Rawbacks trudged through the
lake of gloop to the archway, then back out onto a dry floor, and into the
complex of towers, amid hills of dust and bone.

Katrina walked with Dan. His arm had begun to throb painfully, now
that the adrenalin was leaving his body. Priya didn't have any painkillers
but there'd be medication aplenty on the Rib.

They passed those sad mounds of human bone—their origin, and their
purpose here, still a mystery. They eventually walked by the Tower that had

served as home for a while. Lines of purple still cut through the shadows above their heads. Thunder muttered in deep bass notes that vibrated the bones in Dan's head.

Thankfully, there were no sign of Scarecrows. Either fresh cohorts from the bone mounds, or the ones that had might have recovered after being engulfed by the pink stuff.

Katrina said: "This has been one hell of an adventure."

Dan glanced at Tambara. "Katrina. Are you bringing your sister back to Earth?"

"Yes."

"How are you going to explain Tambara to your family? After all, she died when she was nineteen."

"In the last few years, all kinds of nightmares have happened, haven't they? Millions have been killed by space rocks crashing into the planet. It's time for some good miracles, don't you think?"

"I guess so." He gave a grim smile. "But the entire population of Earth is going to be queuing up to go to Callisto, so that they can Rawback their dead loved ones into living people again."

"Granted. The world's going to have to discuss the whole mass resurrection thing, aren't they?

Katrina slipped her hand into Dan's hand as they walked side by side. Flynn glanced at them from the corner of her eye. She said nothing.

Callisto had another surprise for that group of weary people.

There was the Rib, just a mile ahead of them. The huge structure curved pretty much like a human rib. Dan could see the silvery glint of the Crab, which was fastened to its underside, and he couldn't escape the unsettling synchronicity of the Blisters attaching themselves to human beings. Both were, to put it bluntly, parasitic.

Garner quickened his pace. The man was eager to board the Rib. "When I get back onboard," he declared, "I'm going to have a turkey dinner. Call it an early Thanksgiving. And I'm going to drink the saloon bar dry. Beer, glorious beer."

"Classy," snorted Jellsby from his gaggle of family.

"Yeah, and that comes from the guy who shoots junk into his veins."

The argument might well have developed into a fight. But fate had a shock in store.

There was no sound. And no sudden movement.

The Rib slowly, and smoothly, rose into the air. The purple lightning etched sharp lines that met in the center of the roof. And the Rib continued to ascend with serene grace.

The purple lines became a vortex of rotating smears of light. The Rib entered the lights and, within seconds, had vanished.

Garner stared upward. The man's expression was one of horror. "They've gone. They've left us behind."

He didn't have to say those words. Everyone there knew that their sole means of return to their home planet had left without them.

Gen let out a gasp of shock. "We're stranded here."

Katrina tightened her grip on Dan's hand. Her expression was deeply serious, yet she managed a tiny smile. "We're marooned," she whispered. "But at least we are marooned here together."

The breeze sighed through mounds of bone.

Garner shook his head. Then he turned to Flynn. "Okay, Captain. What the hell do we do now?"

TO BE CONTINUED …

ABOUT THE AUTHOR

SIMON CLARK is an award-winning author who has penned a good number of novels, short stories and scripts. His novels include the post-apocalyptic cult-classic Blood Crazy, which will soon be a trilogy issued by Darkness Visible Publishing, Vampyrrhic, Darkness Demands, Stranger, Whitby Vampyrrhic, Secrets of the Dead, and the British Fantasy Society award-winning The Night of the Triffids, which was also broadcast as a five-part drama series by BBC radio. Weird House Press have recently issued Simon's new collection, Sherlock Holmes: A Casebook of Nightmares and Monsters, and a novel, Sherlock Holmes: Lord of Damnation. He has also scripted an episode of the audio drama Doom's Day, part of Doctor Who's 60th anniversary celebrations.

Simon lives in Yorkshire, England, where he can be seen roaming this legend-haunted landscape with a black and white Border Collie by the name of Mylo.

ABOUT THE ARTIST

ENnie Award winning illustrator **M. WAYNE MILLER** continues his quest to synthesize the perfect blend of science fiction, fantasy, and horror with his work. Primarily focusing on science-fiction and horror imagery for limited edition book covers, lavish interiors, and numerous role playing games, Wayne strives for constant improvement as an artist and illustrator through continuous education, training, and pushing the boundaries of his skill set. One of Wayne's goals for 2022 and beyond is to broaden his artistic reach and expand his illustration work to collectable card games, board games, and other media. His list of clients include Weird House Press, Thunderstorm Books, Chaosium, HeroMaker Studios, Modiphius Entertainment, and Pinnacle Entertainment Group.

NEVER MISS A BOOK YOU WANT!

Join the Weird House mailing list
for the latest news, releases, and special offers!

Scan this code or visit:
https://www.weirdhousepress.com/subscribe/

www.ingramcontent.com/pod-product-compliance
Lightning Source LLC
Chambersburg PA
CBHW030404020726
47493CB00003B/938